THE GERMAN
MUJAHID

Boualem Sansal

THE GERMAN MUJAHID

*Translated from the French
by Frank Wynne*

Europa
editions

Europa Editions
116 East 16th Street
New York, N.Y. 10003
www.europaeditions.com
info@europaeditions.com

Copyright © by Editions Gallimard, Paris, 2008
First publication 2009 by Europa Editions
Translation by Frank Wynne
Original Title: *Le village de l'Allemand
ou Le journal des Frères Schiller*
English translation © by Frank Wynne 2009

The author and publishers gratefully acknowledge the copyright holders
of the following text: Primo Levi, "Shemà" (see p. 61),
from *Collected Poems*, translated from the Italian
by Ruth Feldman and Brian Swann (London: Faber & Faber, 1998).
The publishers guarantee in good faith that serious efforts have been made
to locate and contact the copyright holders to the poem by Primo Levi
without success. The publishers declare to be at their disposal
to clear the necessary permission rights.

Library of Congress Cataloging in Publication Data is available
ISBN 978-1-933372-92-1

Sansal, Boualem
The German Mujahid
This work has been published thanks to support from
the French Ministry of Culture – Centre National du Livre
Book design by Emanuele Ragnisco
www.mekkanografici.com
Cover photograph © dpa/Corbis
Cover illustration © Emanuele Ragnisco
Prepress by Plan.ed – Rome
Printed in Canada

Affectionate thanks to Mme Dominique G. H., my teacher at A. M. who was kind enough to rewrite my book in good French. So good I hardly recognised my own work. It was hard for me to read it. She did it in memory of Rachel, because she taught him too. "The best pupil I ever had," she stressed.

Sometimes I've taken her advice, I've changed names and scrapped some remarks. Other times I've kept to my version, because it's important to me. She says there are dangerous parallels that could get me into trouble. I don't give a shit, I've said what I have to say. Full stop.

MALRICH SCHILLER

Rachel died six months ago. He was thirty-three. One day, about two years ago, something in his head just snapped and he started tearing around all over the place—France, Algeria, Germany, Austria, Poland, Turkey, Egypt. Between trips, he'd hole up in a corner and read, think and write stuff—and he'd rage. He lost his health. Then his job. Then his mind. Ophélie walked out on him. One night he killed himself. It was this year, 24 April 1996, at about 11 P.M.

I didn't know about any of this shit. I was a kid, I was seventeen and when that something in his head snapped, I was into all sorts. I didn't see much of Rachel, I steered clear, he was doing my head in with all his preachifying. I don't like to say it, I mean, he was my brother, but when someone goes all self-righteous on you like that, it does your head in. He had his life, I had mine. He had this big job with this giant American company, he had the girl, the house, the car, the credit cards, every second of his day accounted for; me, I was zoning round H24 with the dregs of the estate. The H24 Estate is classed SUA-1—Sensitive Urban Area, Category 1. There's no room to breathe, you stumble out of one fuckup into another. One morning, Ophélie phones me to tell me what's happened. She'd stopped by the house to check on her ex. "I had this feeling," she said. Momo—he's the son of the halal butcher—he lent me his moped and I bombed down there. There were people milling round everywhere—cops, paramedics, neighbours, rubberneckers. Rachel was in the garage sitting on the ground, his back to the wall, legs stretched out, chin on his chest, mouth open. He looked like he was asleep. His face was black with soot. He'd been there all night, bathing in exhaust fumes. He was wearing these creepy striped pajamas I'd never seen before and his hair was all shaved off like a convict or something. It was freaky. I didn't react, didn't say anything. I couldn't take it in. This paramedic says, "Is he your brother?" I said, "Yeah." He said, "That's it? That's all you've got to say?" I just shrugged and headed into the sitting room.

Ophélie was in there with Com'Dad—he's the area police commissioner. She was crying, he was taking notes. When he saw me, he said, "Come here a minute." He asked me some stuff. I told him I didn't know anything. This was true—I didn't see much of Rachel. I had a feeling he was stressed about something, but I just thought, he's got his shit, I've got mine. It sounds pathetic when you put it like that, but that's life, we've got suicides all the time on the estate. When it happens you're like, What the fuck? You're bummed for a couple of days and a week later you've forgotten all about it. You think, That's life, and you get on with things. This time, it was my brother, my big brother, I had to get my head around it.

I had no idea what had happened to him, I couldn't imagine how far he had come, how far I had still to go. I ran through every possibility, I thought about it for days—girl trouble, money trouble, trouble with the cops, an incurable disease, every shitty thing that can go wrong in life—but I never thought of this. Dear God almighty, not this. I don't think anyone in the world has been through what we've been through.

After the funeral, Ophélie took off for Canada, to her cousin Cathy who got married over there to some fur trader who's rolling in it. She gave me the keys to their house, asked me to look after it. She said, "Let's just see how things go."

When I asked her why Rachel killed himself, she said, "I don't know, he never told me anything." I believed her. I knew just from looking at her standing there shaking that she didn't know anything, Rachel never told anybody anything.

So there I was all alone in Rachel's big house, feeling pathetic. I was beating myself up about the fact that I hadn't been around when Rachel lost it. A whole month I spent going round in circles. I felt like shit and I couldn't even cry. Raymond, Momo and a couple of other mates came round and hung out with me. They'd swing by in the afternoon, we'd talk about nothing much, knock back a couple of beers. That's when I got the job with Raymond's dad, Monsieur Vincent, working in this garage he's got called Rustbuckets' Delight. I was making minimum wage plus tips. I could deal with being on my own. The best thing about work is you forget everything else.

A month later Com'Dad phoned me at the garage and said: "I need you to come down the station, I've got something for you." I went down after work. He sat there staring at me for a bit, clicking his tongue, then he opens this drawer, takes out a plastic bag and shoves it across the desk. I pick it up. Inside, there are four battered notebooks. Com'Dad says to me, "It's your brother's diary. We don't need it anymore." Then he pokes his fat finger right in my face and says: "You should read it. Might knock some sense into you. Your brother was a good guy." Then he starts talking about this and that, the same stuff he's always banging on about: the estate, the future, France, the straight and narrow. I listened to him, shifting from one foot to the other. Then he looks up at me and says, "Go on, get out of here!"

As soon as I started reading Rachel's diary, I felt sick. It was like my insides were burning up. I had to hold my head in my hands just to stop it exploding, I felt like screaming. On every page, I thought, I don't believe this. Then, when I'd finished, I suddenly felt calm, like I was frozen inside—all I wanted to do was die. I felt ashamed to be alive. A week later, I realised that this whole thing, Rachel's story, my story, was all about papa's past, I was going to have to live it for myself, follow the same path, ask myself the same questions, and, where my father and Rachel had failed, I had to try to survive. I felt like this was all too much for me. But I also felt, and I don't know why, I had to tell the world. I knew it was all ancient history, but still, life doesn't change and what had happened to us could happen again.

Before I start, I need to tell you some stuff about us. Rachel and me were born back in the *bled*, in Algeria, in some god-forsaken village in the middle of nowhere called Aïn Deb. When I was little, uncle Ali told me it Aïn Deb meant "The Donkey's Well." I used to laugh, picturing this donkey standing on its hind legs, rubbing its belly, bravely standing guard over the well.

Our parents were Aïcha and Hans Schiller; maman was Algerian, papa was German. Rachel came to France in 1970 when he was seven. His name was actually Rachid Helmut but people shortened it to Rachel and it stuck. I came here in 1985 when I was eight. I'm Malek Ulrich, and that turned into Malrich and stuck too. We lived with uncle Ali, he's a good man, he's got seven kids of his own and a heart the size of a truck. The way he sees it, the more kids around the house, the better. He was from back in the *bled* too, he'd been friends with papa but he was one of the first people to leave and go to France. He worked every lousy job going and managed to build a life for himself here. He's a typical *chibani*—an old soldier—he doesn't say much. I made his life hell, but he'd never complain, he'd just smile and say, "One day, you'll be a man." His own sons disappeared one by one: four of them are dead, illness and work accidents, the other three are out there somewhere, working on building sites in Algeria, the Persian Gulf, Libya, going wherever the work is, chasing after life. You could say they're missing in action: they never come home, they never write, they never phone. They could be dead for all he knows. Now I'm the only one uncle Ali has left. I never saw my father again. I never went back to Algeria and he never came to France. He didn't want us going back to the *bled*, he'd say: "Some day, maybe, we'll see . . . " Maman came three times for a fortnight and spent the whole time crying. It's fucked up, we couldn't even talk to each other. Maman only spoke Berber and we'd be babbling away in whatever random Arabic we picked up on the estate and bits of German cobbled together. Maman never spoke much German and the best we could do was string together what little we remembered, so the three of us would just sit round smiling, saying, *Ja, ja, gut, labesse, azul, Ça va?, genau, cool, et toi?* Rachel went back once, when he came to take me to France. Papa never left the village. It's weird, but family stuff is always weird, there's so much you don't know, you don't think about. After school, where he studied German out of family loyalty and English because he had to, Rachel went to the Institute of Engineering in Nantes. I didn't get the chance, I never got past my first year in secondary school. They accused me of breaking into the principal's office and I got expelled. I made my own way, I hung around the streets, took a couple of courses and a few part-time jobs, did a bit of dealing, went to the mosque, wound up in court. Me and my mates were like fish in a river, sometimes we swam with the current, sometimes against. We got busted all the time, but we were always let off with a caution. We made the most of the fact we were too young to get banged up. I got hauled in front of every youth-offender judge, and in the end everyone forgot about me. I'm not complaining, what's done is done. It's fate, *mektoub*, the old Arabs on the estate call it. Me and my mates would say shit like that all the time: Adversity makes the best teacher, danger makes the man, a man gets his balls by using his fists.

At twenty-five, Rachel got French citizenship. He threw this big fuck-off party. Ophélie and her mother—a hard-core cheerleader for the National Front—had no reason now to put off the wedding. Algerian and German, maybe, but he's French now and an engineer to boot, they told anyone who asked. Another party. Has to be said, Rachel and Ophélie had been together since they were kids and her mother Wenda had run Rachel out of the house plenty of times; but she saw him grow up to be serious and well-mannered. Besides, she couldn't really complain, Rachel had blue eyes and blonde hair, Ophélie was the one with dark hair and brown eyes. Rachel had inherited papa's German genes and Ophélie's Russian blood did the rest. Their life was like some cheesy music box, all you had to do was wind it up and it played. Half the time I was jealous of them, the other half I wanted to kill them just to put them out of their misery. To keep on good terms, I steered clear. Any time I went round their house, they'd flap around like there was a storm threatening the nest. Ophélie was always two steps ahead of me and she'd go round afterwards to make sure nothing was missing.

After he got his citizenship, Rachel said, "I'm going to sort out your papers too, you can't go on like this, like a free electron." I shrugged: "Whatever, do what you like." So he did. One day he shows up on the estate and gets me to sign some papers and a year later he shows up again and says, "Congratulations, you're one of us now, your papers have come through." He said his boss pulled a few strings. He took me to dinner in some big fancy restaurant in Paris near Nation. It wasn't to celebrate me getting my papers, it was to give me a lecture about all the responsibilities that went with it. So, as soon as I'd had dessert, I was like, "Later," and I was out of there.

Monsieur Vincent sorted things out for me, he gave me a month's paid leave. It was pretty good of him really, I'd only ever worked two days here, three days there, and there was a clapped out old wreck I hadn't even finished working on. He sorted things out with social services too, since they were forking out for the apprenticeship.

I needed to hole up, to be on my own. I'd got to the point where the only way to deal with the world is to go off and hide and wallow in your pain. I read Rachel's diary over and over. This shit was so huge, so dark, I couldn't see any way out. Then suddenly, I started writing like a lunatic, me who's always hated writing. Then I started running round like a headless chicken. What I went through I wouldn't wish on anyone.

MALRICH'S DIARY

NOVEMBER 1996

It was hard for me to read Rachel's diary. His French isn't like mine. The dictionary wasn't much help, every time I looked something up it just referred me to something else. French is a real minefield, every word is a whole history linked to every other. How is anyone supposed to remember it all? I remembered something Monsieur Vincent used to say to me: "Education is like tightening a wheel nut, too much is too much and not enough is not enough." But I learned a lot, and the more I learned, the more I wanted to know.

The whole thing started with the eight o'clock news on Monday, 25 April 1994. One tragedy leading to another leading to another, the third the worst tragedy of all time. Rachel wrote:

I've never felt any particular attachment to Algeria, but every night, at eight o'clock on the dot, I'd sit down in front of the television waiting for news from the *bled*. There's a war on there. A faceless, pitiless, endless war. So much has been said about it, so many terrible things, that I came to believe that some day or other, no matter where we were, no matter what we did, this horror was bound to touch us. I feared as much for this distant country, for my parents living there, as I did for us, here, safe from it all.

In his letters, papa only ever talked about the village, his humdrum routine, as if the village were a bubble beyond time itself. Gradually, in my mind, the whole country became reduced to that village. That was how I saw it: an ancient village from some dimly remembered folk tale; the villagers have no names, no faces, they never speak, never go anywhere; I saw them standing, crouching, lying on mats or sitting on stools in front of closed doors, cracked whitewashed walls; they move slowly, with no particular goal; the streets are narrow, the roofs low, the minarets oblique, the fountains dry; the sand extends in vertiginous waves from one end of the horizon to the other; once a year clouds pass in the blue sky like hooded pilgrims mumbling to themselves, they never stop here but march on to sacrifice themselves to the sun or hurl themselves into the sea; sometimes they expiate their sins over the heads of the villagers, and then it's like the biblical flood; here and there I hear dogs barking at nothing, the caravans are long gone but as everywhere in these forsaken countries, skeletal buses shudder along the rutted roads like demons belching smoke; I see naked children running—like shadows swathed in dust—too fast to know what game they are playing; pursued by some *djinn*; laughter and tears and screams following behind, fading to a vague hum in this air suffused with light and ash, merging with the echoes. And the more I told myself that all this was just some movie playing in my head, a ragbag of nostalgia, ignorance and clichés seen on the news, the more the scene seemed real. Papa and maman, on the other hand, I could still picture quite clearly, hear their voices, still smell them, and yet I knew that this too was false, that these were inventions of my mind, sacred relics from my childhood memory making them younger with each passing year. I reminded myself that life is hard in the old country, all the more so in a godforsaken village, and then this tranquil veil would tear and I would see an old man, half-paralysed, trying to stay standing to surprise me, and a hunch-backed old woman supporting herself against the flaking wall as she struggled to her feet to greet me, and I would think, this is papa, this is maman, this is what time and hard living have done to them.

Everything I know about Algeria, I know from the media, from books, from talking to friends. Back when I lived with uncle Ali on the estate, my impressions were too real to be true. On the estate, people played at being Algerian beyond what truth could bear. Nothing forced them to, but they conformed to tradition with consummate skill. Emigrants we are and emigrants we will be for all time. The country they spoke of with such emotion, such passion, doesn't exist, the tradition that is the North Star of their memory still less so. It's an idol with a stamp of tradition on its brow that reads "Made in Taiwan"; it's phony, artificial and dangerous. Algeria was other, it had its own life, everyone knew its leaders had pillaged the country and were actively preparing for the end of days. The Algerians who still live there know all too well the difference between the real country and the one we live in. They know the alpha and the omega of the horror they are forced to live through. If it were left to them, the torturers would have been the only victims of their dirty deeds.

On 25 April 1994, the *bled* was the lead story on the eight o'clock news: "Fresh carnage in Algeria! Last night armed men stormed the little village of Aïn Deb and cut the throats of all of its inhabitants. According to Algerian television, this new massacre is the work of Islamic fundamentalists in the Armed Islamic Group . . . "

I jumped to my feet and screamed, "Oh God, this can't be happening!" What I had most feared had happened, the horror had finally found us. I slumped back, shell-shocked, I was sweating, I felt cold, I was shivering. Ophélie rushed in from the kitchen shouting, "What is it? What's the matter? Talk to me for Christ's sake!" I pushed her away. I needed to be on my own, to take it in, to compose myself. But the truth was there before my eyes, in my heart, my parents, faces, immeasurably old, immeasurably scared, pleading with me to help them, stretching out their arms towards me as ancient shadows brutally dragged them back, threw them to the ground, shoved a knee into their frail chests and slit their throats. I could see their legs judder and twitch as terrified life fled their aged bodies.

I had thought I understood horror, we see it all over the world, we hear about it every night in the news, we know what motivates it, every day political analysts explain the terrifying logic, but the only person who truly understands horror is the victim. And now I was a victim, the victim, the son of victims, and the pain was real, deep, mysterious, unspeakable. Devastating. Pain came hand in hand with an aching doubt. First thing the next morning, I phoned the Algerian Embassy in Paris to find out if my parents had been among the victims. I was transferred from one office to another, put on hold, and I held, breathless, gasping, until finally a polite voice came on the line.

"What was the name again, monsieur?"

"Schiller . . . S,C,H,I, double L, E, R . . . Aícha and Hans Schiller."

As I listened to the rustle of paper, I prayed to God to spare us. Then the polite voice came back and in a reassuring voice said: "Put your mind at rest, monsieur, they're not on the list I have here . . . Although . . . "

"Although what?"

"I do have an Aícha Majdali and a Hassan Hans, known as Sid Mourad . . . Do those names mean anything to you?"

"That's my mother . . . and my father . . . " I said, holding back my tears.

"Please accept my condolences, monsieur."

"Why aren't they listed as Aícha and Hans Schiller?"

"That, I'm afraid, I couldn't say, monsieur, the list was sent to us by the Ministry of the Interior in Algeria."

Rachel had told me nothing. I never watch TV and my mates don't even know it exists. We'd never dream about sitting in a dark room watching pictures and listening to people prattling on. If I did hear about the massacre it was only in passing, and I didn't give a toss. Aïn Deb, Algeria, didn't mean much to me. We knew there was a war on there, but it was far away, we talked about it the same way we talked about wars in Africa or the Middle East, in Kabul, in Bosnia. All my friends are from places where there's a war or a famine, when we talk about that shit we never go into detail. Our life is here on the estate, the boredom, the neighbours screaming, the gang wars, the latest Islamist guerrilla action, the police raids, the busts, the dealers, the grief we get from our big brothers, the demonstrations, the funerals. There are family parties sometimes, they're cool, but they're really for the women. The men are always downstairs, standing outside the tower blocks counting the breezes. If you go at all, it's only to say you went. The rest of the time we're bored shitless, we just hang around on corners waiting for it to be over.

Sometimes, we'll get a little visit from Com'Dad—that's what we call Commissioner Lepère. He always pretends like he didn't know we'd be there: "Hey guys, I didn't see you there . . . I was just passing . . . " Then he'll come over, lean against the wall with us and chat like we're old friends. Meanwhile we're standing there wondering if he's come to phish or philosophize. Both, my brothers, both. Sometimes we'll feed him a scrap, some bit of bogus information, sometimes we'll make out like we're thinking aloud about careers in the service of humanity and the environment. We have a laugh and then say our goodbyes, American style, high fives all round. Com'Dad even buys us all tea at Da Hocine or a coffee at the station bar. Poor bastard thinks it's a good way of getting in with us. It is so lame. But at the same time we pretend to our mates that we've got Com'Dad right where we want him, that we're always feeding him false information and getting him to pull strings for illegals on the estate. As for Com'Dad, he'll turn up uninvited at whatever's going on, he's there at every party, wedding, circumcision, excision, he pops round to celebrate when people get on a course, get out of prison, get their papers, and he never misses the slaughtering of the sheep at Eid. He always leads the procession at funerals. He's part of the new school of policing: to know your enemy you have to live with him, live like him.

In Rachel's garage I found newspaper reports of the Aïn Deb massacre, some from here, some from the *bled*, *Le Monde*, *Libération*, *El Watan*, *Liberté* . . . There was a big pile of them. Rachel had highlighted the stuff about us. It ripped my heart out just reading it. There was something sick about it too, the journalists talking about genocide like it was just another story, but their tone was like: "We told you so, there's something not right about this war." What fucking war is right? This one's just wronger than most. And you end up imagining all the horror, the shame piled up on the grief. I had a film of it playing in my head for days, it made me sick to my stomach. This sleepy old village in the middle of nowhere, a moonless sky, dogs starting to bark, mad staring eyes appearing out of the darkness, shadows darting here and there, listening at doors, shattering them with their boots, inhuman screams, orders barked in the night, terrified villagers dragged out into the village square, kids bawling, women screaming, girls scarred with fear clinging to their mothers, trying to hide their breasts, dazed old men praying to Allah, pleading with the killers, ashen-faced men parleying with the darkness. I see a towering bearded man with cartridge belts slung across his chest ranting at the crowd in the name of Allah, then cutting a man's head off with a slash of his saber. After that, it's chaos, carnage, crying and screaming, limbs thrashing, savage laughter. Then silence again. A few groans still, soft sounds dying away one after the other, and then a sort of heavy, viscous silence crashing down onto nothingness. The dogs aren't barking now, they're whimpering, heads between their paws. Night is closing in on itself, on its secret. Then the film starts up again, only more graphic this time, more screams, more silence, more darkness. The stench of death is choking me, the smell of blood as it mingles with the earth. And I throw up. Suddenly I realise I'm alone in Rachel's house. It's pitch black outside, the silence is crushing. Then I hear a dog bark. I imagine shadows slipping through the streets. I calm myself as best I can and I sleep like the dead.

Rachel wrote:

I've decided, I'm going to Aïn Deb. It is something I have to do, something I need to do. The risks don't matter, this is my road to Damascus.

It's not going to be easy. When I went to the Algerian consulate in Nanterre, they treated me like I was a Soviet dissident. The official stared me in the eye until it hurt, then he flicked through my passport, flicked through it again, read and reread my visa application, then, eyes half-closed, he tilted his head back and stared at a spot on the ceiling until I thought he was in a coma. I don't know if he heard me call him, whether he realised I was worried, but suddenly, out of the blue, he leaned over to me and, just between the two of us, he muttered between clenched teeth, "Schiller, what is that . . . English . . . Jewish?"

"I think you'll find the passport is French, monsieur."

"Why do you want to go to Algeria?"

"My mother and father were Algerian, monsieur, they lived in Aïn Deb until 24 April, when the whole village was wiped off the map by Islamic fundamentalists. I want to visit their graves, I want to mourn, surely you can understand that?"

"Oh, yes, Aïn Deb . . . You should have said . . . But I'm afraid it's out of the question. The consulate doesn't issue visas to foreign nationals . . . "

"Then who do you issue them to?"

"If you get killed out there, people blame us. More to the point, the French government prohibits you from travelling to Algeria. Maybe you didn't know that, or maybe you're just playing dumb?"

"So what do I do?"

"If your parents were Algerian, you can apply for an Algerian passport."

"How do I go about that?"

"Ask at the passport office."

After three months of running around, I finally got my hands on the precious documents I needed to apply. Getting Algerian papers is without doubt the most complicated mission in the world. Stealing the Eiffel Tower or kidnapping the queen of England is child's play by comparison. Phone all you like, no one ever answers, paperwork gets lost somewhere over the Mediterranean or is intercepted by Big Brother to be filed away in a missile silo in the Sahara until the world crumbles. It took me five registered letters and two months of fretful waiting just to get a copy of papa's certificate of nationality. When I finally got the papers, I felt like a hero, like I'd conquered Annapurna. I rushed back to the consulate. The passport officer proved to be every bit as intractable as his colleague at the visa desk, but, in the end, officiousness had to defer to the law. God it must be degrading and dangerous to be Algerian full time.

At the Air France office they looked at me as though I had shown up with a noose around my neck ready to hang myself in front of them. "Air France no longer flies to Algeria, monsieur," the woman snapped, shooing me away from her desk. I went to Air Algérie, where the woman behind the desk could think of no reason to send me packing, but she tossed my brand new passport back at me and said, "The computers are down. You'll have to come back another day. Or you could try somewhere else."

Only when I finally got the whole trip sorted out did I tell Ophélie and, as I expected, she threw a fit.

"Are you crazy? What the hell do you want to go to Algeria for?"

"It's business, the company is sending me to assess the market."

"But there's a war on!"

"Exactly . . . "

"And you said you'd go?"

"It's my job . . . "

"Why are you only telling me this now?"

"It wasn't definite until now, we needed to find someone well connected in the regime."

"Go on then, get yourself killed, see if I care."

If sulking was an Olympic sport, Ophélie would be a gold medalist. At dawn the next morning, while the dustmen were making their rounds, I crept out of the house like a burglar.

The journey itself proved to be much easier than the consulate, the airlines and Ophélie predicted. Getting to Algiers was as easy as sending a letter to Switzerland. Unsurprisingly, Algiers Airport was just as I left it in 1985 when I came to bring Malrich back home. It was exactly how I remembered it, the only difference was the atmosphere. In 1985, it was low-level distrust, now it is abject terror. People here are scared of their own shadows. There's been a lot going on. The airport was bombed not long ago, there's still a gaping hole in the arrivals hall, you can still see spatters of dried blood on the walls.

I found myself out on the street, in the milling crowds, under a pitiless sun. What was I supposed to do now, where was I supposed to go? From my clothes, it was obvious I was a foreigner, so I didn't go unnoticed. I hardly had time to wonder when a whole crowd of guys started sidling past me, staring up at the sky, down at their feet, doing their best to look as though they weren't talking to me: "Hé, m'sieur! . . . taxi? . . . *pas cher* . . . very cheap . . . " they whispered without moving their lips. Clandestine ventriloquists. I adopted the same tactic.

"How much to Aïn Deb?"

"Where?"

"Near Sétif."

A yawning gulf opened up around me. Too far . . . too dangerous. Some of the drivers turned their backs without a word, others looked at me accusingly. It seemed as if my trip was to end here when a young, friendly guy came up to me. Covert whispers were exchanged. He was prepared for take me and quoted me a fare with a string of zeroes—for what he was asking, I could have traveled from Paris to New York in a Cadillac—but danger has a price, and I accepted. I winked discreetly to let him know I agreed. My new benefactor whispered for me to walk some way behind him so no one would realise we were together. The car was parked outside the airport. I stopped short and stared at this rust bucket that looked like it was on its last legs. "Don't worry," he said, "I keep it like this to ward off the evil eye." The car started first time.

The driver's name was Omar. He pumped the accelerator, took off at a hundred miles an hour and, before I knew it, we'd left the city behind us. I decided to call him Schumacher. I told him that I was hoping to get to Sétif in one piece.

"Hé, m'sieur, we need to get to Sétif before dark—after dark is when they set up the fake roadblocks. Tonight, you sleep in a hotel, tomorrow you find a taxi to take you to your *doaur*. If I can find an honest Muslim, they will give me a bed for the night . . . "

"What do you mean I can get a taxi? I've already got a taxi right here, one I'm paying a small fortune for . . . "

"Hé, m'sieur, I cannot take you to some place I've never been to, a place where Islamists slit the throats of everyone in the village, you see what I'm saying?"

"Yeah, you're saying you've ripped me off. But okay, I wouldn't want your death on my conscience, my own will be more than enough, you can drop me in Sétif."

Fear was hacking at my insides. The roads were so deserted it made my blood freeze. Not a soul, not a sound, nothing but the wind whistling around the car, the tires hissing softly like snakes. We passed military vehicles packed with young men armed to the teeth. Whenever Omar saw one, he would ease off the accelerator, look left, look right, look ahead, look behind, then, taking a deep breath and putting himself in God's hands, he'd pull out into the other lane and go hell for leather until we passed them. "Don't worry," he smiled at me, "Those are real soldiers." "What do we do if we run into fake ones?" I asked stupidly. "Nothing," he smiled and flicked his thumb across his throat. We stopped once or twice for petrol, for coffee, for a piss. At the entrance to every village, there was a police roadblock. The routine ran like clockwork: first a machine-gun was trained on us and we were ordered to turn off the ignition, step out of the vehicle with our hands up, leave the doors open and walk to the blockhouse, keeping well apart. Next our papers were checked, then came the interrogation, the body search, the car search. Eventually we would be sent on our way with some helpful nuggets of advice about what awaited us down the road. "When you get to such-and-such a place, be careful . . . If you see a child or a frightened woman hitchhiking, or if you see a man lying in the road pleading for help, put your foot down, it's a trap." Omar knew all about them, he told me stories as we drove. I have never been on such a terrifying journey, though the only people we met were genuine policemen and real soldiers—

all of them as terrified as we were. We covered the three hundred kilometers from Algiers and Sétif in less than four hours, just like you would in France.

As we came into Sétif, the sun, now sinking in the west, still hammered down like a hydraulic press at noon. "You see, m'sieur," Omar got out his best smile: "No problem." "Yeah," I said, "I'm wondering why it cost me so much money. For what I paid the least I'd expect is a couple of murders, a sunset doesn't really cut it."

This didn't sound like the Rachel I knew. Round me, he always seemed so serious, so distant and withdrawn, and he was always acting the big brother—I hated that. Rachel never really fitted in on the estate, with his Swedish good looks and his la-di-dah politeness, his university degree, his big-shot job at a multinational corporation, his little house and his little garden in a posh neighbourhood. The estate doesn't approve of individual success: it breeds jealousy, it rocks the boat, it stirs up a shitload of aggravation. To tell the truth, I was ashamed of him. Everyone on the estate assumed I was loaded. They were always saying, "Why don't you go ask you brother?" He should have moved away, gone to live in Paris. I never understood why he stuck around. To make things worse, Ophélie was the sexiest thing on the estate. All the kids on the estate called her Bump—short for 'speed bump' because everyone slowed down when she walked past—that's how hot she was. After she and Rachel got married, I put the word out: first person calls her Bump is a dead man. After that the guys on the estate called her Rachella. They'd grown up a bit by then, they knew the score, and there were plenty more fish in the sea.

In his diary, Rachel sounds cool, funny, he sounds human. I thought maybe misery made him humble, human, but now I'm not so sure. Everyone on the estate is miserable as sin, but they're not humble and there aren't many like uncle Ali and aunt Sakina who are genuine human beings. Maybe having to question everything is what did it, all the questions he asks himself in his diary. But I think there's something else, I think deciding to go back to Aïn Deb, in spite of the risks and the consequences, was a weight off his shoulders. People say there's a real satisfaction in doing your duty.

Rachel doesn't say what he did in Sétif or how he got to Aïn Deb. I suppose he haggled with a local cab driver and got some all-inclusive deal that covered whatever danger there was out there in the *bled*. Rachel never was much of a talker, but he obviously found people to talk to in Algeria. My mate Momo— his parents are from the province of Kabylia too—says they've got pretty much everything in Sétif: houses and streets and cafés and garages and all that shit. And there's this famous fountain in the middle on the Place de la Fontaine. Momo swears it's the most beautiful place in the world. He says all the men in Sétif are truck drivers or taxi drivers, they're like the cowboys you see in movies who never get off their horses, Momo says they're proud of it, that being a driver is something passed down from father to son for generations, he says that, to them, dying behind the wheel is a glory they all dream about. I'm just telling it like I heard it. I suppose it takes all kinds.

Rachel arrived in Aïn Deb at about 3 P.M. He wrote:

My God, to think I was born here, miles from anything! You won't find Aïn Deb—"The Donkey's Well"—on any map, you're not even likely to stumble on it by accident. There's no reason in the world for anyone to come here. Even someone lost, someone on the run, wouldn't stay here, having more reason than most to keep moving, they'd be out of here as fast as they could. You turn off the tarmac road a couple of miles outside

Sétif and drive along dirt tracks through a bare, rugged, silent wasteland ringed by infinite horizons. You immediately start to feel uneasy, you feel small, forlorn, damned. Much of the time, there is no line dividing earth and sky and everywhere you look is empty, ochre. We drive on towards an infinite, shifting wall of sand, and I feel obsessed by the idea that the map is closing up behind us. In mathematical terms, I'd say that by some quantum shift we seem to have entered non-Euclidean space; there are no signs, no landmarks here that a human being can relate to, there is no sense of time, no possible human compassion, nothing but an insistent drone like the echo of some cataclysm from before the flood. Exhausted from the heat, I start to wonder what terrible danger early man must have been running from to hole up in a place like this. Why did succeeding generations stay here? What enchantment kept them fettered to this place? It seems appalling, but for a minute it even occurred to me that the massacre of April 24 was simply in the nature of things. This landscape is meant be barren, it tolerates man only until it can find some way of being rid of him. But this is where I was born, where I grew up. I played here as a child. I must have loved this place, at that age you're curious about everything, or at least you turn boredom into dreams and take your pleasure in them. If I left, it was because papa decided I should, thereby preempting the judgment of the earth and of Allah's madmen who, in the wasteland of their minds, would come up with the idea of obliterating every trace of life twenty-five years later.

Aïn Deb is wedged at the bottom of a steep valley between four desolate hills. The people who first settled here were clearly trying to hide from the world. Maybe it goes back to ancient times, to tribes exhausted by blood feuds when the weakest hid away, settled out of sight to avoid the constant raids. Or maybe this place was once lush and verdant, capable of sustaining life, perhaps this barren wasteland came later, the result of some great catastrophe, some curse, some strange disease, some nameless mystery. Maybe drought followed hard on its heels like a tornado whipping away the last illusions of those who lived here. Their children would have left for other lands, other skies, taking with them a cruel, bitter memory which, like a self-fulfilling prophecy, doomed them to search in vain to know why they were cursed, while exhaustion, fear and the need to atone ensured they would never feel at peace in their new life. To those who run away, even the idea of a safe haven is dangerous, they see it as a trap where they will be forced to stop running. By some miracle Aïn Deb survived, it had a wellspring and it refused to give up life. And wherever a miracle is born, there is always some fearless donkey to bear witness. It's astonishing how little people know about the history of their country. I wonder how many people in the world are capable of recounting the history of their village, their neighbourhood, even their house without slipping into some convenient fantasy. Fewer still know the history of their own family. And though I didn't know it yet, the mad, nightmarish history of my family was about to blow up in my face and kill me.

I stopped on the crest of a hill. I didn't have the strength to go any further, I felt sick, my eyes were stinging, sweat ripped at my back. Death hung in the air, I could smell it. And yet I could sense some residual force that spoke of life and of eternity. My heart was beating fit to burst, beating out a rhythm to a lament that sprang from the depths of the earth, from the pulsing sun, from the anguished cries of a memory imprisoned in stone. Here, amid this savage beauty, this agony of stone, this harsh light, life and death merged. The question whether to live or to die was superfluous; here opposites converged, here time was as it always was: an infinite silence, a crippling stillness, light rose and fell, the seasons chased each other like brothers and sisters, speaking to nothing but the immutable phases of the solar cycle. I sat on a rock, mopping my face with a handkerchief, and like an old man returning to a forgotten country, memories stirred, images appeared. They were quickly whipped away by what I saw. My memories did not tally with the reality. I dimly remembered a large, immaculate, contented village perched on a hill, and greedy tentacles spilling down, eating into the hillside; what I saw, devastating in its truth, was a pitifully small village which looked as though it vainly struggled to set its roots into the upper slopes. Everything here was hemmed in by steep hills. Two or three houses, rising up to defy the heavens, stood, unfinished, left to wrack and ruin. There was water in the *wadi*, and warty toads, the sort we used to torment during the mating season when we were kids, now there was also a small pool on a bed of powdery rock ringed by deadwood polished by time. In my mind, I remembered a breathtaking forest, but what I saw before me was a dying copse. In my mind, the streets hummed with life, and now, shielding my eyes to look down, all I could see were deserted laneways, cracked, crumbling walls, a flea-bitten mongrel wandering, a lone chicken scavenging, a donkey staring out and . . . there, yes . . . there in the courtyard, on the terrace, in the shadow of the mosque, people, women, children! I leapt to my feet and bounded down the hill like a mountain goat.

It is astonishing how life endures. Many villagers had survived the carnage by disappearing into the thick night, hiding as best they could, others played dead, while others still did not know by what miracle they survived. They recognised me as soon as they saw me. "It's Rachid," they cried, "Cheïkh Hassan'sson!" They rushed over and crowded around me, the children going through my pockets as though I was some wealthy uncle coming home. I couldn't shake off my stilted politeness, I stood stiffly, head high, glancing around me, stammering words that sounded strange and grating to my ear. I listened as I idiotically babbled "*Salam, salam!*" I was welcomed, fussed over, thanked, congratulated. Normal roles had been reversed, the poor were comforting the privileged. For my part, I was shell shocked. I barely recognized my childhood friends, they looked so old, so pitiful it was unbearable, they looked almost like bedridden invalids you take outside in the morning so they can sit in the sun, and bring in again when night falls. The sight of them, with stumps for teeth, grey hair, deep wrinkles, hunched backs, made me feel guilty. Their hands looked thick and arthritic, the story of their short lives could be read in the ridges and their calluses. Those who had been old when I had first known them looked exactly as they always had, though maybe more alive than their children. When death comes knocking, life suddenly revives. We talked and talked some more, we talked for three whole days. The little Arabic I learned on the estate in Paris was useless. I babbled away in a mixture of French, English, German and what crumbs of Arabic and Berber I remembered, and we quickly bonded. We understood each other perfectly. To tell the truth, there wasn't much to say: a smile, a few gestures, a few bows said all that needed to be said. Conversation is all in the mind, you carry on a conversation with yourself, answer your own questions, while a look, a gesture, is enough to sum it up to others. When it came down to it, all I was trying to say was, "I'm very well, thank you, *Allahu Akbar.*" Then I moved on to the next person, said the same things, drank some more coffee. I went from house to house, rediscovering the places, the smells, the mystery of a childhood suddenly rekindled. I wanted to run, to nose about, to steal, to plot, to invent great new secrets I would never tell to a living soul. We talked about that terrible night. They had all lost someone close to them—a relative, a friend, a neighbour. It had happened much as I had imagined it. Crime is not difficult to understand, it is something we know intimately, something we can easily imagine, something we see, we hear about, we read about all the time. Crime is our totem pole, planted in the earth, visible from the moon. It is the history of the world. And Algeria had written a special chapter for Aïn Deb and those who lived there.

Everyone in the village came to visit me in our family home which was now filled with emptiness, with memories of which I knew only the smallest part. But childhood memories are extraordinarily powerful. The people of Aïn Deb fed me, went without so that I could eat, worried about me, watched over me in the heavy afternoon hours as I slept, and when night began to weigh on me, the last of them would quietly creep away carrying their sleeping children in their arms. I was pleased to find that my father had been respected here and my mother thought of as blessed. I felt flattered. They say that the reputation the dead leave behind is ruthlessly judged by those who survive them. My parents had had their quietus.

The victims of the massacre had been buried in a section of the cemetery marked out with whitewashed stones, elevating them to the status of martyrs for God and the Republic. A marble slab set into concrete inscribed in Arabic says as much. I counted thirty-eight graves in neat rows. To a small village, this brutal loss had been devastating. Carved into the gravestones were the names of those who had died, a verse from the Qur'an and a little flag. The regional administration had planned and funded the memorial. The inauguration ceremony attracted officials from civil, military and religious authorities and a national TV crew. They arrived in a cortege, and left trailing a glorious cloud of dust, leaving behind the village which had served them as a film set and the villagers whose walk-on parts they had momentarily upstaged. I had been worried that my father, a Christian, would be buried elsewhere, something that would have upset me, but his grave was next to my mother's in the martyrs' section. On their headstones were the names Aïcha Majdali and Hassan Hans known as "Si Mourad." This strange anomaly again. It was only now that I found out that papa had converted to Islam in 1963. After Independence, he decided to settle here in Aïn Deb. At first, the villagers found it strange, even inappropriate for a German, a Christian, to decide to live among them, but since papa had fought in the War of Independence and earned the title Mujahid, and since he was an Algerian national, they felt honoured. Three months later, charmed by the young and beautiful Aïcha, the daughter of the village cheïkh, papa converted to Islam in order to marry her and took the name Hassan. He was forty-five, she was eighteen. When the old cheïkh died, the villagers conferred the title on papa. It was a formality, really, since everyone already referred to him as Cheïkh Hassan. They came to consult him, to listen to him, he had a solution for everything, they were amazed by the changes he made to the village. Strangers passing through—admittedly, as infrequent as the rain—used to go away astonished, half-believing Aïn Deb was not in the same country. Papa's wisdom, his experience, his flair for organisation and natural authority had argued in his favour without any need to plead his case. This was something else I didn't know. Though, as I child, I heard people call him Si Hassan, I thought it was just a nickname. They called him Si Mourad too, the name he used in the *maquis* during the War of Independence, later they called him Cheïkh Hassan, but I just assumed it was a mark of respect for his age.

Having made my pilgrimage, and having been so warmly welcomed, I soon felt at peace again. My breathing slowed, each breath now filled with courage, each sigh with noble self-denial. Everyone I met offered me words of comfort that harked back to that ageless, tragic condition of man, the essential humanity without which he would be nothing more than an automaton wandering in the desert, rusting without knowing it: "To God we belong and to Him we return . . . We are but dust in the wind . . . No one can knows what lies beyond death . . .

Believe in God, he is the resurrection and the life . . . Allah never forsakes his own . . ." Here in this sacred atmosphere, in this place where death had passed like a blast of the apocalypse, these phrases resonated oddly with me. Being so far from everything in this devastating but exhilirating emptiness, borne up by this sense of time passing unhurriedly, by these infallible memories, by words which have crossed the centuries, questioning and humanizing the unknowable, fosters a sense of infinite and unshakeable patience, of transcendence. You do not see yourself moving towards this blessed state, but suddenly you are someone else, someone who observes the world serenely, asks no questions, feels no fear. It is wonderful and terrifying at the same time. You spurn life, rise above it, look on it as inconsequential, ephemeral, illusory, even as life—indefatigable, magnificent, eternal—crushes us like grains of sand and sweeps us under the carpet.

I was worried when I read this part of Rachel's diary. I've cut out a lot of stuff and kept the best bits, the rest is the sort of bullshit you hear in the mosque. I've had my fill of sermons like that. Back in the day, I was a regular in the basement of Block 17, where the jihadists had a mosque for anyone who wanted to come. You're hooked before you know it—it only takes three sessions, and there are five prayers a day and you don't get any days off. This is the sort of stuff they talk about all the time there: "real" life, paradise, *djina*, they call it, the *houris*, the Companions of the Prophet, the saints of the Golden Age, God's perfect system, Brotherhood, then everyone smiles that merciful smile and hugs like veterans of some holy war, thinking hard about Jerusalem—*El Qods*, they call it. At first, it was cool—me and my mates went because we enjoyed going. Then a bunch of other people showed up with this new imam who was a leader in the AIG—the Armed Islamic Group—and the whole laid-back vibe turned into this terrifying madness and we were all caught in the headlights. Suddenly the only thing anybody talked about was *jihad* and the martyrs of Islam, about *kaffirs* and hell and death, about bombs and rivers of blood, about the end of the world, and noble sacrifice, about exterminating the other. Even outside, after we'd been to the mosque, we talked about it all the time. Then, the next time we heard the muezzin, we'd head back down to the basement wearing a black band round our foreheads, bloodthirsty and ready for action. When I got expelled from school, the new imam was delighted. According to him, school was a crime perpetrated by Christian dogs, the mosque was the future. I'd never really had much time for school, but I'd never thought about it like that. The imam said, "I will teach you what Allah expects of you, I will open the gates of paradise for you." I made my excuses, said I had some training course to do and got the hell out of there. Momo kept going, he was really into all that shit, but when he got to Taliban level, he found out the meaning of pain. When you get to be a Taliban—a student of Islam—leaving is considered desertion. The jihadists caught up with him and beat him to a bloody pulp. He would have died if we hadn't got him to hospital. We told the doctors he'd been run over by a truck. Momo spent two weeks in there being spoiled by the nurses. The jihadists were planning to finish him off in hospital but they didn't get round to it and then they ran out of time. It was round about then that Raymond, who'd been going round calling himself Ibn Abou Mossab, asked his father to help get him out of there. Raymond was in deep shit by then, he already had his plane ticket to Afghanistan and the manual for the training camps in Kabul. He was only seventeen, but on his fake papers they'd added ten years and a big beard. After he got his son out, Monsieur Vincent set up a neighbourhood watch committee and that's when all hell broke loose. They managed to get the mosque in Block 17 closed down for health and safety reasons, but the

jihadists just set up again straight away in the back of a Moroc-
can grocery shop. Com'Dad is in there all the time, he's big
friends with the owner.

In his diary, Rachel says that he came back from Algeria a
different man. He mentions taking me to lunch in some posh,
boring restaurant. I don't remember. He says that was when
he decided not to tell me about the massacre, about our parents, about his trip to Algeria and all the secrets he dragged
back with him, the whole tragedy going on in his head. He
probably thought I was too dumb, too insensitive, that's what
he usually thought about me. Or maybe he was worried the
whole thing would send me further off the rails. He wrote
some nice things about me, the sort of things you say to people who aren't nice because you know they'll never really
understand.

Poor Malrich. Life hasn't been easy on you. I feel like I'm to
blame, I've never really made the effort to get to know you. I'm
not trying to make excuses, I'm not saying it was because of
school, or my exams, or the four years I spent in Nantes, or
working 24/7 for a multinational that only cares about the bottom
line, or even life with Ophélie—though you know better than
anyone how difficult she can be—or the responsibilities society
imposes on everyone. I've used every possible excuse I could
think of to justify my indifference to you, to poor uncle Ali who
opened his home and his heart to us, to his sons whom life
chewed up and spat out before they had a chance to find out
what any of it meant, to our parents whom I put out of my mind
and never gave a second thought. Now I realise that what I
thought was intelligent conversation was just pompous preach-
ing, that even as I claimed I was doing things for your own good
I was putting you down. The worst thing is, I know you don't hate
me for it. You think I'm a good person, you defend me with the

same excuses I used to use: he's the serious type, he's studying for his finals, he's looking for a job, he's travelling for work,
Ophélie is giving him grief, he's part of a world with its own rules.
What's done is done and there's no way now to make amends.
If I were brave enough, I would go and tell you that I love you,
that I'm proud of you. After we left the restaurant, I felt so
ashamed, for saying nothing, for being a coward. I'm not looking
for another excuse, but I was honestly trying to spare you the
pain. Our parents died in terrible circumstances and what I know
now, this thing that's eating away inside me, would have hurt
you, in time it would have destroyed you. I decided the best
thing was to keep you at arm's length. Some day, you'll read this
diary and you'll understand and I know that you'll forgive me.
Time will have done its work.

Things with Ophélie got worse. Rachel wasn't the same any
more, he spent all his time brooding, he was reading way too
much and travelling all the time, running around all over the
place, and every time he came back he was worse. Ophélie has
always been controlling. Her life has to be perfect—she can't
stand anything getting in the way of her happiness, anything
that throws sand in her perfect routine, anything that sends
clouds over her perfect little garden. She got her idea of life
from playing with Barbie. And she's always been a bit of a
snob. Poor Rachel, she nagged him and pestered him, she'd
pick fights, make snide comments, throw tantrums, she'd sulk
and slam doors, and she'd leave him, regular as clockwork. She
always was high-strung. She'd usually go round and stay at her
mother's and it would take a UN peacekeeping force to get her
back. Love is stupid and dangerous. Ophélie's mother completely spoiled her, she never really had a chance to grow up,
become a woman, accept the fact that problems and worries
and trouble are just part of life. But I do feel kind of sorry for
her, Rachel never talked to her, just like he never talked to me,

he kept everything bottled up. Nobody likes being treated like they don't exist. Especially not Ophélie. When I think that he never told me about our parents being murdered, I could kill him. I would have given anything to go to Aïn Deb with him, visit their graves. We might finally have gotten to know each other.

So, anyway, that's the first part of our diary. Rachel came back from Algeria completely changed. He was physically different. I didn't see much of him back then, he was always travelling and, anyway, I had my own shit to deal with—I'd been hauled up before the courts again and this time it was serious—but even *I* noticed he'd changed. I saw him a couple of times at the supermarket, trailing around behind Ophélie, who was as excited as a bee who could smell flowers a wing-flick away. I always make a quick getaway. I hate talking to people in supermarkets. Just watching them pushing their shopping trolleys around like rats in some air-conditioned maze, talking about property prices and home improvement, makes me want to throw up. My attitude to supermarkets is to get in and out as fast as possible—I take what I want and use the emergency exit checkout. Supermarkets are so fucking hideous, I think it's completely reasonable to steal from them. I remember laughing to myself and thinking, God, Rachel's looking old, that multinational of his is obviously getting its money's worth. This was the beginning of the end. The reason for the change was in the little battered suitcase Rachel brought back from Aïn Deb, the suitcase that contained all papa's files. His past. The rest of it, Rachel found out from books and from his trips to Germany, Poland, Austria, Turkey, Egypt and all over France.

I've tried to think what must have been going through his mind when he first opened the suitcase in our old house in that *douar* in the middle of nowhere. The way I imagine it, it's dark, sleep has abandoned him somewhere along the way so he gets up, makes a cup of tea and sits drinking it, thinking about papa and maman, about what happened on 24 April, or maybe he's thinking about Ophélie waiting for him back at home, and suddenly the business about the names on the Ministry of the Interior's list starts bugging him. He's thought about it before, asked at the embassy. I've thought about it myself. Why do papa and maman appear on the list under different names—the names are real enough—Majdali was my mother's maiden name and Hassan was the name papa took when he converted to Islam. But why list him by his first name rather than his surname? And why does the name Schiller not appear on the list at all? The names on the gravestones were the same, but who decided what to write? Was it some bureaucratic fuckup? A political decision—I know that's what Rachel thought—was the government worried that a foreign name on the list of victims would set off a diplomatic incident? If the European press, the German newspapers in particular, got hold of the story, questions might have been asked of the Algerian government, and their reputation isn't exactly squeaky clean, given that they've been accused of genocide, crimes against humanity, torture, systematic looting and I don't know what else. Anyway, this whole business is bugging him so he gets up and wanders around the house and ends up in our parents' bedroom, he's looking for something though he doesn't know what, then he finds this suitcase on top of the wardrobe or under the bed. An alarm goes off in his head. I heard it myself the first time I picked up the suitcase. Rachel hid it in the tool cabinet in the garage, the one place in the house he knew Ophélie would never look. And I did what he had done two years before.

When you're faced with an box you know is full of secrets, you feel scared. It was easier for Rachel, he wasn't expecting to find anything out of the ordinary in this suitcase. Every family has a shoebox, a folder, a suitcase like this full of papers and photographs, letters, bits of jewelery, charms and talismans. Uncle Ali has one—one of those huge trunks you take when you're emigrating, tied up with ropes and big knots, in it there are hundreds of certificates, all the paperwork from a lifetime spent slaving at temporary jobs, there are a couple of talismans he brought back from the *bled* and a huge collection of gris-gris he bought from the Senegalese griot in Block 14. But from reading Rachel's diary, I already knew what was in this suitcase, what horror was waiting for me. There were papers, photos, letters, newspaper cuttings, a magazine. Yellowed, tattered, stained. There was a stainless steel watch from the last century which had stopped at 6:22. Three medals. Rachel had looked them up, the first one had the symbol of the *Hitlerjugends*, the Hitler Youth, the second was a medal from the Wehrmacht for bravery in combat, the third had the insignia of the Waffen SS. There's a piece of tissue paper with a skull and crossbones, the *Totenkopf*, the emblem of the SS. The photos were taken in Europe, Germany probably, papa is wearing his uniform, there are photos of him on his own and some group shots. In some of the photographs he's very young and he and his mates are built like athletes, proud of their uniforms, happy to be alive. In others, he's older-looking, very serious, wearing a black SS uniform. He's leaning against a tank or posing in a huge court-yard, or sitting on the steps of some house. In one of the photos he's wearing civilian clothes, he looks handsome and elegant, all dressed in white with a big moustache, it was taken somewhere in Egypt, he's posing beside the great pyramid, smiling at a couple of elderly English ladies who are smiling back. There are more recent photos of him from when he was in the *maquis* in Algeria, wearing fatigues and a safari hat. He's put on a bit of weight and he's really tanned, which suits him. In one of them, he's standing in a forest with two young guer-rillas who are sitting on the ground, there are guns spread out on a blanket. He's doing weapons training. There's an Algerian flag on a makeshift flagpole. In another photo, he's standing next to some tall, bony guy with a haunted look wearing battle dress, smiling like his teeth hurt. Rachel figured out who the other guy was, he calls him Boumédienne, he was the leader of the *maquis*. There are newspaper clippings in English, French, Italian. The French article is from some magazine called *Historia*. I read it. It was about the Nuremberg Trials of the Nazi leaders: Bormann, Göring, von Ribbentrop, Dönitz, Hess, von Schirach, and that lot. It talks about the ones they captured later—Adolf Eichmann, Franz Stangl, Gustav Wagner, Klaus Barbie . . . It goes on about the ones who are scattered across the world to countries in South America, the Arab world, in Africa. It mentions Brazil, Argentina, Columbia, Bolivia, Paraguay, Egypt, Turkey, Syria, Nigeria, Ethiopia, Rhodesia and a couple of others. There are lots of letters in German, one in French, signed Jean 92, dated 11 November 1962. You need to know code to work out what it says, because it sounds like a letter from a burglar to a fence. It reads like it's nothing important—this Jean 92 mentions a number of valuable items recently recovered, some other items that have been traced and are likely to be recovered soon, then says that no one knows where the rest of the loot is hidden, so it must be in a safe place. He mentions a high-powered investigator called SW, some group known by the initials BJ and another one he calls N which seems to be linked to an incredibly dangerous organisation he calls M. He mentions some woman called Odessa who's looking after the objects and having them transferred to a safe place. Rachel worked it all out, he did a lot of research. The mysterious Jean 92 signs off: *HH, your star of better days*. I think this is the letter that sent Rachel racing around Europe, and from there to Egypt. He talks about it a lot in his diary. But he doesn't explain everything, or maybe you need to know other stuff, stuff I don't know yet, before you can understand.

*

There are two Algerian documents. The first one, dated 17 June 1957 and signed by Colonel Boumédienne, Chief of Staff of the *Armée des frontières*, reads:

> This is to attest that Si Mourad has been appointed to the training corps of the EMG as an advisor on logistics and weaponry.

> CC: BE, SBLA, head of the CFEMG, heads of the technical and operational units of Wilayah 8 (communications, transport, engineering . . .).

The second, dated 8 January 1963, is signed by the General Secretary of the Officer Training Academy in Cherchell:

> 1) This is to confirm the appointment of the aforementioned Mourad Hans, a temporary civil instructor.

> 2) The chief of service of personnel shall be responsible for implementing this decision.

> CC: personnel department of the Ministry of Defense.
> For information only: Office of Military Security, district of Algiers.

There is a battered little booklet: papa's military record. The writing on the front is in this really impressive German gothic type. The first page lists his personal details: Hans Schiller, born 5 June 1918 in Uelzen, son of Erich Schiller and Magda Taunbach. Address: 12B Millenstraße, Landorf, Uelzen. Education: Chemical engineering, Johann Wolfgang G o e t h e -Universität, Frankfurt am Main. His regimental number is stamped in a little box, and at the bottom of the page is the signature and the stamp of the recruiting officer: *Obersturmbannführer* Martin Alfons Kratz. The rest is a complicated list of the postings, transfers, ranks, promotions, citations, medals and injuries he received during his career. The pages are peppered with stamps. Papa reached the rank of Captain, he was a big shot. And he was a hero too. He was wounded a bunch of times and he was mentioned in dispatches and decorated over and over! He was posted to Germany, Austria, France, Poland and other places which would have meant nothing to me without Rachel's notes: Frankfurt, Linz, Grossrosen, Salzburg, Dachau, Mauthausen, Rocroi, Drancy, Auschwitz, Buchenwald, Ghent, Hartheim, Lublin-Majdanek. Some of the places were extermination camps. These were top-secret places where the Nazis exterminated the Jews and other undesirables. Rachel says hundreds of people died and the article in *Historia* says millions. Fucking hell, I thought.

I had already read Rachel's diary over and over and I had found out a lot of stuff, but holding papa's medals, his military records in my own hands, seeing the names, the documents, the stamps on them with my own eyes really fucked me up. I felt sick. This meant papa was a Nazi war criminal, he would have been hanged if they'd ever caught up with him, but at the same time it didn't mean anything. I refused to believe it, I clung to something else, something truer, fairer, he was our father, we are his sons, we bear his name. He was a good man, devoted to his village, loved and respected by everyone, he fought for the independence of his country, for the liberation of a people. He was a soldier, I thought, he was just obeying orders, orders he probably didn't understand, orders he didn't agree with. The leaders were the guilty ones, they knew how to manipulate people, get them to do things without understanding what they were doing, without thinking. Besides, I thought, why stir up all this shit now? Papa dead, his throat cut like a sheep at Aïd, murdered along with maman and all their neighbours by *real* criminals, by the most brutal bastards the earth has ever produced, criminals who are supported, cheered on, even helped by people, in Algeria and all over the world. These criminals speak at the UN, they have ads on TV, they insult whoever they like, whenever they like, like the imam in the mosque in Block 17, always jabbing his finger to heaven trying to scare people, to stop them thinking for themselves. I can understand Rachel's pain, his whole world falling apart, I can understand why he felt guilty, tainted, why he felt that somehow, somewhere, someone had to atone. Rachel was the one to atone, though he had never hurt anyone in his life.

I know it sounds incredible, but I didn't know anything about the war, the extermination. I'd heard bits and pieces, things the imam said about the Jews and other stuff I'd picked up here and there. I always thought it was like a legend, something that happened hundreds of years ago. But the honest truth is I didn't think about it much, I didn't care, me and my mates, we were young, we were broke, all we cared about were our own lives. Rachel wrote terrible things. Everything was boiling over in his mind—words and phrases I'd never heard before cropped up again and again: *the final solution*, *gas chambers*, *Kremas*, *Sonderkommandos*, *concentration camps*, the Shoah, the Holocaust. There was a phrase in German, I didn't know what it meant and Rachel didn't translate it but it sounded like a curse: *Vernichtung Lebensunwerten Lebens*. And another one that I recognised straight off: *Befehl ist Befehl*. That means "orders are orders." When we were little, living back in the *bled*, papa used to say it under his breath sometimes if we argued back. Then, in French, or in Berber, he'd say, "We're not at the circus!" It's like what Monsieur Vincent used to say when we tried to get round him: "Just do what I told you to do, if there's time later, we'll talk about your ideas."

I guess after he read all this stuff, Rachel sat up all night. Reading what he wrote about it did my head in. Rachel was clever, he could always see the big picture, he understood things. I'm not like that, I need explanations, I need time to get things straight in my head. If I'd been Rachel, the stuff in the suitcase would have meant nothing to me, all I would have thought was: my parents have been murdered and I'll never see them again. I'd have thought: papa was a soldier back in Germany, then he came here to train the *maquis*, end of story. The only thing that seemed weird to me was that with all the experience he had, papa ended up in a godforsaken hole like Aïn Deb. I'd have been off to California, I'd have been a stuntman in Hollywood or a bodyguard to some rich heiress. But that was papa, he was a bit of a poet, a bit like those weirdos who get up one morning, sell their big city apartments and head off to the mountains to raise sheep that wolves will end up eating before they do. Papa went a lot farther, he went to Aïn Deb. It was the perfect place, really—even Algerians have never heard of it. Or at least they hadn't until 25 April 1994.

I'm going to finish with something Rachel wrote, I think about it all the time: "Here I am, faced with a question as old as time: are we answerable for the crimes of our fathers, of our brothers, of our children? Our tragedy is that we form a direct line, there is no way out without breaking the chain and vanishing completely." There's one more thing. I've made a resolution: someone needs to put a stop to the imam from Block 17 before it's too late.

Tuesday, 22 September 1994

Face pressed to the window, I stare out at the carpet of clouds. Everything is white, the clouds and the sky, motionless, flickering fit to blow a fuse. I close my eyes. My thoughts are waiting for me, dark and murky, ready to drag me under. I feel exhausted. I open my eyes and look around. The plane drones gently, it is packed with passengers glowing with health, the light is mild, the temperature milder still. The passengers bury themselves in their newspapers, whisper to each other or doze. They are Germans, for the most part. This is their regular commute. When I was checking in at Roissy, I noticed most of them didn't have any luggage, just a roll-on Samsonite, a briefcase, a couple of magazines tucked under their arm. This is routine to them, they could do the trip blindfolded. They're freshly scrubbed, well-groomed, long-suffering as Buddhist monks. They're tired, but they never let it show. It's a matter of habit and considerable self-discipline. There is something terrifying about the deathly daily commute that passes for life in Paris. Somehow on a plane it's even more depressing. Airports are the anthills of the third millennium, high-surveillance hubs with their business hotels like glass prisons, the hidden loudspeakers spouting counter-fatwas born in the bellies of all-powerful computers. When they arrive, there are the buses, the metros, the trains, the lines of taxis waiting to shuttle them onwards until at last everyone disappears into their hermetically sealed homes. Anonymity is daunting, definitive, spanning the planet and the movements of capital. These people arrive in Paris every morning, attend their business affairs, then take a plane back the same night or the next day, and by the time they land there another flight is waiting for them. They come and go and all they need to pack is a toothbrush. I'm just like this when I travel on business—a robot, all I need is an oil change and a socket to plug in my electric razor. I arrive, do what I have to, go back to the hotel, pick up my things and head back to the airport. Now and then we let our hair down. With the Italians, the Spaniards and the Greeks, it happens all the time, it doesn't matter whether business goes well or badly. Mediterraneans like to party, we can be crude, rude, tell each other anything—that's how we relax. The Germans, the Austrians, the Swiss and the English are different, work is their religion and their hobby. We might take time off for a coffee break occasionally, talk about the weather. The most thrilling places to me are the former dictatorships still riddled with red tape, violence and corruption. I love the film-noir feel of these places, they still cling to the best of socialism, the conspiracy, the cloak and dagger politics, but have adopted the choicest parts of capitalism, its killer instinct. All these hopeless people who shuffle along, and the others who are constantly chasing some insistent rumour that will not let them rest until they're dead. The murkiness, the mystery, the frenzy, the misery. And the joy when—by the purest fluke—you stumble on some nameless civil servant, some nondescript hanger-on who, with a magician's flourish, makes one phone call and breaks the impasse in a public finance contract someone has just sworn would never be resolved. That's when parties start, the endless round of formal ceremonies, not to commemorate a successful conclusion to an honest negotiation or the miraculous release of a bank transfer—that would be tasteless—no, to celebrate the friendship between our two great countries, the *entente cordial* between their great leaders. By the time you get home, you have lots of stories to tell your friends, and you can exaggerate as much as you like without the fear of overdoing it: a spy here, a

hit man there, an assassination attempt in a hotel lobby, the minister who strangles his secretary in the middle of negotiations for
leaving out a zero in a memo, the minister who pisses on lobby-
ists who are not from the same tribe as he is, the leader who
gasses a rebel village then flies around in his Sunday best apol-
ogizing and proclaiming a new world order. You hear a lot more
than you ever see. In these countries of constant mourning,
rumor and gossip are the lifeblood of every day, every minute.
I've never quite understood how our bosses manage to make
any money out of these power-mad lunatics desperate to keep
every penny to themselves, but then again, we sell pumping systems, something people can't live without, and even if we're
motivated purely by greed, it will never be as big as their
appetite. We've got pumps in all colours, to suit all tastes, horizontal and vertical, manual and remote, tiny pumps the size of a
marble and vast installations you'd need to build a hangar to
hide. We're the market leader, we have something to tempt even
the most difficult customers.

I miss Ophélie, even if she is the most difficult woman in the
world. I want so much to be home, to go back to our boring sub-
urban routine, anything for a quiet life. But she's probably lying
on the sofa over at her mother's place right now, crying and ranting about me and about men in general, but especially Algerian
and German men since we're born stupid and cruel. I know how
eloquent she can be on the subject, though not as eloquent as
my mother-in-law. By now, the two of them will have flayed our
relationship to the bone. God himself could not save us now.
Ophélie and I don't talk anymore, she sits in her corner sulking
and I sit in mine thinking. We're past the stage where some
grand gesture could bring us back together more passionate
than ever; and although we have both stopped digging, coldly,
inexorably, the hole we are in just keeps getting bigger. The war
is almost at an end, the silence of this phony ceasefire simply

heralds the breakup. It's probably for the best. I'll never be a normal man, a dutiful husband again. I've left her the bedroom and the living room, now I sleep in a corner of the mezzanine and I spend my evenings in the garage. I've set up our camping stuff and a bookcase out there. Everything is in that bookcase, all thirty volumes of it, the extermination of the world and the glacial silence that followed. I don't know why I haven't told Ophélie about this. Shame, maybe, the fact that I don't understand it myself, fear of the consequences. There is a difference between saying to yourself, "I am the son of a war criminal," and hearing someone else say, "You're the son of a war criminal, a man guilty of genocide!" Besides, we'll only end up talking about me, about us, about our insignificant domestic problems, and I don't want to talk about what we need to do to "sort things out" when in my head I'm trying to sort out something that is beyond me, beyond us, something that will always be beyond us. Ophélie has always been pretty good at substituting one problem for another, with no regard for the nature or gravity of the original problem. She flits from subject to subject like a butterfly and, in the end, everything always comes back to her. But right now I'm trying to come to terms with the Holocaust, something that would try the patience of God himself, and behind it all is the figure of my father.

While I was thinking about my work and my personal problems, the plane had landed and was now taxiing along the runway towards the terminal of Hamburg airport. I've been through this airport so often that I hardly notice it. It's just another glass and steel box with flickering fluorescent lights. In the crowd, no one notices me, I'm just another passenger, just another German. If they do notice me it's only because, like all Frenchmen abroad, I draw attention to myself. That's how we are, we complain whenever things don't go our way in foreign countries. Today, however, I felt tense, I felt scared, I shuffled forward in a daze. People jostled me, gave me strange looks, talked behind my back in German, in English, in Japanese, some of them frankly sneering, which should give you some idea of the state I was in. Until now, I've only ever travelled for work—where everything is pre-planned, every minute timetabled, I am met at every airport—or with Ophélie, who anticipates every problem before it happens. I am lost, searching for myself, I am travelling back through time, peering through shadows, exploring the greatest atrocity the world has ever known and trying to work out why I am carrying the weight of it on my shoulders. In fact, it is because I already know that what I am doing is so painful. It would be impossible for me to grasp the enormity of this tragedy and emerge unscathed. I am terribly afraid I will come face-to-face with my father in some place where no man can stand and still be a man. My very humanity is at stake.

Hamburg, it has to be said, is in rude health. A very Teutonic health. Behind the beautiful façades there is something substantial, there are pleasing depths. Compared to Germany, our beloved *Frankreich* looks like a badly run campsite. In France, we see healthiness as a sin, with all its connotation of money, monopolies, class struggle, and the exasperating exuberance of nouveau riche nonentities. If we spend so much time and money on our bodies it's probably to purge our bourgeois sins. We have become overweight, chubby-faced, bright-eyed dyed-in-the-wool revolutionaries. With my haunted look, my deathly pallor, my face unshaven, I looked obviously French, something that clashed with my glaringly robust Nordic physique. I tried to make up for it, but I couldn't: I'd forgotten how to be exhausted and hide it, how to get annoyed without losing my temper, how to be completely lost but walk as though I knew exactly where I was going. I rented a car and set out. All I wanted was to be alone. More alone than anyone in the world.

Deepest darkest Germany is really dark and deep, much more so than France, which is open to the four winds, bounded by the seas and the mountains, its last hidden beauty spots ruthlessly exploited by tour operators and estate agents. Tourism is a tragedy for any country. The hidden depths of a country need to stay silent and hidden; if not, they're just cardboard sets for open-air theatre. In the hidden depths of Germany, which are vast and deep and Lutheran to boot, there is a mesmerizing stillness, a dread that harks back to earliest times where everything was in the mystery of stones and the contemplation of souls. What we see here seems set down for all eternity, and for those of us afraid to face tomorrow, that is the worst thing we can imagine. I drove through still suburbs, past still villages, still meadows, saw people standing motionless in their doorways, in their fields, hunched over motionless machines. I saw solemn black-frocked crows perched high in hieratic trees and, in the distance, through the mist, empty roads disappearing into the beyond. Movement is confined to the *autobahn* but the *autobahn* is obviously not a part of the country, it is a late addition, a concession to the foreigner and, above all, a means of keeping him at arm's length. I had come to look deep into the eyes of Germany and already everything seemed infinitely remote, irrevocably secret.

Then, suddenly, I happened on people—people moving, talking, laughing loudly, eating heartily, walking briskly, scolding their sulky children or lecturing them in voices that were not bullying, but simply unequivocal. The German language lends itself to certainty and quickly oversteps the mark: "*Befehl ist Befehl.*" The scene seemed so alive, so familiar, so ordinary, so colourful, so utterly in keeping with the country I have visited so often. But hardly had I left the petrol station, the restaurants, the shops, when stillness and silence closed round me again. I felt obscurely angry that, for a while—the time it took me to eat lunch—these Krauts had made me believe everything was normal, mundane, predictable, when even they, with their bulbous beer-drinker's noses, did not believe it. They sat at their tables, staring, wondering what this pretentious, pathetic *Franzose* was doing so far from home just as I was wondering how they could seem so cheery in this landscape heavy with significance. And then I realised: I carried the mystery inside me, my point of view was defined by my investigation, I was an investigation, *the* investigation. I was looking at this country through the eyes of a wounded man whose very existence was threatened by the history of their country. It was hardly surprising I seemed strange to them.

Hamburg, Harburg, Lüneberg, Soltau, Uelzen. Four short hops for an honest traveller but a yawning chasm for a broken, half-dead man, a man travelling back through time in search of his own humanity. Every mile was grueling, my breathing felt laboured. As I arrived in Uelzen, the town where papa was born, my heart was pounding in my chest. Since leaving Hamburg, I had been steeling myself for the shock, but when I arrived I realised once again that in life, the more you prepare yourself, the less prepared you really are. You conjure so many mental images that reality comes as a complete shock. When torn from our everyday routine, we're like blind men deprived of our white sticks. Uelzen looks just like every other town in Germany, in Europe. A feeling of déjà vu follows me like my own shadow, whispering in my ear. Uniformity is the future—something business travellers like me have long known—it had been stupid to imagine things would be different, but I felt cheated that this town was so unlike what grief and distress had led me to expect. I'd been expecting a village out of the 1930s, all misery and rage, crushed under the weight of unemployment, tormented by primitive demons, hordes of officious, swastika-wearing party workers teeming through the streets, the Devil himself writhing at the heart of humanity. In reality, Uelzen is pristine, charming, welcoming, with every amenity a tourist could wish for, the people are warm, hospitable, the embodiment of cheerful artisans happy with their lot. The town that papa was born in is gone, swept away by the war, buried beneath the reconstruction. Everything I see speaks of the new world, a world of brilliance and soaring heights, a miracle of urban planning which has slowly grown to encompass new buildings and the great ideas of generations of town planners. Its suburbs are like any other suburbs, the pedestrianised town centre is like any other, but the beating heart of Uelzen is the financial district with its suited businessmen and hollow-eyed security guards. I was everywhere and nowhere, everything looks like everything else, the tsunami of globalization has swept away our heritage, erased individual traits such that we no longer recognise our own or those of others. Uelzen is a product of post-war urbanization. Millenstraße no longer exists and Landorf—which I had expected to be a patch of countryside in the town, or a scrap of town set in countryside—looks just like the Paris suburb I live in, though half the size and ten times as sturdy. We all live on the same quiet streets, with the same neatly trimmed hedges, in tidy little houses so similar we can barely tell ourselves from our neighbours. There is a vast Plexiglas shopping centre painted in bright colours to reassure the poor, the working classes, that they are on the right track, that wealth and happiness are waiting round the corner just as soon as the mortgage is paid off. How did Landorf look when papa pounded these streets? Was it all misery and rage or was it an idyll of bucolic tedium? I wandered the streets, sniffing the air in the hope that instinct might speak to me; I talked to strangers in the streets, the bars, especially to old people, who carried their memories around like libraries. Nothing. "Millenstraße? Never heard of it." The name Schiller rang no bells either, except for those few who immediately thought of Friedrich Schiller. The Germans are an obliging race, too obliging, they feel frustrated and humiliated when they are unable to help. But they don't give up easily: they direct the lost soul to someone who might know. "Try the post office," they said, "they'll know where it is," or "Let's ask the woman who runs the delicatessen, she knows everything." Checkmate: at the post office, the woman asked me to submit my request in writing; at the deli, the woman suggested I might ask at the police station. This was something I had no intention of doing, talking to the authorities, since I would have to answer their questions and I simply did not have the strength. You wouldn't risk it in France, life's too short for regrets. I was looking for my father and no one could help me. I was a lost child.

It was pointless traipsing around here. Racing around all Germany. The terrible history I was looking for had been erased, forgotten, swept under the carpet. I was just about to turn back. I had come completely unprepared, I had nothing to guide me but grief and a battered military record. But I hadn't reckoned on fate, which suddenly intervened. Taking the sandwich I bought at the delicatessen—my way of thanking the owner—I went and sat in a small park for the mothers and children of Landorf. It was empty. I was grateful. I needed to be alone. I already felt more alone than anyone else in the world. Then an old man in cap and slippers, unshaven, came over—the poor creature was just looking for some company. Old men are the same the world over, always looking for someone to talk to, always quick to spot a straggler. "*Guten appetit!*" He had his opening gambit prepared. "*Danke*," I said in the same cheery tone, hoping he might leave me in peace. He sat down next to me and rolled a cigarette, slow as a wet weekend. By the time I finished my sandwich and he stubbed out his cigarette, we knew all there was to know about each other—by which I mean nothing. We looked like tramps sharing a park bench. We talked about the weather, about life, about the Franco-German alliance. His position was straightforward: he had never believed any of that rubbish. To him the French franc was just monopoly money, but he worried about the mighty Deutschmark, the bedrock of German power, and bitterly resented the rise of the European Union which was slowly but surely chipping away at it. "The only ones who make money out of it are conmen and feckless idlers," he concluded. I was well used to this kind of right-wing diatribe, Ophélie's mother comes out with this stuff all the time. "Not to mention all the illegal immigrants!" I egged him on. When I casually mentioned I was part German, part French and part Algerian, his mouth dropped open. What can you say to a chameleon without riling him? You talk about this and that, you chat as though you have all the time in the world. He'd been retired for years, he told me, his beloved Hilda had died in her sleep at seventy and his one dream was to see the Château de Versailles again before he died. I told him I had been in Hamburg on business and had come down because I'd always dreamed of seeing Uelzen, especially the beautiful suburb of Landorf where my father, Hans Schiller, had been born seventy-six years ago. Papa's name clearly rang a bell. The old man's face lit up. "Did you say Hans Schiller?" I believe that this man was sent by heaven just as surely as I believe that two plus two equals four. He had known papa, and papa's family and his old friends. Best of all, his memory was perfect, accurate, encyclopedic. I could not let him get away. I took him to a café for some hot chocolate and bombarded him with questions. Actually, he asked most of the questions, I played it safe, I wasn't about to wade in and start talking about papa's past, I wanted to find out who this man was—was he a former Nazi, a victim of the Nazis or just some poor devil who had come through it all without knowing anything? I wanted to know what his politics were. I played the dutiful grandson listening wide-eyed to his grandfather's stories. I let things roll. Nudging him gently, I managed to get him to reminisce, persuaded him to trust me. I painted him an idyllic picture of the Schiller family, the perfect blend of Germany, Algeria and France—three countries with a long history of mutual friendship and mutual slaughter—three countries which had produced my father, my mother, my wife and all the principles I held dear. I made it sound as poetic, as exotic, as I could. A quick brush-stroke transformed my Paris suburb into a haven of tranquility, another transformed Aïn Deb into a glorious oasis where old men basked like lizards in the sun, listening to the song of the wind, watching the dance of the dragonflies. This was how I had imagined Aïn Deb before the massacre of 24 April 1994. "Hans Schiller's son!" Over and over the old man clapped me on the back. "It's a miracle . . . "

"The real miracle is meeting one of papa's friends on a park bench . . . Who would believe it?"

After this, and after another hot chocolate, we picked up the thread of our conversation.

"Good old Hans! What did he die of?"

"Oh . . . you know, he was old . . . he hadn't been very well, but his death was very sudden."

"*Ach, das tut mir leid . . .* he should have stayed here in Germany. The fresh air here is like a fountain of youth. What was he doing over in Africa? Where did you say he lived?"

"Algeria. He was a weapons instructor, he trained soldiers . . ."

"*Ach* . . . that is not good . . . these countries, they do not need armies, it sucks the blood from them. There is war in Algeria, *nicht war*?"

"Yes, a brutal war, but it is fought in the name of *Allahu Akbar* and His Holiness the Raïs, so that justifies the exterminations and the rest of it. Tell me what Landorf used to be like, tell me about you and my father and his friends."

"Back when?"

"During the war . . . "

"*Ach* . . . that's all so long ago. They're all gone now, I am the last and . . . well, you can see for yourself, we don't really lead an exciting life."

Silence. His face clouded over. Selective amnesia. It

seemed clear to me that he and his friends went the same way as papa. Or maybe the opposite. Boys are like that, they follow each other blindly, hopping on the first bandwagon without looking to see where it's headed. The estate Malrich and I grew up on is just the same, it's like a station where all the trains read *Destination: Paradise* and they go straight to hell. You have to dodge the fare to get off.

"You were saying . . . ?"

"Hans was a good boy, he was loyal, he did his duty, we all did . . . that's all there is to it."

"Papa used to talk to us a lot abut his duty, he'd tell us stories about his time in the *Hitlerjugends*, the pranks he and his friends used to play, the parties and the torchlight processions. He talked about his time in the *Wehrmacht*, too, about the war . . . all of it. In fact, when I was a boy, back in Aïn Deb, I was in the youth wing of the FLN, the *FLNjugends*, and I was a real activist. I miss it sometimes, we were obsessed with it, we were always arguing about this and that, we drilled morning, noon and night, we were passionate about purging the ranks and we celebrated our victories howling with the wolves . . . "

"The wolves?"

"Figure of speech."

"What is this FLN?"

"The National Liberation Front, the National Socialist party of the great leader . . . you haven't heard of it? Anyway, we were talking about you, about the Reich."

"There's nothing to tell, *Jugend*, it's ancient history. When the war came, we all went our separate ways, we all did our duty, that's all there is to say."

"That's it?"

"I didn't see your father after that. The last time I saw him was in Paris . . . June 1941. We took some leave so we could spend time with our old friends, then we all went back to our units. When I came back here after the war, Uelzen was nothing but rubble. My family and your family and many other families had died in the bombings . . . "

"Just like Aïn Deb, the village I come from. And the war in Algeria is only just starting."

"Hans is buried there?"

"Yes, with my mother and all our neighbours."

Silence. A nod. The man was lost in memories of the past, now was the moment to strike.

"After the Wehrmacht, papa joined the SS, he was posted to Dachau, Buchenwald, Auschwitz . . . Did you know about that?"

The old man looked at me for a long time, then shrugged in what might have been a yes or a no. I whispered, "Were you one of them?"

Silence.

"Was that part of your duty?"

Silence.

"Please."

Silence. A shrug of exasperation.

I don't know why I did it, but I took papa's military record out of my pocket and gave it to him. He didn't know what to make of the gesture. He hesitated for a moment, then took it, turning it over and over in his hands, then he set it down on his lap, put on his glasses and leafed through it infinitely slowly. His hands were shaking, his lips quivering. I knew it had been a mistake, I knew that he wouldn't say any more now.

I said again, "Please."

Silence.

"You were talking about duty . . . "

"Duty . . . duty is something that must be done, there's nothing else."

"Whatever the circumstances?"

He got up from the table, muttering to himself.

"It's time I was going home."

He looked out at the blue sky, out towards Germania as

though looking for some answer, then he looked me in the eye again and said, "Your father was a soldier, that's all there is to say. Never forget that, *Jugend*."

And he left, shuffling away like an old man scared of his own shadow. I pitied him, picturing him going home, climbing into his lonely bed and dying of a sudden fever in the night. What had he meant when he invoked duty as the sole justification for the workings of the world? Was he talking about papa? About himself? Was he talking about me? The word "duty" can be made to hide a multitude of sins, whole peoples can be dragged into it and hurled into the abyss. That's all there is to it.

I went down to the toilets and took a leak and washed my hands slowly. "You were right," I said to my reflection in the mirror, "What you've been thinking since Aïn Deb, papa was just obeying orders, he was doing his duty." To the bitter end. "*Meine Ehre heißt Treue*"—"My Honour is called Loyalty." I felt like throwing up.

Shemà

You who live secure
In your warm houses
Who return at evening to find
Hot food and friendly faces:

    Consider whether this is a man,
    Who labours in the mud
    Who knows no peace
    Who fights for a crust of bread
    Who dies at a yes or a no.
    Consider whether this is a woman,
    Without hair or name
    With no more strength to remember
    Eyes empty and womb cold
    As a frog in winter.

Consider that this has been:
I commend these words to you.
Engrave them on your hearts
When you are in your house, when you walk on your way,
When you go to bed, when you rise.
Repeat them to your children.
Or may your house crumble,
Disease render you powerless,
Your offspring avert their faces from you.

                         Primo Levi

To this poem, Rachel had added the verse:

Your offspring do not know;
They live, they play, they love.
And when what was appears to them;
The tragedies bequeathed by their parents;
They are faced with strange questions,
Glacial silences,
Nameless shadows.
My house has crumbled, grief has made me powerless;
And I do not know why.
My father never told me.

WEDNESDAY, 9 OCTOBER 1996

M omo and Raymond swung by the house and told me some horror story, the fuckers were talking like it was something they saw on TV. I nearly didn't listen when, actually, it was a real tragedy. And I know all about tragedy, I'm up to my neck in it in Rachel's diary. "And you only come and tell me now," I yelled. "The moped was fucked," Momo said, the liar. It was about Nadia, a sixteen-year-old Arab girl, worked as a trainee at Christelle's salon by the RER station, The Golden Scissors. She'd disappeared. I'm sure I probably knew her, but all those girls look exactly the same, same hair and everything, I can never put a face to a name. They should be forced to wear something so you can tell them apart; because you never know, I mean this is the proof. "Who's Nadia?" I said. "Just some girl," Momo says, the fuck-wit. "She lives in Block 22," Raymond says. "Her old man's Moussa, works in the steelworks, you know the guy who drives the green Ami 6." The men all look the same to me too, Moussa, Abdallah, Arezki, Abdel-Ben-some-shit. Anyway, you never hardly see them, all they do is work and sleep, they're up at the crack of dawn and working half the night—except Sundays, the Lord's day, when they all hang out in lame cafés, eaten up by nostalgia and gambling on scratch tickets or the horses. Even when you do see them, they're just crooked shadows appearing and disappearing into the darkness. Anyway, the whole estate was mobilised to look for Nadia—parents, kids, police, fire brigade—everyone running around. The women

were out on the balconies wailing and praying and yelling at
their husbands. At first everyone said she'd run away, then they
were saying she'd been kidnapped, since yesterday they're saying she was murdered. A bunch of TV crews showed up and
set up their cameras in the skankiest part of the estate—the
sort of no-go area even people on the estate never set foot in.
Someone said they'd seen some girl getting beat up by some
guy with a beard, a young guy from Block 11, some big shot
always banging on about how he's been to Kabul and London
and Algiers, calls himself Allah's Terminator. Apparently he
didn't like the way she dressed, didn't like her day-glo hair or
the fact she hung out with boys—and not just any boys—*kaffirs*—unbelievers. So he slapped her about, spat in her face,
pulled her hair and yelled, "Last warning!" It all went down in
the stairwell of Block 22, some kid coming downstairs saw it
and he told his mates, they told their mates and so on until it
got back to Moussa. Moussa didn't stop to think, grabbed a
knife and headed out looking for the guy with the beard. The
neighbours grabbed him as he was leaving the block, took
away the knife and marched him off to see Com'Dad. The two
of them had a little chat round the back of the supermarket—
no witnesses. The guy with the beard was busted and twenty-
four hours later he was out again. No corpse, no crime; no
crime, no perp. The Terminator's lawyer—some guy with a
beard and a three-piece suit—knew how to play the system, he
got to faxing and phoning every association, every Islamic consulate, every brotherhood, every *marabout* and every sleeper
network—even woke up the Minister for the Interior. The sky
was black with fax toner and thundering with righteous anger.
Com'Dad was purple with rage when he got a call politely suggesting he release the killer and reopen the mosque in Block
17. Don't rock the boat—the whole city is happy to think she's
run away. The Terminator was giving it large about how he'd
got his ticket to paradise—*djina*, they call it in Arabic—put

one over on the cops and heroically confirmed his status as Emir of the estate. Then, this morning—shock, horror—they find poor Nadia in the basement of some shop that's been boarded up for years, all naked and tied up with barbed wire, her face and body burnt to shit with a blowtorch. The parents identified her straight off. It was their little girl, they just knew it. They put the cuffs on the Emir as he was coming out of the mosque. Apparently he was spitting fire at Com'Dad: "Allahu Akbar, your day will come." The Imam immediately announces there's going to be a big service on the esplanade between the tower blocks to honour the hero, support his worthy parents and raise money for the cause. It's going to be on Friday at 8:30 P.M. And he issued a fatwa saying anyone who doesn't show is a sinner and Allah will not fail to punish them. To forsake a Brother in Islam when he's attacked by *kaffirs* is among the greatest of sins. The place will be rammed. I'm planning on being there. It's not some spur-of-the-moment decision, I swore to myself I'd cut the throat of that SS fucker who's trying to turn this estate into an extermination camp, and now's the time.

We headed out and did the tour of the estate, rounding up the posse—Cinq-Pouces, Garcon-de-Café (we call him Bidochon) Togo-au-Lait, Manchot, who's only got one arm, and Idir-Quoi, who can barely get a sentence out he stutters so badly—then we all went up to offer our condolences to Moussa's family. There were crowds milling outside Block 22 and all the way up the stairs. We waited our turn. Fuck sake, it was tough . . . You had to feel for Nadia's mother, she just sat there, saying nothing, staring down at her hands clasped in her lap, whimpering like a cat that's been run over, Moussa just stared at us and nodded, and we stared back at them, holding our breath. After that we went over to Christelle's salon, where Nadia worked. The minute she saw us at the window, Chris-

telle flinched and reached for the phone. Since I'm the only
one with blonde hair, I went in on my own and told her why
we were there. She came out and listened to us blethering on
about how sorry we were. We didn't know what to say.
Besides, she was crying so hard she couldn't hear a word anyway. It's weird, offering condolences to people you don't even
know. When we saw her crying, we started crying, we looked
like fucking idiots standing there trembling in the wind. Eventually we stopped crying and headed off to the cafeteria in the
train station and held a meeting in the upstairs room. We had
to do something, we had to show we had balls, we had to save
the estate. The cute couple making out by the window left as
soon as we piled in—there were eight of us and we did look
pretty dodgy. The owner came over with his big backstabbing
smile, brought us our drinks then went back and stood next to
his panic button. Pretty quickly we all got angry. A bunch of
the guys, that gimp Momo was one of them, reckoned there
was nothing we could do, then there was Raymond (we call
him Sting-Ray when he gets riled), who suggested we start a
counter-*jihad*. One extreme to the other, same old, same old. I
said, "We have to cut off the head, and the head, that's the
imam."

Silence. Whispers. *The imam, fuck, that's heavy . . .*

"What the hell is with you guys? They've fucked every single one of us over—they fucked me up, and you Momo, and
you Raymond, going around calling yourself Ibn Abû-some-
shit, all ready to fly off and gun down a bunch of Afghans. And
what about you, Cinq-Pouces, down at that mosque from four
in the morning until midnight bowing and scraping . . . "

"I . . . I . . . I . . . I think we sh . . . sh . . . should t . . . t . . .
talk to our pa . . . parents."

"Idir, if you can't think of anything sensible to say, then
don't say anything. Our parents will say we should talk to the
police, the police will say we should talk to the judge, the judge

will say we should talk to the government, the government will say that it has to be referred back to the mayors and you know what the mayors will say: fuck off!"

"So it all comes down to us?"

"Too right it does, Bidochon . . . and the first thing is, nobody says anything to anyone about what we're planning."

"But what can we do? The jihadists are all over the estate—they're the ones with the money, the lawyers, the connections, they're the ones with friends in high places, all those ambassadors and shit . . . "

"Counter-*jihad*, it's the only way. We give them a taste of their own medicine—set up our own cells, infiltrate the . . . "

"Yeah sure, all eight of us! And this counter-*jihad*, what religion were you planning to fight in the name of?"

"Hey Manchot! Are you with us here or are you dreaming about that missing arm again?"

I'll stop there, I just wanted to give you an idea of the discussion. By the time we finished, we'd come up with three mutually exclusive angles: "We're fucked and whatever we do we're still fucked," (Momo and his lot); "The only way to fight *jihad* is counter-*jihad*" (Raymond and his lot) and "We need to waste the imam" (me and my lot). The last one is what I planned to put into action.

After the meeting, we headed back to my house and picked up a couple of six-packs at the supermarket along the way. The eve of battle was going to be a long night.

Thursday, 10 October

We spent the day just hanging out. The whole estate was in mourning. The men were hanging around outside, propping up the tower blocks. Little groups united in their grief and their passivity. What were they talking about? What were they thinking about? About Nadia? About what might happen to them? They probably weren't thinking about anything. They looked like concentration camp prisoners waiting for time to pass, for something to turn up, waiting for the ground to open up and swallow them, for someone to come tell them to get home now because their favourite soap was starting. They looked so crushed, so sheepish, it disgusted me. The jihadists were down in their mosque making plans, their *Kapos* out patrolling the camp, looking at people like they were worthless prisoners. There was a fleet of cars parked outside Block 17, all brand new, all clean and polished, so they obviously didn't belong to anyone on the estate. We were just about to head off when—surprise, surprise—Com'Dad comes out of the basement with a bunch of people, some guys from the city council, some from local organisations and some people I didn't recognise. That evil fucking imam had his arm round Com'Dad's shoulder, like they were best mates and he was just giving him a few gentle reminders. Fucking fuck. The French authorities in talks with the SS, and in their own bunker too—that takes balls! Because we know what Com'Dad is like, he's new-school police, you make friends with enemies and you all play nice together. Fuck the rest of us, we're dead, France is marching backwards with a truncheon up its arse.

Friday, 11 October

7 A.M. I've never seen anything like it. The whole estate is deserted: the esplanade, the alleys, the balconies, the car parks. Not a soul. Not so much as a shadow. Not even the old African guys in their Turkish slippers who sit out sunning themselves even when it's pissing rain. If you wanted to make a movie about the end of the world, this would be the perfect film set. I never realised the estate was so ugly, so depressingly cold, so

completely fucked up. Before all this happened, it all looked normal, everyone kind of liked the estate, we all came and went, we never noticed anything. Whenever I heard people complaining about the noise and the dirt, I felt like thumping them, it was like they were dissing us.

So there we were, the eight of us, looking like a right bunch of fucktards. We'd come to fight a war and the other side hadn't even shown up. We'd been so sure how things would go down. The jihadists are pros, when they organise something, they're up and out at dawn, straight after the first prayer—*Fajr*, they call it—they've got their *Kapos* running round from shop to shop, from block to block, dragging people away from whatever they're doing and bringing them along in their wake. An hour later, everyone's been rounded up, herded onto the esplanade, packed in like sardines, and after a few cries of *Allahu Akbar* over the speaker system, they've got them all fired up. By the time they turn them loose, there's no stopping them.

8 A.M. Sick of waiting, we headed over to the mosque. It was closed. We were pissed off the jihadists had backed down. Were they the ones running scared now? Did they back down because of the support for Nadia and her parents? They're better informed than the CIA, maybe they figured out people wouldn't stand for it. Honouring a murderer, celebrating his crime and praising Allah in the same breath was going too far—the estate wouldn't stand for it. It was a matter of decency.

But then I realised there was another reason the jihadists hadn't shown: riot police. There were CRS crawling all over the place and we hadn't even noticed. They were waiting in their unmarked SUVs all over the estate. The bastards had screwed up our revenge, this was supposed to be between us and the jihadists and from the silence all over the estate it was clear that we were winning. Now the jihadists could claim they were men of peace and had only called off their demonstration so as not to give thugs and troublemakers and Islamophobes the opportunity to hijack their ceremony to honour the victims. Islamists are expert spin doctors, they could make a crocodile blush.

I was just about to track down the imam and carve a swastika into his forehead when I heard someone calling me: "Malrich! . . . Malrich! . . . C'mere a minute . . . Get over here now!" It was Com'Dad. He was stepping out of an unmarked car. I wandered over, hands in my pockets.

"Come here!" he said, dragging me by the arm, then he had me spread my arms and frisked me to see if I was carrying a knife or a rocket launcher or something. He gave my mates a look that told them to stay where they were.

"Don't even think about bullshitting me, I know what you and your bunch of Looney Tunes are planning."

"We weren't planning anything . . . We were just heading over to see if—"

"Shut the fuck up!"

"Honest to God, officer—"

"Listen up, I'm not going to say this twice, the imam is our problem, not yours. If you so much as say hello to him, I'll have you hauled in for attempted murder. And I don't want to see you and your idiot friends hanging round the mosque like you were yesterday, get it?"

"No, I don't get it . . . So people aren't even allowed to walk around the estate now?"

He grabbed my elbow again and slammed me against the car.

"Listen, Malrich, I know where all this is coming from. It's your brother's diary. But you don't understand, he didn't go killing people just because other people did . . . He tried to understand . . . "

"Yeah . . . and he died trying."

"Go on, fuck off home, and take your gangsta mates with

you. I want you in my office at 6 P.M. . . . and take your hands out of your pockets."

We headed into Paris, we were sick of hanging round the estate. We wandered round Châtelet, then down to Beaubourg, we traipsed halfway up the Boulevard Sebastopol to one of Togo-au-Lait's cousins who does hairpieces and makes carcinogenic beauty products. It's the family business. Then we went down to the river for something to eat. After that we headed up to the Champs-Élysées. It's like a different world, makes you wonder if you're still in France. Finally, we went back down to the Tuileries and sat in the gardens to talk. I had a question I needed to ask.

"Obviously someone here is a snitch and I want to know who it is. Momo? Or maybe you, Togo? I mean you voted with him, you were all up for wimping out and doing nothing."

After an hour of everyone throwing accusations around, I realised any one of them could be the snitch, or it could be some friend they'd mentioned our plans to, or even the guy at the station cafeteria, he'd been listening in. It was even possible that that Com'Dad just guessed what we were planning when he saw us outside the mosque at 7 A.M. We're nocturnal creatures, everyone knows that.

"Well, I'm heading back, I'm freezing my balls off here and Monsieur le Commissaire is expecting me for tea."

6 P.M. The police station is a fortress of breeze blocks and bulletproof glass planted right outside the estate, one side overlooking the estate, the other overlooking the neighbourhood where Rachel lived. All the cops know me. Babar, the desk sergeant, jerked his thumb towards the hall. "Yeah, yeah, I know—chief's office is down the end of the hall. The one with the padded door." Com'Dad has been around for, like, ten years. He and I showed up about the same time, me from

Algeria, him from some sink estate up north. He's an expert in Sensitive Urban Areas. I don't know if he's made any difference to ours. I don't think so. It's the same as it ever was except the kids have grown to be gangsters, the gangsters have grown old and fat, and the old guys walk round flashing their battle scars like they're vets back from the war. Everyone else—the families, the ordinary people—just get on with life same as they always did. Some of them have jobs, some are on welfare, some are on disability. The kids are either with social services or at school or somewhere in between. The only thing that changed was when the jihadists started showing up. It's something to do with the war in Algeria, apparently, or the war in Kabul or the Middle East or I don't know where. They use France as a safe haven, as a base for operations. Whatever the reason they're here, they've fucked everything up for everyone, that's why we're wandering around till we can't take it any more. Before anyone knew what was happening, these death-dealing fuckers had taken over. If you blinked, you'd have missed it: everything changed, the clothes and everything. After that, the estate started to empty. The local economy packed up and moved out, the shops, the offices, the cash-in-hand work that keeps the jobless afloat. That's their strategy: block the escape routes, make lots of noise, keep people poor—that way they're one step closer to paradise. They treat people like sheep. And we fell for it, me, Momo, Raymond, all of us—mostly because we believed the Führer's spiel: "Join the Brotherhood, you can have everything, you can have money and *djina*," partly because they were constantly tugging at our *djellabas*, we couldn't set foot outside without one of them jogging over and reciting the ten commandments of the suicide bomber. The Brotherhood and their fucking *djina* got us in big trouble, we were in and out of the police station, dragged up before the courts, forced to do community service. The only thing left for us was jail. We were branded for life. We had Com'Dad on our backs 24/7. But later, when he saw we were getting out of all this fanatical end-of-the-world bullshit, he put in a good word for us with the authorities, had us sent on training courses, got us apprenticeships. We were even taken on tours of parliament and got to meet our *Député*. It wasn't going to change anything, but it was something to do.

"Come in. Take a seat. Do you want a cup of tea?"

"No."

We talked: he did most of the talking, pacing round the office, and I was only half listening. As usual, he started out with all the stuff he cares about—the estate, the future, the Republic, the straight and narrow—then he got to talking about me, like he was a mate who was only looking out for me.

" . . . you need to know, your brother was a good man, a very good man. Given all the stuff you know now . . . about your father, Rachel did the only decent thing a man can do, he tried to understand. Doesn't matter if you're dealing with a crime committed yesterday or crimes committed years ago, that's where you have to start: *the first thing you have to do is understand*" (he said it slowly, dragging out every word), "you can't just rush in and judge things. When you were running around in you *djelleba* with that ratty little goatee beard, I could easily have thought: he's a fundamentalist, a terrorist, I'm taking him down. But I didn't, I tried to understand, to get to know you, and I decided that you weren't one of them, you were Malrich, you were a good guy just trying to live your life like everyone else. Nothing is ever simple. Your brother's suicide proves that. He tried to understand, but sadly he gradually started to believe that he was guilty, he felt he was to blame for what the Nazis—what your father—did to the Jews during the war. He hated your father but that still didn't change the fact that he was your father, and like everyone, Rachel wanted a father he could look up to, a father he could be proud of. And it was worse for him, because you guys didn't live with your parents, because you missed him, because of the terrible way your father died—his throat cut by Islamic fundamentalists with your mother and all those poor souls with only the sun to light the day. But the more research he did, the more he learned, the more he suffered. Something inside him snapped, he turned everything on its head and started to hate himself. Rachel couldn't help but think of your father as a war criminal, but mostly he thought of him as his father, someone who had fought for Algerian independence, someone loved and respected by the people of his village; Rachel saw your father as a victim of the Islamic fundamentalists and of the Algerian political system that fosters these monsters. It was too much for him, he started to feel guilty, he was ashamed of his success, of what he saw as his selfishness towards you and the rest of your family, of his affluent lifestyle. That was when he started to cut himself off from everyone—from you, from his wife, from his adoptive parents. It was his way of trying to protect you. In the end, he took it all on himself, he passed judgement on himself in his father's place. Suicide was his last resort, the only way he could reconcile the irreconcilable, do you understand?"

I don't know what I said. Nothing, probably. I was tumbling into a black hole. I could see shadows . . . my father, my mother, Rachel spiralling into madness, poor Nadia screaming as she died, the emir burning her with a blowtorch, the shadow of the imam looming over the estate; I thought about the massacre in Aïn Deb, about . . . I don't remember. I remember yelling, "What are you telling me all this for? What's it got to do with me?"

He leaned over and said, "It's got everything to do with you. I know what's going on in that head of yours. You're confusing the past and the present, you're comparing yourself and Rachel, your father and the imam, you're thinking about the Nazis who stole your father from you and used him as a tool in their genocide, you're thinking about the Islamic fundamentalists who murdered your parents, who murdered poor Nadia, you want revenge, you want to take down the imam because he's the leader, the Führer, because you used to belong to his Brotherhood of pathetic losers busy trying to wipe out humanity and you think this gives you a way to redeem yourself, to see your father differently, to forgive him. Do you understand?"

"This is bullshit. Can I go now?"

"Sure, you can go. But read your brother's diary again, maybe you'll realise something that even Rachel didn't realise, though it was staring him in the face: you can't get justice for a crime by committing another crime, or by committing suicide. We have laws to do that. For the rest, we have to rely on memory and wisdom. But the most important thing you need to learn is this: we are not responsible for the crimes of our parents."

"Can I go now?"

"My door is always open, come back if you feel like it."

I went up to see uncle Ali and aunt Sakina. I was planning to sleep at their place that night, I felt terrible, I hadn't seen them in over a month. Actually, I was scared to be alone in Rachel's house, I didn't know what I might do. But there was another reason: there was something I wanted to ask aunt Sakina, something that hadn't occurred to me before, or to Rachel—at least there was nothing in his diary about it: how did papa and uncle Ali meet? It's weird the stuff you don't know, that you don't even think about. Ten years I'd been living with uncle Ali and aunt Sakina and I didn't know anything about them, I didn't know how they knew papa.

Uncle Ali and aunt Sakina are exactly like you'd imagine, they're immigrants who've stayed immigrants. Their life in France is the same as if they still lived in Algeria, it would be exactly the same if they lived on another planet. "Allah decides all things," they say, and that's all there is to it. They're good people, they don't ask for much out of life: enough to eat, somewhere to sleep, a little peace, and now and then some news from the *bled*. They love getting letters. I used to have to read the letters to them and write the letters back. Back then I thought it was a pain, but now I look back on it fondly. Papa used to send them standard-issue letters: *Dear Ali, just a few lines to let you know that I and the family are well. I hope that you, your wife and your children are well. We send you our love.* Then he'd write a bit about life in the village, about the weather. Uncle Ali would write back: *Dear Hassan, thank you for you letter which we received. We are happy to know that you are well. Allah be praised. Everything here is fine, the children send their love. Please write again soon. The peace of Allah be with you. I have sent the medicines you asked for, I hope they will arrive safely. If you need anything else, let me know.* Then he'd write a bit about life on the estate, about the weather. I wrote dozens and dozens of letters, every one of them exactly the same—the only thing different was the date, the weather and the names of the medicines.

Now that I finally wanted to talk to them, I realised I didn't know how to begin. We'd only ever talked in set phrases. Me saying, *Hi uncle Ali, Hi aunt Sakina, I'm hungry, I'm going out,* and them saying, *Hello, Hello, Are you hungry? Can I get you some coffee? Put a coat on, you'll get cold, God go with you.* The rest was silence, politeness, the routine clichés of family life.

"*Am'ti*, how did papa and uncle Ali meet?"

I have never seen my aunt Sakina look surprised by anything. She answered perfectly calmly.

"They were in the *maquis* together during the War of Independence, they became great friends, they were like brothers."

"Is that it? What about afterwards?"

"When independence came, times were hard, everyone was poor, people were sleeping in the streets while our leaders were feasting in the palaces left by the colonists and killing each other over who should take power. Your father and uncle Ali were disgusted by what was happening. Ali came to France, he couldn't bear it. As soon as he found a job, he went back and asked for my hand, and I came back to France with him. Allah has watched over us, we have never wanted for anything."

"What about papa?"

"He had problems with the new leaders, I know that. There were people who wanted him to leave Algeria—they threatened to kill him. But there were many people who wanted him to stay so he could go on training army officers."

"Why did some people hate him?"

"I don't know. Your Ali would have been able to tell you, but the poor man is not himself anymore. I do know that he hid your father for many months in our village in Kabylia. Later, after we left for France, your papa went into hiding in Aïn Deb with a friend from the *maquis*. Tahar, his name was, he was your uncle. Your father married his sister Aïcha. Tahar died long ago, before you and your brother were even born."

"Why did papa never come to France?"

"I don't know, *oulidi*. He had fought the French in the war back when he lived in Germany, and when he came to Algeria he was afraid he might be arrested."

"But uncle Ali fought against the French, and he came to live here, and he never had any problems."

"Well, I'm sure your father had his reasons, but I don't know what they were."

"Why did he send us here to live with you in France, why didn't he want us to stay with him and maman? I mean, is that normal?"

"Don't judge your father, *oulidi*, he was thinking of you, of your future, he wanted you to study, to be successful, to live in peace. Why are you asking me all these questions?"

"No reason, *am'ti* . . . no reason."

"You're not well, *oulidi*, ever since your brother died, you haven't been the same. You are not happy, you spend too much time thinking. But it will pass, you are young, Allah watches over you."

That night I slept like a baby. It was the first time in a long time.

My life is a living hell. Everything is going wrong. Ophélie is always nagging me, she won't give me a minute's peace, she wants things to go back to the way they were, she wants me to be the man I was when we first met. I know now why women love soap operas—they tell the same stories over and over with the same dialogue, the same sets, actors who barely age a day in twenty years. The characters never change. Maybe this is their way of taking revenge on life. But I can understand Ophélie. Her whole world has been turned upside down, she's living with a stranger, an intruder, an impostor, someone who is not interesting or exciting, some lunatic who is constantly brooding about horrors from another time, another world. This is not the man she married, this stranger has no business being in her life, in our soap-opera love story. I've tried to keep things to myself, but it's getting harder and harder. I've tried hiding behind my work, I've made up emergencies, deals going south, I've blamed the recession the economists are always talking about, I've blamed tough negotiations, I've blamed the Chinese and the Indians and the Koreans for underbidding and stealing our market share, senior management for their obsession with endless meetings, flurries of last-minute orders, endless seminars and conferences, the unions terrified of losing their benefits just making things worse. I talk to her about these things the way you might explain a war film to a pacifist or a conscientious objector, I try to keep up the suspense, putting in just enough high-minded principles to justify the ruthlessness of our reactions. Our jobs are on the line, we're fighting for our lives, for her. But she doesn't care about any of this. In her eyes, none of these things can justify my silence, my constant absences, the bags under my eyes, my lack of interest in food, in sex, and nothing can justify my obsession with those books—*those vile books*, she calls them—about the war, the SS, the deportations, the extermination camps, the machinery of death, the post-war trials, the worldwide hunt for war criminals. In fact, she once threatened to throw them in the fire, but one look at me and she knew it wouldn't be a good move. I moved the books out to the garage and put a lock on the tool cabinet. Sometimes she said things that were really hurtful, though I knew it wasn't really her, it was her mother talking. One day she said to me, "You're all the same, you half-breeds, it's all six of one and half a dozen of the other, you have no idea what you want really." I said, "You can tell your mother from me that six of one and half a dozen of the other are not the same thing, though that's what the expression is supposed to mean." Ophélie sulked for a whole week because I corrected her, and her mother phoned me and screamed that she wasn't about to take French lessons from a foreigner. I didn't know what she was talking about, but I said, "It's all relative. A foreigner is only foreign to a foreigner. In the absolute he is just a person and there's no law that says he can't read Molière and Maupassant." She slammed the phone down. One night, when I came home with a pile of new books under my arm, Ophélie, with an ingenuousness that scared me, said, "It's not like *we* killed the Jews, I can't see why you're so obsessed with this whole thing." This was the last straw. I answered with the same chilly detachment, "You're right, it wasn't us, but it could have been us!" I didn't try to explain and she quickly changed the subject. "My mother's coming over for dinner tonight, so do me a favour and snap out of this mood."

My mother-in-law is really something. I don't mind that she's fat, ugly, eccentric and her taste in clothes might best be described as garish. It's quite funny watching her play at being the diva. My problem is she has a poisonous tongue and a stare that could turn a nest of rattlesnakes to stone. When she's around, I can't breathe without her thinking the worst.

"I'm very disappointed in you, Rachel, you've really changed, you've completely let yourself go. In my house, we don't . . . "

"Well, I'm delighted to say that you clearly haven't changed at all. But may I remind you that we are not in your house, this is *my* house . . . "

With that, dinner came screeching to a halt. My mother-in-law stormed off spluttering, her daughter threw her napkin in my face and went after her. A minute later, the front door banged as though a hurricane had ripped it from its hinges, the whole house shook. I sat by myself, finishing my dinner, delighted at the thought that I had spared at least a few rattlesnakes.

The next morning, there was a shitstorm waiting for me at the office. Another one. When it rains it pours. I was summoned to see the boss and, from his secretary's tone, I knew he was going to tear me off a strip. I'd been expecting it. It was all over the office, people had been talking behind my back for months. Whenever I walked into a room, everyone suddenly changed the subject. I was worried, but not too worried. My boss, Monsieur Candela, is a friend, he's like a brother, he hired me, he showed me the ropes, and whenever this magnificent money-making machine kicked me in the balls, he was the one who helped me up again. We had two things in common: Nantes, where both of us had studied and where he had once taught fluid mechanics; and Algeria, his birthplace and that of all his tribe going back generations to some distant Basque forefather. The minute he saw my CV, he decided to hire me. He needed a fellow student, a fellow countryman to help him run his kingdom: the largest sales force in Europe and Africa. And he needed a talented engineer, something I believed I could become. I was twenty-four, I had a brand-new degree and a head full of new ideas. The job was a gift, I had made a good friend and had gained the prospect of travelling. Six months later, I moved into our dream house and—with her mother's rose-tinted blessing—I married Ophélie, the only girl I've ever loved. They were good times, our feet only ever touched the ground when we needed to walk somewhere.

Monsieur Candela was sitting at his desk with the sullen, scornful glower of a manager expecting an underling who has suddenly fallen from grace. Playing bad cop doesn't suit him, he has a sunny, cheerful Mediterranean disposition. I hadn't even closed the door when he ripped into me. "Are you planning to keep up this shit?" This is how he always talks at work, very American, shooting from the hip, straight to the point, no pussy-footing. It makes sense, after all we are here to make money and the company article of faith can be summed up in three words: *Time is money,* our god is the Almighty Dollar. The company is 100 percent American, the only thing foreign about it is the market. And the staff—the pissant, prolix, profligate Frogs, though at least they get to pay us in French francs—they consider to be infidels.

"I'm going through a bad patch."

"So what else is new? Is it Ophélie?"

"Not really."

"What then? Is Monsieur having a crisis of conscience?"

I told him the whole story, about the April 24 massacre, about papa's past. I gave it to him in bullet points like it was a corporate debriefing. I skipped over my crisis of conscience. He skipped over his shock and his questions.

"Let's go to the café, we can talk there. But I'm warning you, the boss wants your hide—or my head. Your sales figures for the last six months are a disaster, and he's obviously got someone keeping tabs on every day, every minute, you're out of the office. Congratulations. You've set a new world record! I've put in a good word for you, but this is a company, not a church, so you're going to turn this fucking thing around right now or three months from now you'll be clearing your desk. Is that clear?"

It was clear. I was going to be fired. My stay of execution was complicated by other factors, the union wouldn't get involved, there were too many human-resources hoops to jump through, too much red tape. The company was doing well, but per capita revenue is per capita revenue. It's a principle we've been taught to carry around like a sick man carries a thermometer. The company philosophy is simple as a biblical exhortation: Better we throw out one bad apple rather than risk infecting the whole barrel. The "we" in that sentence is a formality—the rank and file swallow management decisions hook, line and sinker and parrot them as their own. It's inevitable, given our profit-sharing system. How was I going to break the news to Ophélie? She wouldn't believe it. Say nothing, tomorrow is another day, sufficient unto the day is the evil thereof . . .

Monsieur Candela has a flair for understanding things without anyone needing to explain. Our conversation was brief; in his half-closed eyes I saw all the wisdom of the world. I also saw the swift hand that wise men raise to ward off evil.

Stirring his coffee, he said, "Listen to me, Rachel, I know about these things, in my family, we've seen it all, hardship, war, deportation, more war, exile, contempt, loneliness, you name it, so listen up: you have to draw a line through this whole thing right now or it'll destroy you. First of all, you're grieving for your parents, and feeling sorry for yourself isn't going to bring them back. You need to do what any good son would do—visit their graves once a year and pray for the repose of their souls. Thank them for the gift of life they've given you and let them know that you are making the most of that gift. As for the rest of it—the Holocaust and all the other atrocities in this world—pray to God they never happen again. That's all you can do. Read if you have to, campaign if you have to, make what little difference you can. Anything more is the devil's work, anything more means letting your hatred and your thirst for revenge get the better of you. If you let evil in, it will only breed evil, and without realising it, you'll become a monster. Okay, now, let's get back to the office. Work is therapy."

Another favourite Americanism. You wipe the slate clean, spit on your hand, get back behind the wheel. His advice seemed to be to deal with evil by forgetting, which is the worst evil. I was disappointed, but not very. I had expected Monsieur Candela to enlighten me and he had. But was light enough?

Later that afternoon, he phoned and told me that if I needed him he was there for me, then abruptly hung up like a real boss who's said what he has to say. I wanted to say thank you, but he caught me unawares. Besides, when it comes to expressing my feelings, I take the Buddhist approach: the less you say, the better.

After work, I went to a bookshop. There was a book I needed to pick up. This would be the last book. A man can't live off welfare even with a couple of hundred share options. We have a lot in common, me and the guy who owns the bookshop. As he gave me book, there was a gleam in his eye. "This is the book you should have started with," he said. It was true. It hadn't occurred to me. Urged on by horror, I had started at the end, with the Nuremberg Trials, and slowly worked my way back to the beginning, the hunt for war criminals, the discovery of the camps, the Normandy landings, the war itself, the phony war, etc. All the way back to the source. And this book was the source. When I'd asked him to get me a copy a couple of weeks earlier, he shook his head. "It might be tough to get hold of. It used to be banned. I'll do what I can, otherwise, you can try secondhand bookshops . . . I'll give you a few addresses." In the end, he managed to track down a copy of the book which had unleashed the most terrible tragedy on the world. On me. *Mein Kampf*.

I don't know how many times I read it. Angrily, compulsively at first, then more calmly, finally with an increasingly anxious serenity. I was looking for the key, the spell that had persuaded intelligent, able-bodied men like my father to shed their humanity and become killing machines. There is nothing in this book, nothing but dishwater, the ramblings of a hick from the sticks, the pretentious claptrap of tin-pot chiefs who dream of being immortal dictators, slogans for election posters in a slave republic. "God helps those who kill the Jews; An Aryan in the hand is worth all the Jews in the world; Preserve the bloodline, beware of contamination; Is your neighbour sick or handicapped? Kill him." If this was all it took for evil to sway the Germans and turn them into Nazis, you had to hand it to Hitler. I had been expecting some irrefutable line of reasoning, an alchemy of complex arguments, devastating revelations about a worldwide conspiracy against the German people, a chain reaction linking one chapter to the next, extraordinary circumstances skillfully orchestrated, I had expected Satan to have penned certain passages supplying the ink and the details for the rest of it. But there was nothing. All it had taken for evil to triumph was a beardless, blustering soldier, a depressive, syphilitic housepainter, a few well-turned phrases, a muscular title—*My Struggle*—and a socioeconomic context that fostered grievances, condemnations, recriminations and hyperbole. There were, of course, other factors: the history of the country, its roots in centuries-old sects, in age-old myths filled with vague esoteric ideas, echoes of this or that, far-fetched theories, rediscovered mythology, new philosophies born in the heat of action, dreams of glory that might have come from an inmate at the local lunatic asylum or a drunk in the bar next door, and the lust for power that technical progress and scientific advancements inspire in a society desperate to reassert itself. You didn't have to look too hard. What country doesn't have demons locked up in its ancient cellars, what country doesn't have warmongers, dreams of immortality, what people doesn't have a few genes damaged by history, what people is not exposed to life's slings and arrows, what religion hasn't been rocked by scientific discoveries? There is but one humanity and evil lurks within us, in our very marrow.

I was sinking, I knew that. Worse still, I was gappling with trivial details when what I needed to do was cling to the simple facts. There was no reason for what had happened. To try to find a root cause for evil was absurd. Evil is. It has existed since the dawn of time. Looking for a means to analyse it or a ready-made explanation is pointless, and weighing every detail in the balance is self-defeating. I believe that evil is an endlessly recurring accident that sends good and bad drivers alike crashing into a wall. Good has meaning only at funerals, it is only at such moments that we see ourselves for what we truly are: dust which will be swept away with the next breath of wind. This, I firmly believe, is what goodness means. There is no better deterrent, there is no more salutary lesson. If this person has died, we too will die, there is nothing more to it. But there is no good, evil reigns supreme. What happened to my father happened to others in Germany and elsewhere, yesterday and the day before, and it will go on happening tomorrow and the day after. For as long as the earth revolves around the sun, for as long as life—this sweet madness—keeps company with its antidote mankind—this furious madness—there will be crimes and criminals and victims. And grief beyond measure. And accomplices. And bystanders. And despots who wash their hands of our suffering. And yet, this crime is not like other crimes, and it is this uniqueness I must face. Alone. More alone than anyone in the world.

Rereading what I have just written, I realise I've missed the most important point. I've ducked the issue, what I've written is just gobbledy-gook and cheap philosophy. I have to face the facts. They are what they are, nothing and no one, not even God, can go back and deal the cards again. My father did what he did of his own free will, he acted according to his conscience, the proof being that others refused to do what he did and paid with their lives, or managed to emigrate in time. The other, irrefutable proof is that he kept his files like sacred relics, his military record, his medals, that fucking SS Death's Head, preserved like blessed sacraments. When you can do nothing in the face of totalitarianism, when you are already caught in the trap, there is still one last means of self-preservation: suicide. It is our last resort, our wild card, invisible, invincible. It is why when the wolf, that magnificent beast, gets his paw caught in a trap, he gnaws on it, he chews it off and finds his freedom, whole, intact, troubling as Psyche herself, struggles on to the last drop of blood and dies of exhaustion and overwhelming relief. Even after the crime was committed, papa still had this recourse, to give himself up, demand justice in the name of his victims, become again the man he had been, regain his dignity. Instead he ran away, he hid, he lied, he disowned himself and, in doing so, left his crime unpunished, silence was his refuge. He consecrated it. I would have preferred him to have appeared before a jury of his peers with the *Bonzen* of the Third Reich, Hess, Rippentrop and the rest of them. Solemn judgement gives the crimes back their full horror and restores to the guilty some part of their lost humanity. Silence perpetuates a crime, gives it new life, closes the door on justice and truth and throws opens the door to forgetfulness, to the possibility that it might happen again.

One question drives me mad: Did papa know what he was doing in Dachau, in Buchenwald, in Majdanek, in Auschwitz? I can't think of him as a victim anymore, as some fresh-faced innocent unwittingly infected by evil. And even if he was, there comes a moment, a split second, some event, however trivial, some unexpected, fleeting series of terrible images which lead to realisation, doubt, revolt. At that moment something within us cries out, it must do, if it did not then there is nothing, no God, no man, no truth. How could anyone fail to react, if only with an imperceptible shudder, when faced with the haunted eyes of a sickly child shivering with cold in the desolation of a death camp, with a naked woman hiding her pudenda as she is dragged to the gas chambers, *a woman without hair or name, with no more strength to remember, eyes empty and womb cold as a frog in winter,* with a man clinging to a dignity long since destroyed even as the last tatters of humanity are stripped from him, a man *who dies at a yes or a no.*

I tell myself: if a single crime goes unpunished on this earth, if silence prevails over anger, then men do not deserve to live. In a better world, I would have given myself up, put on my black suit, stood before a judge and confessed: "My father tortured and killed thousands of people who never did him any harm and he got away scot-free. By the time I knew what he had done, he was dead, so I have come here in his place. Judge me, save me, please." But in this world, I wouldn't even be thought of as laughable, I would be thrown out of court, I would be summarily ejected, lectured. My God, they might wink at me! All I can do is deal with this thing alone. But I don't know, everything is shocking, secret, squalid, everything in this world that has survived the end of the world is governed by prevarication and procrastination; once again we have come to believe that a lie is a necessary social protection for a people, a useful gift for an unruly child, a comfort for the anxious. I tell myself all sorts of things, I am drowning in a nightmare of horror, I have no raft to cling to. I am alone. More alone than anyone in the world. This world that to me seems so remote, deceptively preoccupied, obsessed with itself, its vague desires, its inconsequential joys, its follies, feeding on them as a cannibal feeds on himself, obsessed with its own time, its own tragedies, its dreams, its powerlessness.

I'm struggling. Usually, I've got no time for self pity, for inter-
minable obsessions. I remind myself that all this is simply history, that history belongs to the past, that the past is dead, we
have forgotten, we no longer know, we have put things in per-
spective, that we live in an age that has its own problems, problems that are so great, so terrible, we cannot see our way out,
while tomorrow, our only choice in life bears down on us with all
its cruelties and sorrows. To me, it is an entire world that has collapsed on my head, it is the entire history of evil that stares me
in the face, probes at my heart, my guts, steals into my memory, asks to be remembered, tells me endlessly how things were,
who we were. The image haunts me, the fog suffocates me, my
head aches, my ears are ringing . . . I hear a commotion . . . I
see the dreary camp . . . watch the procession of shadows . . .
men, women, children, all skin and bone, numberless, naked,
marching obediently towards a vast inferno beneath the watchful eye of the SS officer . . . *help!* . . . I peer further into this horror . . . I scream for help, I look around for my father . . . *Where
are you, papa? What are you doing?* I need to find him, to wake
him, I need to wake up . . . to save my father . . . my father who
is lost . . . who has ruined us. *My house has crumbled, grief has
made me powerless; and I do not know why, my father never
told me . . .* There he is, papa, immaculate in his black uniform,
wearing the famous red armband . . . He smiles at me, tender
but stern, the affectionate smile of a father . . . I don't know how
it happened, but he is here with me, just as he was in our house
in Aïn Deb. We are living in a beautiful house just outside . . . the
camp . . . the *Konzentratzionlager* . . . Nearby is a beautiful forest, glorious flowers, shimmering colours, and behind the hill . . .
that *place*, all black, all grey, the place where I am not allowed
to go . . . I play with the other boys, the officers' children and with
children they bring over from that *place* to keep us company, to
play games, to be our playthings, our whipping boys when we're
angry, to serve our whims . . . but we hate these children, they're

scrawny and sickly, flea-ridden and scrofulous, they have no hair, no teeth, they don't know how to play, they're silent and stupid and we don't understand them. All they can think about is eating, keeping warm, sleeping . . . we shout at them, we hit them but still they don't react, they just curl up like hedge-hogs . . . Around us, inhuman wretches with sunken eyes shamble through the pretty village, pretending to till the ground, rake the gravel, paint the fences. They are our prisoners, these creatures who have maimed our country, incensed our Führer, they wear filthy striped pyjamas, they are ugly, foul-smelling, deceitful, fawning, ungrateful, they steal whatever they can—cigarette butts, scraps of papers, stale crumbs of bread, the sight of a rusty nail can make their eyes pop out, the sight of a bone can have them slavering like dogs, they poke through our garbage, stare at us enviously . . . Sometimes they stop pretending to work, they look up, look out into the distance, past the camp, past the hill . . . to the tall column of oily fetid smoke that rises into the sky . . . *Oh, that scream!* . . . the sky is dark with wheeling carrion crows, filling the air with their baleful cawing . . . *Get out of here! . . . You too, you fucking kikes* . . . The prisoners stare up at the sky. They seem constantly surprised by the sudden whirr that sometimes wakes us in the night, at dawn, in the cold, a grinding noise that grows louder, a series of dull metallic sounds, chains clanking, the slamming of heavy metal doors, the quiet fitful hiss of the pumps, the sudden drop in voltage that makes the lights flicker . . . screams, perhaps . . . a ghostly clamour that grows louder and louder, then gradually dies away, leaving a haunting silence . . . *My God, how strange this silence sounds, how painful* . . . people who . . . more shaven heads appear by the foot of the hill . . . another column of smoke advances stolidly . . . emerges from the darkness, trudges through the dull grey day to disappear into the night . . . it is far away . . . the wind is blowing in the other direction . . . the prisoners stop, lost in contemplation, so our *Kapos* rush over and knock them to the ground, lice hopping from their clothes as the *Kapos* lash out with clubs and guttural roars *"Arbeit! . . . Arbeit! . . . Schnell! . . . Schnell!"* We roll on the ground laughing. Ha ha ha! Ha ha ha! . . . It's strange that flayed and wasted as they are, the prisoners feel nothing, say nothing, do nothing, some laugh, baring their horrid teeth, staring up at the sky, they look as though they might sing . . . They are fascinated. Then, when they are ready, they scramble to their feet, pick up their tools and pretend to till the ground, rake the gravel, paint the fences, check that everything is spick and span. Infuriating automata, they look as though all their lives they have done nothing but make these same gestures, as though they were born to this. Sometimes, there are two or three still sprawled on the ground but their comrades do not see them, pretend not to see them. The *Kapos* bark orders and they are carried off on stretchers past the camp, over there, past the hill . . . Officers laugh or yell angrily, their whips whistle, slapping against their boots . . . the *Kapos* laugh, they bow and scrape . . . the *Kapos* are favoured prisoners, they have some flesh on their bones at the expense of their suffering brothers . . . they speak a language I don't understand, or barely. *"Gut, gut, Juden kaput, fini, Konetz, danke, Dûkuji, merci beaucoup, dobrÿden."* Papa calls me inside for something to eat . . . I . . . I . . . the wind has shifted, the air is suddenly rank and muggy . . . We go inside and close the windows.

I feel like screaming, like ripping my skin off. I don't know, I don't know what to do, I feel crushed by the silence, this terrifying silence, it is impossible for me to tell things apart. Dream, nightmare and reality have merged. There is no way out.

I woke up sweating. It was—I don't know, it might be night, it might be day. I called out for Ophélie. I shouted again, "Ophélie, Ophélie!" I heard a noise in the kitchen, a dull drone . . . the hiss of gas expanding . . . the fridge. "Ophélie . . . Ophélie!" She isn't there. She hasn't come home. She has left me. The silence is preternatural . . . I can hear it, it smells of burning, it clings to your skin. Something falls off the sofa. *My God, the noise!* A book . . . *Mein Kampf.* I take it into the garage and burn it.

I found Jean 92. It was easy. I simply turned up at the return address he wrote on the letters he sent to papa. He lives in a tumbledown shack at the end of a dark alley in a dismal part of a village somewhere near Strasbourg that has shrivelled away as families have died out. Driving from the urban masterpiece that is Strasbourg to this hamlet which appears on no maps and whose name, out of humanity, I won't mention, I felt as though I might reach the end of the world and bitterly regret it. In France there are still godforsaken places so out of the way you wonder where you are. My Renault 4 didn't know the place, though I rented it in Strasbourg and it must have roamed this hinterland often enough. Coming in to the village, a surly farmer jerked his thumb towards the arse-end of the street when I stopped and asked, "Could you tell me where I might find Ernest Brucke?" There seemed no point thanking him, he'd lost the power of speech, he would have been incapable of saying, "You're welcome, monsieur."

After scaring three miserable old witches leaning on their brooms, and setting a pack of stray dogs yapping, I finally found the place. It was the last house in the village. Beyond, there was nothing but a wall of wild vegetation.

I had been expecting to be met by an old man and was worrying whether he would still have wits enough to understand my questions; what I found was a man of indeterminate age wearing a curious getup, his belly swollen and distended, his face as mottled and pockmarked as that of only the most dedicated alcoholic. His fly was gaping open but he clearly didn't care. He was sitting outside in a tiny garden full of flaking, peeling junk— a handkerchief-sized wasteland. He sat at a rickety metal table on which stood a bottle of schnapps; there was a chipped glass whose existence was nominal, fused as it was to the table, half-filled with an oily liquid on which floated leaves, pine needles and dead flies; and there was an improbable ashtray buried under a mound of ashes, cigarette butts and cremated insects. The man stared straight in front of him, saying nothing. He did not even see me arrive.

I felt a surge of pity. Here was a human wreck on the brink of extinction. An image flashed into my mind and I was convinced that this was what would happen: the man would die here, covered in lichen, glued to his chair, the bottle within easy reach, thinking nothing, saying nothing, seeing nothing of what was around him. I found it difficult to imagine papa—a picture of austerity, a very German austerity—being friends with such a man. But a lot of time had passed, I thought, and maybe this man had had his day in the sun. However, a little mental arithmetic persuaded me that he and papa did not know—could not have known—each other. It was a matter of age and circumstance. Papa hadn't set foot outside Algeria since 1962, at which point this man would have been playing cowboys and Indians with the dirty little village pigs or playing hide-and-seek in the bushes with the sheep before he and his *Kameraden* discovered alcohol. Now, the man was about fifty years old—clearly fifty years too many—but a far cry from seventy-six, the age my father had been when he died. I didn't even consider the possibility that he had been to Algeria and had met my father there. They don't stand for any bullshit in Algeria, they have a border, they have fearsome guards and draconian laws, no one is allowed to visit and there is no question of making exceptions. There are places like that, places where you are not allowed to enter, to leave, or to know why. Perhaps alcohol had preserved him, or prematurely aged him, or maybe it had given him the means to become a different person. There was obviously something I didn't understand.

The man finally looked up and saw me. His brooding eyes and tremulous lips, like a rapacious old pervert, made me uncomfortable. I felt like a cornered child. I took a deep breath and adopted the posture of a boy accustomed to terrorizing girls in pigtails. I didn't want to put his back up, the way I had the old man in Uelzen, by asking awkward questions.

"If you're Ernest Brucke, aka Jean 92, I'd like to shake your hand and thank you on behalf of my father Hans Schiller."

The man sat lost in thought for a moment, then, exhausted by the sheer effort, stretched his hand past the bottle and said in a gravelly voice, "Schiller? . . . Who's Schiller? You're the son?"

"Too right I'm his son! On his deathbed, my father asked me to come and say goodbye to some old friends, people who helped him when times were . . . "

"Hold on a minute, I'm not Jean 92 . . . "

"Then who might you be, monsieur?

"I'm Adolph, his son . . . the old man kicked the bucket years ago . . . "

"Oh . . . "

"So what did you want with the old man . . . apart from to say thank you?"

"I just wanted to talk about old times . . . "

"Really? What for?"

"I'm, um . . . I'm looking for stories, background stuff, I'm writing a book about my father's struggle, his fight to save humanity, as far as I know Neo-Nazism is alive and well."

"Yeah, you look like a writer."

"If you don't mind, I'd like to interview you, for a chapter I'm writing about your father, and about you, obviously . . . "

Bingo. I'd hit the jackpot. This drunken slob could see himself at the top of the bestseller list. He sat up, cleared his throat and looked at me a little more warmly. It hadn't occurred to me—I'd forgotten that this sickness was still out there, this smug self-righteousness, the overweening pride that goes before a fall. I wasn't about to let this guy slip through my fingers, the wonderful Jean 92 Junior.

"Maybe I didn't mention it, *mon cher* Adolph, but I've already got a publisher, they pay well . . . you'll get a cut."

"How much?"

"It all depends on the sales, but it could be a nice little earner. Here, here's a hundred francs, call it an advance."

It was a done deal. We sat back and chatted like partners in some lucrative scam. It was pretty futile, as it turned out. And it was hard work. The drunken slob kept trying to sideline his father and hog the limelight. He wanted a chapter to himself. He told me about his childhood, about his grandmother Gertrude who taught him to speak German, his military service in the "fucking French army," the little wars in Africa where he did a little nigger-bashing to make up for the shame of having to fight for France, some bitch named Greta who ruined his life, some cousin Gaspard or Hector who ripped him off, his aunt Ursula who lived in Brazil with some guy called Felix who trafficked diamonds or maybe it was emeralds, how his house was falling down around his ears, how the village was under threat from some urban renewal scheme, how the fuckers at the city council, etcetera, etcetera. And he told me everything about his work with his Nazi father. Just paperwork at first, a little spying on the neighbours, watching the comings and goings from the post office, his role as acolyte at the shadowy ceremonies and, later, when he attained the age of unreason, the endless get-togethers, the secret meetings of freaks and failures, the summary justice dealt out to traitors and revisionists, the beatings meted out to local hooligans, the altercations with the local police, the winters spent drinking with old veterans depressed at how the world had changed. All in all, a rewarding catalogue of misery. He even showed me his files. I was surprised he was capable of standing up. He had a whole cupboard full of documents and I fell on them like a man possessed. An hour later, I was covered in dust and smelled of rotting flesh. I felt ashamed to be human. I poked around through the sort of jumble and clutter you would expect to find in the attic of a former torturer who has finally gone to meet the Prince of Darkness. It reeked of old men, of misfits, mildew and madness, of futility and horror. Dead or alive, a torturer is still a torturer. Poor Jean 92 should have died at birth. There were grubby posters, tattered books, a book of hours in a linen slipcase, hunters' catalogues, faded pennants, hideous letters and even more appalling photographs, bile-filled notebooks and nauseating tracts. Adolph offered to sell me the lot for 200 francs. It was a lot of money for such unspeakable shit, but I had come here in search of the roots of evil. There was a pistol, too, and some copper bullets grey-green with age. "A Luger—best gun in the whole world," he said, gripping it proudly. "You said it," I nodded. "My old man swore by his." What with Adolph and his Luger and me carrying a sheaf of Nazi pamphlets and pennants, we looked like we were about to take on the whole world. Any young firebrand who saw us would have signed up to fight with us.

Trying to find out about past wars is hellish, a series of dead ends, of paths that disappear into darkness, suppurating cesspits shrouded in mist, dust rising like curtains of smoke as you grope your way through the void. I'm beginning to understand the problems faced by people responsible for investigating war crimes that are inevitably shrouded in silence, amnesia and collusion. It's impossible, the truth is always buried, mislaid in a pile of dossiers and reports, hushed up, covered up, doctored. Then there is the silence, the selective amnesia, the half-truths, the carefully rehearsed lines, the pleas by devil's advocates, speech after speech, the worm-eaten papers. And above the chatter howls the wind of shame, sweeping aside our best intentions, and so we close our eyes, we lower our heads. Victims always die twice. And their executioners always outlive them.

"Papa never did tell me what 92 meant . . . "

"That was the code name for the organisation the old man set up. Unit 92, everyone in the unit had an alias, Jean 92, François 92, Gustave 92. We had to watch our backs, we had the French authorities on our backs, the Yids, the . . . "

"But why 92?"

"It was . . . Hitler came to power in '33, Pétain signed the armistice in 1940, the same year my father joined the Gestapo, he was nineteen . . . if you add them up, you get 92. Clever bastard, the old man. That's what the unit meant, loyalty to the Third Reich."

"*Mein Ehre Heißt Treue.*"

"Exactly! So anyway, when the old man died in 1969, I took over and renamed it Unit 134 . . . I was born in '42, you see, 92 plus 42 equals 134, get it? But by that time there wasn't much to do, by then most of the *Kameraden* were living it up in Santiago, Chile and in Bangkok somewhere over in China . . . you know?"

"Yeah, yeah I know . . . it's near Thailand somewhere . . . So it was Unit 92 that managed to get my father . . . ?"

"Absolutely. At the end of the war, when *Kameraden* were forced to go to ground, the old man and a bunch of his friends set up Unit 92 to help get them out of Germany to friendly countries. Later on, he hooked up with ODESSA, you heard of them?

"Sure . . . ODESSA, the Franciscan network, the Vatican Refugee Organisation, the phony papers supplied by fellow travellers in the Red Cross, the Ethiopian line, the Turco-Arab escape routes, and the rest."

"Anyway, the 92, we mostly looked out for the SS officers who ran the Death Camps. They were the elite, you see, the guys that had to be saved for the future. You've got to put all this in the book, the old man did good work, he saved dozens of officers from those bastards. You can see all the names there in the little black book. You father must be in there somewhere . . . What was his name again?"

"Schiller . . . what bastards?"

"The Russkis, the Yanks, the *Engländer*, the backstabbing French cunts and those vermin the Yids. Can you believe it, there were still some left? The old man had a rough time, what with Nakam and the fucking Jewish Agency who exploited all the upheaval to get their hands on Palestine and France, and then there was Mossad and that bastard Wiesenthal who was lining his pockets . . . and that's not counting all the people who turned traitor overnight, some of them members of the 92. We didn't know what was going on, we had to keep tabs on what they were planning, tell the *Kameraden*, set up the networks, protect the lines, raise money, forge papers . . . I can tell you, I worked like a dog . . . I miss it, really. Back then, people were prepared to go to any lengths for the sake of honour . . . These days . . . "

I listened without really listening. I knew a hundred times more than he did about all this. But seeing him, hearing him, smelling him, squelching with him through this fetid mire, I experienced what it was like after the war, that end of the world unlike any other, the ruined wasteland stretching to the horizon, the scrawny hordes of dazed, half-dead people, bulldozers clearing the towering heaps of corpses, madmen wandering through the ruined countryside, surreal scenes, the wind carrying the stench of rotting flesh, the feckless already haggling, wheedling, testifying, making provisions for the future and, over this bedlam and confusion, excruciating, maddening, this haunting silence, this fog that chokes me even now.

"So . . . what's the story now, uncle Adolph?"

"It's all over now, *Jugend*, the Jews have won."

"But Hitler will come back . . . or someone else, someone more p . . . someone as powerful."

"Yeah, yeah . . . Dream on."

"It could be a Frenchman, someone like us . . . "

"Don't make me laugh. You ever see a Frenchman with balls?"

"Pétain had balls, didn't he?"

"Yeah, but he didn't have Hitler's genius. The sort of guy we need can only come from Germany."

"But what about Stalin and Pol Pot, Ceauşescu, what about Mao, Kim Il-sung, Idi Amin and . . . the other guy, you know, with the moustache, the one who gassed all the . . . "

"Scum, the lot of them, nothing but Commies and niggers and gooks, they don't count."

"An American would be good, I mean they exterminated the Indians—though I admit they didn't do such a great job with the Blacks. And they dropped a couple of atomic bombs on the Japs."

"Bullshit! They're all Jews in America, they should be wiped out, the whole lot of them."

"Maybe the Arabs . . . what do you think? I mean they've got the rhetoric . . . "

"The what?"

"The spiel, the shtick, they've got a coherent ideology . . . "

"Fucking Yids just like the rest of them, they're only good for making charcoal, and not even decent charcoal."

"Hey, maybe that would solve the energy crisis they're always busting our balls about—we'd get a cheap renewable source of energy out of burning them, we'd never have to worry again . . . "

"Ha, ha, ha! You're your father's son all right! Ha, ha, ha! Ha, ha, ha!"

In other circumstances I would have been only too happy to wander through his brain, I'm sure I would have found charming grottos and ravines the bastard didn't know he had, there's clearly no end to cretinism, what I had seen was only the tip of the iceberg. I felt like . . . like . . . nothing. You don't kill madmen, you don't exterminate the mentally handicapped, you pray for them. But for all his madness, his sickness, he managed to hurt me with that line: "You're your father's son all right!" It was like an electric shock to my heart. I thought of him as his father's son, offspring of Jean 92, good Samaritan to Nazi fugitives, saviour of murderers, and he had reminded me that I was my father's son, offspring of SS Gruppenführer Hans Schiller, the angel of death.

On the train back to Paris, the phrase ran through my mind— *I am my father's son . . . I am my father's son . . .* —over and over, to the steady monotonous clacking of the train, until it deafened me, devastated me, until I fell asleep. I think I might have said it aloud, might have shouted it. I was caught between two nightmares, two spasms, two impulses: to die here where I sat, or later, when I had drained the cup to the dregs. I thrashed about in darkness. But I know I heard a voice from somewhere in the carriage whispering to his neighbour, "The fact he needs to say it means he must have doubts," and another voice reply, "The question is, does his father know?" And suddenly all these good people, the tourists and travellers, started laughing, giggling behind their hands, chuckling behind their newspapers, others snorting half-heartedly. I laughed myself. It was a good joke, these were good people, but just as the laughter petered out into hopelessness I got to my feet and, addressing the assembled company like a prophet of doom, I whispered, "Let he who knows where his father is raise his hand." A chill ran through the carriage. It brought me back to life.

I don't know why, but I thought about that Jewish joke: Moishe is lying on his bed kvetching, tossing and turning like a devil in a baptismal font. It's after midnight and he has promised to pay back the money he owes his friend Jacob by noon. Moishe hasn't got any money. He imagines himself disgraced, thrown out of the merchants association, vilified by the rabbi. His tossing and turning wakes his wife and she asks, "Moishe, what is it?" "I owe Jacob twenty roubles," he tells her, "but I have no money. What shall I do?" "Is that all?" his wife says then gets up and bangs on the wall and shouts for all the neighbours to hear, "Jacob! My Moishe still owes you twenty roubles? Well, he isn't giving them back!" then climbs back into bed and says to her flabbergasted husband, "Now go to sleep, let Jacob stay awake!"

The rest of the journey passed without incident. I picked up the newspaper and caught up on what was happening in the world: everywhere, with giant steps, war was gaining ground.

31 OCTOBER 1996

I don't understand Rachel. He really pisses me off. He talks like papa was a murderer or something, he bangs on about it, it's insane. So what if Papa was in the SS? So what if he was posted to extermination camps? There's no proof that he actually killed anyone. He guarded prisoners, that's all. Not even that, they had the *Kapos* to do that—German convicts and deserters, Rachel says himself they were dogs, they're the ones who guarded the prisoners, who beat and robbed and raped them, forced them to work, clubbed them to death and dragged them feet first, tossing them into the furnaces. Papa was a chemical engineer, not an executioner. He worked in some laboratory way outside the camp, he oversaw the preparation of chemicals, that's all. He didn't know what people were planning to do with them, how could he know? The gas chambers were run by the *Sonderkommando*, the death squads, the *Einsatzgruppen*, not the laboratory. Papa's responsibility ended at the point of delivery. The trucks showed up, picked up the canisters, the paperwork was signed and the drivers drove off to God knows where. How could Rachel, who was so impressed by the way the Germans organised things, possibly think that the *Bonzen* would have had a scientist like papa working as a common killer, stoking furnaces, fuelling gas chambers, locking doors, turning levers, watching dials? Rachel and me are *Hälfte-Deutsch*, he knew as well as I do Germans are sticklers for regulations. That's what Papa was like, you didn't joke around with him except when it was time for joking around. Rachel lost it, he forgot everything we learned. He was angry and upset and he let his imagination run away with him. He was sick to his stomach like I am whenever I think about us, about the Islamists slitting our parents' throats in their sleep, about our godforsaken rathole of an estate, the people living there constantly harangued by the imam, surrounded by jihadists in *djellebas* and black jackets, with *Kapos* snapping at them like pitbulls, when I think about uncle Ali wasting away like a prisoner in a concentration camp and aunt Sakina who just waits, never surprised at anything, when I think about poor Nadia burned to death by the Emir. I think about my father. How did you get mixed up in this shit, papa? Did you know what was happening? You had to know something. In the camp, everyone eats together, the officers all in the officers' mess, you talk about work, about the things that go wrong, brag about the stuff you've got done. Then there's the meetings, you listen to the Führer's speeches, read the official communiqués from Himmler himself, you talk deadlines, figures, technical problems, you bawl out the slackers, praise the high achievers, get this week's orders. And there are the loudspeakers, those awful megaphones hanging over the prisoners' heads, tormenting them, driving them insane, the unemotional voice drowning out the howling wind, forever ordering them to assemble, to submit, to surrender, spelling out the horror line by line, verse by verse, transforming a monstrous crime into the simple implementation of a policy. And in the evenings, after dinner and the obligatory toast to the Führer, everyone sits around the stove, relaxing, listening to music, playing cards, drinking, daydreaming, thinking about their families, talking about hunting trips and fishing trips with friends, about the battles being fought elsewhere. Eventually, they get round to talking about the camp, the stories, the jokes, the racketeering, the gossip, the horrible diseases, the pitiful scams, the prisoners who arrived that morning welcomed with full military fanfare, still clinging to hope, to their dignity, to their battered suitcases, apprehensive but not scared, still believing in God, in reason, in the impossibility of the incredible. Everything is fine, they're thinking, as they line up outside the camp. They cling to the idea—as old as the world—that submissiveness will save them, will make their masters think well of them; the *Bonzen* look so powerful, so impressive that it's impossible to imagine they could lack nobility, compassion. The sight of the pristine camp, the disciplined *Kapos* running it, reassures them, persuades them that death is not the certainty some pessimists predicted during the long, agonising journey in the cattle trucks, it is merely a possibility that can be evaded with a little luck, a little cunning, if they swallow their pride. The worst is over, they have been quickly separated into groups: men, women and babies, children, the old and the crippled, the beautiful girls like Nadia. They will not hold out for long. In a little while or maybe tomorrow at dawn, after disinfection, the worthless, the *Lebensunwertes Leben*, will be sent to the gas chambers. The able-bodied will be assigned to the *Arbeitkommandos* and the *Strafarbeitkommandos*, the brothels for the *Kapos* and I don't know what else. The camp is just like our estate—everyone knows what's going on, what people are doing, what they're thinking, what they're hiding. People gossip, they watch each other, they get together for parties, funerals, marches on the town hall, campaigns to clean up the stairwells, patrol the car parks. We all know who the Islamists are and what they're planning, and we know the people who aren't and what they're afraid of. We know everything there is to know about each other. And at the same time we don't know anything, we're strangers, we think we know each other but we're all living inside our own heads, we know what we think, but other people's thoughts are vague or hearsay. On the estate, just like in the camps, people speak fifteen different languages and at least as many dialects, we can't possibly understand all of them. We fake it, we mumble. Besides, we've got nothing to talk about except the weather, we say the same things we said yesterday, the same shit we'll say anther thirty times by the end of the month. The people who live on the estate know where Paris is and the people who live in Paris know that the estate is somewhere in the suburbs—but what do we really know about each other? Nothing. We're just shadows and rumours. Between us there's a wall, barbed wire, watchtowers and minefields, fundamental prejudices, unimaginable realities. In the end, papa knew and didn't know, that's the truth of it. Rachel was my brother but I knew nothing about him and his diary is like a shield that stops me seeing him. Poor Rachel, who are you? Who was papa? Who am I? I get so fucking angry I want to scream, to cry. I'm trapped, the whole world disgusts me, I disgust myself. I'm losing my mind just like Rachel did. I hardly set foot outside the house anymore, I spend all day reading and rereading his diary, his books, or slumped in front of the TV, I go round and round in circles, cramps in my stomach. At night I go out and I walk and walk as far as I can. Alone. More alone than anyone in the world. *Like Rachel. Like poor Rachel.*

I need to know, I need to understand. Rachel made a mistake, he got caught up in his grief and it destroyed him, just like his boss Monsieur Candela told him it would. You have to try and put things in context, like Com'Dad said to me, "First you have to understand." Com'Dad thinks Rachel understood, but he's wrong, Rachel wanted to understand to take away the grief—or maybe so he could finally grieve. He became obsessed with evil and he turned it on himself. He got so caught up in it that he tried to take papa's guilt upon himself. He even imagined he'd lived in the camps, imagined himself as an SS officer's son playing with other kids, beating and killing poor little bastards who never did anything to him. The most dangerous traps are the ones we set for ourselves. Rachel even imagined putting on his black suit and going before a judge to confess to every crime committed in the Third Reich. I think what really finished him off was that poem by Primo Levi that starts off blaming the readers: "*You who live secure / In your warm houses, / Who return at evening to find / Hot food and friendly faces: / Consider whether this is a man . . .*" It was like the poem was describing Rachel's life, he's trundling along with no real worries, and then he suddenly finds out about the massacre in Aïn Deb, finds out our parents have been murdered, then he discovers papa was an SS officer who worked in the death camps for the Third Reich. When it came to me, I got straight to the point. I asked myself, what has papa's past got to do with us? That was his life, this is ours. How can we be blamed for that war, that tragedy, the Holocaust, what they call the *Shoah*? Ophélie was right: "It's not like we killed the Jews, I can't see why you're so obsessed with this whole thing." History is like that, it's a steamroller crushing everyone in its path, it's horrible, it tragic, but what can we do about it? Like Monsieur Candela said to Rachel, "Your grieving for your parents and feeling sorry for yourself isn't going to bring them back." I can't rewrite history, and feeling sorry for myself won't bring anyone back—not my parents, not Rachel, not poor Nadia, not the millions of people I didn't know who died in the gas chambers. I need to do something. To act. But do what? "Read if you want, campaign if you want, make a difference however you can. Anything else you do is the devil's work." That's what Monsieur Candela said, and he'd seen enough of life to have more faith in the devil than he had in God. And I remembered something Monsieur Vincent used to say when he'd see us scratching our heads over some clapped-out old banger: "If you stop thinking so hard, you might see things better." And a lot of the time he was right: we'd push start the old rust bucket and it would be fine. People are always making problems for themselves and then wondering why they end up with a headache.

Over and over I ask myself the same question: where in all of this is papa—the man I knew, the man who married maman, the Cheïkh of Aïn Deb, the man everyone loved and respected, uncle Ali's oldest, closest friend? Because he did exist, the father we spent all those years missing, he had two healthy sons, Rachel the brainy one and me who was never much good at anything, but I'm smart enough to know right from wrong. Am I supposed to believe the man I called papa and the SS officer are really the same person? How is it possible to blame one and honour the other, to hate the killer he was—a man I never knew—and love the father, the victim he is now, a victim of the same terrorists who are gunning for us? Did my father pay for his crimes? What about us, are we paying because we are his sons? Is this fate, *mektoub,* is it a curse? *"I commend these words to you. / Engrave them on your hearts / When you are in your house, when you walk on your way, / When you go to bed, when you rise. / Repeat them to your children. / Or may your house crumble, / Disease render you powerless, / Your offspring avert their faces from you."* That's what Primo Levi says: the children are doomed from the start because parents never tell their children about their crimes, if parents told their children everything it would be like killing them in the womb. This Primo Levi guy is crazy. I refuse to believe that God is more evil than man, that children are doomed to their fate.

Some of my mates come by the house from time to time, they say they do it just to annoy me, but actually they're shit scared that I'm losing it. They come right out and say it too, but when they see how I react, they start joking around, grabbing each other by the sleeve, by the neck, by the dick, calling each other wacko. The crazier you are, the more you laugh, they say, laughing like lunatics. You can't choose your friends. I play along just to get it over with. After they've trashed the place, we collapse on the sofa and talk. We talk for hours. It's always the same conversation. It starts with me. Why don't I go out any more? Why am I always going round with a face like an undertaker? Why am I always reading? And what the fuck am I writing in this notebook? Then they start with their stupid questions: Am I eating properly? Who washes my clothes? Who does the cleaning? Who takes out the rubbish? Who's paying the electric? I don't bother to try and explain, they've all got mothers and sisters who do everything for them. I can't imagine Bidochon—who's done, like, three days of work in his whole life—or Momo, who lives off the halal meat from his father's butcher's shop, know what a direct debit is, or how to wash a pair of boxers, make an omelette, cut a slice of bread, clean up after themselves, flush the toilet. All they've ever done is sit back and wait for everything to be done for them. The only one who can actually think is Idir-Quoi, but he can't tell you what he thinks because the minute he opens his mouth he starts stammering. There's no point even talking about Togo-au-Lait, he's black as the ace of spades, he's got his hair in cornrows like some gangsta and he thinks he's clever as a monkey. When you see the way he rolls his eyes as soon as he sees a question mark, you realise he doesn't know anything about monkeys—a lot of them are incredibly stupid. Raymou's got two brains that don't connect, a brain full of working-class common sense he inherited from his dad, and his own brain, which chews up common sense and spits it out. How much sense you get out of Raymou depends on whether you're talking to the father or the son. Or the Holy Ghost. At the end of the day, Cinq-Pouces is the only one of the lot of them with a clue, his nickname means he's all thumbs, but he's a hard worker. He's the only one of them who's ever held down a job. He used to work with his father and he can turn his hand to pretty much anything. The things at the end of his arms aren't hands, they're Swiss army knives. Like I said, you can't choose your friends. But I love them the way they are, crazy, dumb, ungrateful, awkward, useless, infuriating, and all out of bene-fits, even the benefit of the doubt. They're prisoners. Yeah, I love them.

When they came by today they said they had news—some good, most bad. The good news is that the imam from Block 17 was arrested as an accessory in Nadia's murder. "That calls for a beer," I said. "The thing is," they said, "now the whole estate has gone to shit, we couldn't stand it anymore, we had to get out." This was why they had come round, they couldn't breathe there. On the one hand, you've got the people living on the estate playing dead, waiting to see what happens before they make a move, on the other hand you've got people running round all over the place: the imam's suicide bombers, his sleep-er cells, Com'Dad's informants, the cops, the CRS, people from all kinds of organisations, reporters, academics, rubberneckers, counsellors from City Hall, representatives from Sensitive Urban Areas all over France and one or two from Belgium. We're all over the news. When the sink estates in Paris catch a cold, the whole of France ends up spitting blood. Everywhere you go on the estate you get ambushed. On their way here Momo and the guys were stopped and full-body searched thir-ty times, questioned fifteen times, interviewed seven times, called in as backup three times, and once they managed to slip through the cordon. They came up with a brilliant way of get-ting rid of the TV reporters: whenever a journalist tried to talk to them they shoved Idir-Quoi to the front, stood well back and pissed themselves laughing.

"When was the imam arrested?" I shouted.

"Yesterday," someone, I think it was Momo, said. "Some crack squad from the Rapid Response Unit they sent in from Paris pulled him in."

"They've got him bang to rights, he'll go down for at least

ten, that's what Babar down the police station said to Rabah—you know, the guy who works in the supermarket."

"Yeah sure, dickhead!" said Raymou. "My dad says that politicians are bound to get involved, I wouldn't be surprised if he wound up getting a medal."

"One of Togo-au-Lait's cousins who works as a cleaner for some government minister said they're planning to release him. Apparently banging up an imam is like setting some pedo loose in a primary school, it's just asking for trouble. Locking them up apparently just turns out more suicide bombers, meanwhile the imam's inside phoning round every sleeper cell in France and getting them out on the streets, that's right isn't it Togo?" said Manchot.

"Yeah, swear to God, my cousin heard the minister talking on the phone to some guy and pleading with him to make a conciliatory gesture."

"What does that mean?" asked Momo.

"It means what it means," said Manchot.

"They should just kill the fucker," concluded Momo.

"I agree, Momo, you're a butcher like your father, I've no bone to pick with you."

"They j . . . ju . . . just going to c . . . c . . . cover up the in . . . in . . . "

"Cover up the incident?"

"Y . . . yeah."

"We'll make them fucking sit up and take notice if they try. They've got him, they can keep him."

"They could send him back where he came from with only one eye."

"Or one arm, like Manchot here."

"Well, if that's the good news, the bad news must be a world fucking war. Spill . . . " I said.

"The first thing is there's a new emir on the estate, a guy called Flicha."

"Recruitment is obviously booming."

"And we've got this new one-eyed imam. They call him Cyclops. Aren't one-eyed people bad luck?"

"No, fool, that's hunchbacks you're thinking of."

"Bullshit, hunchbacks are supposed to bring good luck."

"This just gets better and better, now we've got gimps casting spells. Anyone else?"

"These guys are no-bullshit, they're from the AIG, they were sent in from Boufarik, that's where they've got all the Taliban training camps. The day they showed up they issued a fatwa. First: anyone who's not with them is against them. Second: girls aren't allowed out on the street anymore. Third: we're forbidden from talking to Jews, Christians, animists, communists, queers or journalists. Fourth: they've banned speed, blow, cigarettes, beer, pinball, sports, music, books, TV, movies . . . I don't remember the rest . . . "

"Wanking in public."

"Wanking in private."

"Farting in the direction of the mosque."

"Shaving your d . . . "

"You fuckwits think this is funny?"

"Yeah . . . no . . . we're just having a laugh!"

"What about the people on the estate, what are they doing about it?"

"Same old same old, they just play dead."

"What about you guys?"

Silence. Whispering.

"What about you guys?" I repeated.

"What do you expect us to do?" Raymou was angry.

"Nothing. Same old same old."

"You can talk, you the one who never leaves the house, what about you?"

It was my turn to tell them a few things. I told them what

I'd been thinking. I couldn't believe it, they actually listened from start to finish, except Momo who got up halfway through and said, "Hang on, I've got to piss, don't say anything till I get back."

He came running back, stuffing his water pistol back into his pants.

"Okay, you can go on now . . . "

I started with a question.

"How much do you guys know about Hitler?"

Silence. Looks. Whispers.

"Okay, none of you knows anything much, that simplifies things . . .

"We weren't born in Hitler's time, most of our parents weren't born, except my father, who was a fifteen-year-old sports freak when he came to power. Hitler was the German Führer, sort of like an all-powerful imam in a peaked cap and a black uniform. He had this thing called Nazism which was like a new religion. All the Germans wore swastikas round their necks, a swastika was a symbol that meant: I'm a Nazi, I believe in Hitler, I live through him and for him. He outlawed loads of things, just like the imam with this fatwa he's issued, then when Hitler had the Germans well trained, when they were proper Nazis obsessed with this new religion, with their Führer, he declared that all Jews, foreigners, immigrants, cripples, people with one arm, like you, Manchot, brainiacs like Togo, prodigies like Cinq-Pouces, motormouths like Idir-Quoi, people who were a bit soft in the head like Raymou here, mixed-race kids like me and halal butchers' sons like Momo should all be wiped out. He said they were impure, an inferior race, said they didn't deserve to live, and he said the parents that had given birth to them were to die in the fire with them. Hitler ordered all the Jews in Europe, including the ones here in France, to wear a yellow star on their chest so it would be easier for the cops to haul them in. And he had millions of people burned in furnaces. Not little ones like the one near the old train station, vast incinerators, bigger than the ones they use to burn the rubbish on the estate, and much better organised. You get the picture? Millions of men, women and children snatched off the streets, dragged to some nearby stadium where they were branded with a red-hot iron, then packed into cattle trucks and shipped off to extermination camps where they wait around for days, weeks, even months, barefoot in the snow, for someone to come and burn them. Every day, the Nazis pick some random group, tie them up with barbed wire and dump them on a conveyor belt that went more or less right to the mouth of this huge furnace. The prisoners are so scared, they don't even scream, and it doesn't matter even if they do, because there's no one to hear but themselves. And it's not just Nazis who are in charge, some of the people doing the work are prisoners—mostly young, fit guys like us—called *Kapos*. While they're waiting their turn, they work as guards, shovel coal into the furnaces, check the thermostat, keep track of the number of dead, rip out the prisoners' hair, their teeth—and know what they do with the ashes? They make fucking soap and candles for the soldiers. And it goes on and on like this, day after day, for months, years . . . "

Whispers, the guys shift in their seats, cough, I've never seen them so quiet.

"What I'm telling you here is the bare truth, it's all here in these books, I can show you the photos if you promise not to look at them for more than a second, because otherwise they'll fuck you up for the rest of your life. You won't be able to believe you're really men, that your parents are really human, that your friends are really friends, good guys like you lot, like me. Rachel checked it all out, he did research, he went to Germany, to Poland, he saw the furnaces, saw them with his own fucking eyes."

Idir-Quoi asked a question.

"What did he do it for, Rachel, I mean?"

"I'm getting to that . . . " I said.

"One day, the whole world got together and declared war on this madness and they killed the imam, the leader, the Führer and all his emirs and they took over Germany. That's when they found the extermination camps. There were dozens of them and millions of dead and survivors that looked like so much like corpses that they didn't know what to say to them. When my parents and everyone else in Aïn Deb were murdered by the Islamists, Rachel got to thinking. He figured that fundamentalist Islam and Nazism were *kif-kif*—same old same old. He wanted to find out what would happen if people did nothing, the way people did nothing in Germany back in the day, what would happen if nobody did anything in Kabul and Algeria where they've got I don't know how many mass graves, or here in France where we've got all these Islamist Gestapo. In the end, the whole idea scared him so much he killed himself. He thought it was too late, he felt guilty, he said that by saying nothing it was like we were colluding, he said we're all caught in this trap and if we go on doing nothing, go round pretending like we're talking about things intelligently, we'll wind up being *Kapos* without even realising, and we won't even notice that everyone around us has turned into a *Kapo* already.

"That's bullshit—we're not *Kapos*!" Raymou yelled.

"Really? A while back we were all on their side and we didn't even know, remember?"

I didn't have to say any more, they remembered, they'd been up to their balls in it.

"So, what? You're suggesting we all top ourselves like Rachel?" Raymou asked.

"No, we're not going to die, we're going to live, we're going to fight."

"How?"

"I don't know, we'll have to see . . . "

"Fuck's sake, all this bullshit and now he says he doesn't know!"

"Why don't we set up an anti-Islamic league?" suggested Bidochon.

"Islamic or Islamist?" asked Raymou.

"Who cares? It's the same difference."

"Bullshit, it's not the same at all, my parents are Muslims, Islam is the greatest religion in the world!" shouted Momo.

"My mother does the *Salat*, and she wouldn't hurt a fly," added Idir-Quoi.

"It's Muslims that end up becoming Islamists, though, isn't it?" said Manchot.

"No, there's Christians too, like Raymou," said Idir-Quoi.

"Okay, Momo, look it up in the dictionary, tell us the difference."

"There's no difference if you ask me," said Bidochon.

"Just look it up, Momo . . . under I, no that's J . . . it's comes before that . . . Idir-Quoi, you look it up."

Idir-Quoi might have trouble saying words, but when they're on a page he's a genius. It took him two minutes to find the definition but it took him ten minutes to read it out, so I'll skip the stammering.

"*Islamic: of, or relating to, Islam*, and Islamist means . . . um . . . I can't find it. It's not in here, it doesn't exist . . . what the fuck?"

"That's an old dictionary, they didn't have Islamists back then."

"No, it was published in 1990, we had jihadists back then."

"Yeah but dictionaries are serious, they don't just put every single word in there."

"Okay, let's say anti-Islamist."

"And what exactly is it supposed to do, this league of yours?"

"Take down the Islamists."

"How?"

"We'll run them off the estate!"

"How?"

" . . . "

An hour later we still hadn't got anywhere. The conversation went off in all directions, but every time we hit a brick wall. We knew what the problem was, we just didn't have the solution. Stopping Islamism is like trying to catch the wind, you need a bit more than a sieve or a bunch of muppets like us. It wasn't enough to know. It wasn't enough to understand. It wasn't enough to want it. What we didn't have the Islamists had in spades: determination. We're like the concentration camp prisoners, caught up in the Machine, paralysed by fear, fascinated by evil, clinging to the secret hope that passivity will save us.

I didn't tell them about papa, about his past. They're my friends, I didn't want them spooked, didn't want them running out on me. And besides, they are what they are, they're harmless enough but they get wound up easily. They might start thinking their fathers were hiding some terrible secret in their past. I didn't want Togo suddenly remembering his great-grandfather was a cannibal and that the only way they cured his father was by feeding him raw steak from the day he was born—it would kill him. *My father never told me anything*, Rachel said. It's true, fathers never have anything to say.

Momo, who's always been too curious for his own good, gave me this weird look. "Your father was German, wasn't he . . . was he a Nazi?" I said, "Don't be so fucking stupid, he emigrated to Algeria, he was fighting with the *maquis* for your country's independence . . . and he died a martyr."

It was midnight by the time they left. I could tell just by looking at them that this whole conversation had scared them, they didn't say anything, they were shuffling along, not looking at each other. They pulled their jackets tight around them and disappeared into the freezing shadows. I felt sorry for them, they looked like prisoners dragged back to camp after a botched escape attempt. Tonight, they would come to know the nightmare that has haunted me since Rachel's death. In a couple of months I've aged a hundred years. I wouldn't wish on them what the camp prisoners had to live through every moment of their short, endless lives. I wouldn't wish it on anyone except the imam from Block 17 and his emir.

SATURDAY 2 NOVEMBER 1996

First thing this morning, I had a visit from Madame
Karsmirsky, Wenda Karsmirsky—Ophélie's mother. In
another life she was a white Russian, in this one she's a
die-hard French bigot who's completely forgotten her roots.
I'd had no idea, but the way she leans on the doorbell is
enough to wake the dead—a brutal, non-stop, angry ringing—
only cops ring doorbells like that. One minute I was sleeping
and next I was standing in front of the door wondering who I
was. The panicked reflex of a sleeper. As I opened the door I
still had my eyes closed. "Young man," her harsh voice spat in
my face, "the least you could do is look at me when I'm talking to you." That was Madame Karsminsky for you. The Diva,
Rachel used to call her. "*Bonjour, madame,*" I said, rubbing my
eyes. She shrugged and marched past me trailing a sickly cloud
of perfume. I'm not sure what happened, but I ended up in the
living room staring at the ceiling while she nosed about
upstairs. I listened as she whirled around like a tornado, high
heels clattering. Then she came downstairs and stood in front
of me and started yelling: "My God, this place is a pigsty!" She
gave me the morning to tidy the place up, pack my stuff and
move out. From what she didn't say, I worked out that Ophélie
had decided to stay in Canada permanently and had asked her
mother to sell the house and send her the money. "I've got
power of attorney," she told me, taking a piece of paper out of
her bag and waving it triumphantly under my nose. I had to
believe her. I said, "Is it okay if I take Rachel's books?" She

gave me a look of withering contempt. "Much good they'll do you!" I went into the garage, filled a cardboard box, heaved it onto my shoulder and headed for the door. "Who's going to tidy up this mess?" she yelled after me "It looks tidy to me." I said, and I left. She ran after me and said, "You can take Ophélie's car if you want." "I don't know how to drive," I said. "And anyway, I haven't got a licence." It was only the third time I'd seen her; the first was at the party Rachel threw when he got his French citizenship, the second was the day he married Ophélie, today was the end of the story in which we had played minor but important roles, she the overbearing mother-in-law, me the little brother who'd gone off the rails.

She called me back again, rummaging through her handbag. "I forgot," she said, "I don't suppose it's important, but Ophélie sent you a letter. I haven't read it—you can see for yourself, the envelope's still sealed." I said, "Thank you, madame," and I left.

I headed back to the estate. With a big box on my back and a face like death warmed over, I looked like a burglar heading home after a hard night's work. If the cops had stopped me, I'd have been screwed, I'd have had a hard time explaining my obsession with books about exterminating the Jews. But the cops round here know me; I thought, to cheer myself up, we'd just shoot the shit for ten minutes and I'd be off.

Standing at the entrance to the estate, looking up at the tower blocks rising into the sky, I felt dizzy, I felt sick. My life as a recluse was over. I was like a convict finally released just as he realises he doesn't want to get out because he knows that on the outside, with his friends and family, he'll be a true outsider. I was terrified, I knew nothing would be like the way it was before, not me, not the estate. I knew I'd have to find somewhere else to live, I'd be a real exile, with no past, no future.

Books are heavy and, I tell you, walking up ten flights of stairs takes it out of you. The lift packed up so long ago people forget it's even there. On the estate, we live like mountaineers, we climb up and toss a rope down to help the old folk stuck on the ledges. By the time I got to the tenth floor, I was practically crawling. I rang the doorbell, polite as I could. Aunt Sakina said, "Sit down, I'll get you some coffee." I set down the box and collapsed into a chair. Uncle Ali was sitting in his favourite chair, staring out the window, he was off in his head somewhere. It was nice, I realised, to come home, to be with your family, to see them getting on with life as though nothing had happened.

I opened Ophélie's letter. There was a piece of card and . . . ten $100 bills. *In God We Trust* was printed on each one. I read the letter as I drank my coffee. I'd forgotten what it tasted like. Ophélie wrote:

Dear Malrich,

I hope you and your family are well. I've decided to stay here in Canada and I've asked maman to put the house up for sale. Thanks for looking after it for me all this time. I hope you weren't too bored living there, and that you weren't too scared sleeping there at night. And I hope you remembered to water the plants! I'm sending you $1,000 for your trouble. By my reckoning, you should get 5,162 francs for them at a bureau de change. *If they offer you less, take it to a bank, their rates are usually better. You'll need some form of ID, so don't forget to bring your identity card. If you want anything from the house, the TV or Rachel's clothes, feel free, I've told maman to let you take whatever you want.*

I send you my love. Be good. Find a nice girlfriend and be happy.

Ophélie

P.S.: I'd rather you heard this from me: I've met someone else, we're getting married.

I thought about Rachel: Poor bastard, must be turning in his grave.

This sudden downpour of dollars is a blessing—now I can finally go to Aïn Deb. Like Rachel, I'm going back to the source, back to my childhood, to our house, our parents. Back to my father. To say a prayer at my parents' grave. I'm scared to death but I'm happy. I feel it's a journey that I need to make, one I would have had to make sooner or later. I need to feel Algerian soil beneath my feet, feel it hold me up like an insignificant insect. Not because I used to live there as a kid, not because my mother and my grandparents were born there or because my father spent most of his life there. None of these things are as important as the fact that my parents are buried there. I don't know how to explain it, I've always had trouble putting things into words, I can't do it, so I just write down the facts, but that doesn't explain what I feel. I never was very good at school. What I'm trying to say is that death expresses truth better than life. I think nothing connects a man to the earth more than the graves of his parents and his grandparents. That's only just occurred to me, I'll have to think about it, because it sounds strange to say death binds us to life when we know that death is the end of everything. Rachel used to say home is where you live, which is true—but he was talking about the emigrants who stubbornly go on living as emigrants and who end up not living in their own country or their adopted one. Rachel was right, it's psychology. They're just thinking about themselves, about their deaths, about the grave waiting for them back in the old country, they're not thinking about the children they're leaving dangling over the abyss. It's hardly surprising that when they fall, they break their necks. Imagine if Togo-au-Lait's parents had raised him to be like his great-grandfather, he'd have eaten the lot of us and he wouldn't even feel sorry. But I also think that home is the country where your parents are buried, that's why I felt I needed to go and see that land, walk on it, soak up some part of the mystery fed by generations of souls. "A riddle wrapped in a mystery inside an enigma," to quote Churchill, who Rachel thought was the greatest hero of the war against the Nazis. That's what a country should be, a mystery. But still I wonder why I've never been interested in Germany. My father was born there, my grandparents are buried there, so some part of my soul must be over there in what Rachel called the mystery of deepest, darkest Germany. Is it because of the war? Because of Papa's past? Is it because I've never been there? Rachel says it's beautiful, incredibly well organised, he says the people are really helpful. I'll go there some day.

From what Rachel says in his diary, the officials at the Algerian consulate in Nanterre aren't likely to be much help. I can't trust them, I'll have to see if I can find someone on the estate who's got some scam going with the passport officer, it will save a lot of time and a lot of money.

In the end, it was easy. Momo steered me in the right direction, his father had been involved in some dodgy stuff back in the day, back when Algeria was just coming out of the socialist terror and everyone thought they'd be able to come and go whenever they wanted. Passports were selling like hotcakes, you'd hand over your cash in the morning and you'd get your *Ausweis* delivered to you at Café Da Hocine the same night. But it only lasted a couple of months before the doors slammed shut again, the socialist dictatorship in Algeria came back with a vengeance and this time got into bed with two other dictators—corruption and religion—and Momo's dad had to stop trafficking in passports because he was no match for the new regime, so he took all the cash he'd made and set up as a halal butcher and pretty quickly he got the reputation of being the best halal butcher for quality, value and strict adherence to Qur'anic law. He does a lot of his business at Eid, he goes all round the estate slitting sheep's throats, for a whole month he's up to his elbows in sheep's blood. So I got myself a brand new green Algerian passport, same day service, and all it cost me was five kilos of prime fillet steak. Poor Rachel had to slog his guts out to get his. It was weird, having the passport made me feel like an illegal immigrant. That's the thing about being mixed-race, you're not one thing or another. What I need is a French-Algerian-German passport. But you have to make do with what you get in this life, as Monsieur Vincent used to say when he'd see us drooling over a brochure for some shiny high-tech equipment.

This was the first time in my life I ever saw aunt Sakina surprised by anything. When I told her I was going back to the *bled*, she looked at me like she didn't understand what I'd just said. "Where did you say you were going?" she said, her voice cracking. I kept right on, pretending I hadn't noticed how worried she was. "To Aïn Deb, just for a week or so, I want to go and see papa and maman's graves, catch up with some friends from when I was a kid." She thought for a moment, then she said, "I've got a little money put by, I'll buy some things for you to take to the children there, I'm sure there's a lot of things they need."

She packed a suitcase for me, the biggest one she could find, the suitcase of an emigrant coming home, a poor man's Santa Claus.

When I told my mates I was going back to the *bled*, as we stood freezing our balls off in a stairwell in one of the tower blocks, they didn't pull punches.

"What are you, sick in the head? You'll get your throat cut."

"Have you forgotten what they did to your parents?"

"Fuck sake, don't be stupid, stay here with us."

"You don't speak Arabic, you don't speak Berber, how are you supposed to talk to people?"

"Pretend you're deaf and dumb . . . "

"Dress like a Taliban, that way no one will notice you."

"Steer clear of the red-light districts."

"Steer clear of the *banlieues*."

"Watch out for the cops, everyone says they're like the mafia."

"Keep away from the jihadists."

"They'll roast you like a Jew."

"There's no way they're going to let you come back."

"They'll arrest you, they don't like the French over there."

"They'll never let you in, they fucking hate French Arabs."

. . .

I waited till they were done, then I said, "Thanks for the support, guys, but I'm going anyway. I'll be back in a week. Meet me from the plane at Orly."

The night before I left was a long one. Aunt Sakina kept coming and going, she'd check to make sure the suitcase was properly closed, then she'd open it and put something else in, close it again, zip it up tight, go back to the living room, then come back to check it again. Uncle Ali was in his bed, staring at the ceiling, off somewhere in his head.

In my room, I read and reread the part of Rachel's diary about going back to the *bled*, the airport, the security guards staring at everyone, snapping their fingers and dragging anyone suspicious out of the line, the atmosphere in the streets of Algiers like a concentration camp, the undercover taxi drivers who dump you in the middle of nowhere, the fake roadblocks, the guards holed up in their blockhouses, the desolate, dying landscape. It was weird, but the black picture he painted of it encouraged rather than discouraged me. I'd never thought that going back to the root of things would be easy. Everything has a price, and I was prepared to pay. Rachel says something about the road to Damascus, I don't know what it means but I'm guessing that's what the road to Algiers must be like.

Aunt Sakina didn't get a wink of sleep that night. She didn't move from the living room. She was turning things over in her mind. I'm the only child she's got now; when uncle Ali is gone, she'll only have me. I have to come back.

I didn't sleep either. I read for a bit, then I turned off the light and stared at the ceiling, trying to think. I had all this stuff going round and round in my mind. I'd tried to deal with each worry as it popped into my head, but the more I tried, the more there were. There were so many, I couldn't think, and in the end I dozed off. Suddenly I saw myself in a long, dark hallway, terrified as a prisoner on death row, I was struggling against something, I don't know what, something pushing me into the darkness, then suddenly these two guys in balaclavas jumped out of the darkness, grabbed me by the arms and dragged me off, panting for breath. My legs were kicking into thin air. They threw me into this huge stadium where the terraces were already teeming with prisoners who looked weird, haggard and silent. Just as I was about to get to my feet and run away, these terrifying men appeared out of a tunnel and surrounded me, chanting my name in hoarse, frenzied voices: Schiller! . . . Schiller! . . . Schiller! . . . they stretched their arms out towards me: *Sieg Heil! . . . Sieg Heil! . . . Sieg Heil! . . .* The silence on the terraces was more intense and I was crying in pain. I woke up with a start, turned on the light. *Maman*, where am I? I put my head in my hands. I looked down at the suitcase on the floor. I didn't remember leaving it there. It was a stupid place to leave it, anyone might trip over it, I would have pushed it against the wall or under the bed, or put it on a chair. I couldn't take my eyes off it. It fascinated and terrified me, then I smiled to myself, it's just a thing, a box, a suitcase that needs to be strapped up so it doesn't burst and spill everything everywhere. It seemed strange, taking clothes when you're going nowhere, when you're going to spend a week with friends in your other home . . . But caught up in Rachel's stories of the Holocaust, the suitcase reminded me of the concentration camps, of the life we leave behind.

This is no time to get spooked, I thought, in a couple of hours I'm flying off to a country where there's a real war on, where no one can be sure they'll make it through the day alive. Fuck sake, I grew up on the H24 estate, I've seen enough to take on the devil himself! But every time I managed to calm myself down, it started all over again. I'd read a bit, turn off the light, stare at the ceiling, determined not to think about anything. I'd try to think of the best way of not thinking about things and suddenly all the same thoughts would come flooding back. Suddenly I'm drugged and thrown into that stadium with the same zombies still chanting my name. It's a vicious circle. In the end, I got up, pushed the suitcase under the bed, sat on the floor next to the window with my back to the wall and kept watch until morning. I didn't feel safe until I heard the usual racket of the town blocks. It was four in the morning, the old African men in their Turkish slippers were getting ready for their daily migration across the savannah, the faithful were feverishly performing *Wudu*—their ritual ablutions—and every kid on the estate, ripped suddenly from their nightmares, was screaming loud enough to burst a deaf man's eardrum. Then all the TVs and the radios came on at once. By this time, aunt Sakina had already settled uncle Ali in his chair by the window, cleaned the apartment and made breakfast. I checked my papers five times and drank endless cups of coffee while I waited. I was shaking. This would be the first time I'd been on a plane since I'd left Algeria, the first time I'd left France since then, the first time I'd faced the unknown, the first time I'd ever felt death at my elbow. And it was the first time in my life I would ever carry a suitcase. I was scared shitless.

Rachel's Diary

June–July 1995

I've been wandering around Europe for more than a month now, still retracing my father's footsteps. I was travelling back through time. It was the story of my life. I can't cope with being in France, with being at home, with the day-to-day routine. Too much has happened. The company finally fired me, Ophélie finally left me, my health wasn't too good. And there was nothing I could do about any of it. To be honest, I had seen it coming but I did nothing, I just let it come. On a battlefield, such stoic acceptance and self-sacrifice would have marked me as a hero, but I did nothing because in the situation I was in, there was nothing to be done—the evil came from within. Everything inside me was broken. I was like one of those hopeless people whose great love has died, like someone who has survived a terrible disaster and goes into mourning never to come out. I had lost my place in the social order, in life, I was a pariah, I was my father's son—I had been told as much by my friend, that ruin of a man, the great Adolph, aka Jean 134, son of the no less-remarkable Jean 92. At work, it was like I didn't exist: no projects, no meetings, no phone calls. The paperwork was in hand, just waiting for a signature, everyone was waiting. There was nothing to be done, the CEO was constantly on the move, looking for some new El Dorado. When the paperwork finally arrived, I left, and it was as though I had never worked for the company. One signature wiped away ten years of loyal service. All anyone remembered were the last six months, which, admittedly, were catastrophic compared to the successes of my first nine and a half years there. Monsieur Candela shook my hand, squeezed my shoulder, said, "Drop by the house anytime." He even had a tear in his eye, he's always been a straight-up guy. I promised to drop by and I left. I've had enough of selling pumps and sluices, of cavitation problems that are always the fault of the manufacturer, never the fault of the client, I don't give a damn about the terrible quality of their water, their oil, their milk, I can admit that now I've been relieved of my duties. Ophélie had reached the point of no return; in her mind, she had already left me, now she could breathe easily as she slowly packed up her things like we were moving house. I didn't say anything. From time to time, she would look at me, head tilted back, eyes half-closed, then she'd shrug and go back to her packing. That's how she's always been, more worker bee than wife. Then, one day, she walked out. She left a note on the kitchen table. I read it and put it in a drawer. I knew that she was only doing what she had to do, I didn't blame her. I couldn't expect her to go on living with this frightening stranger. And she had no idea what was really going on, she didn't know the stranger she was living with was the son of a monster who at any moment might turn into an SS officer and stuff her into the gas cooker. My body no longer sent out alarm signals, I had long since passed the danger point, now I didn't feel anything except a slight sclerosis sometimes, a sudden confused urge to tear off my skin. I was distanced from life, and the distance had grown wider, the haze had thickened, the silence had deepened, the empty hours passed, the emptiness ever deeper. I was like the outsider the prescient Camus describes, an alien on earth, everything is here but nothing means anything. Perhaps I was dead but didn't know it. How could I know, since in my state everything was relative and therefore equally unimportant?

This is the nature of great tragedies, they hatch in the bowels of the earth, one day a small crack appears, at night you hear a rumbling and wonder whether it might be an earthquake, then just when you begin to think there may be hope, the world caves in and crumbles into rubble. An immense column of pain rises into the sky. Silence falls and with it a colossal emptiness. You are shocked, crushed, shattered, your dignity is torn from you and you slump into prostration, into autism, one step closer to the end. This is where I was now, in utter darkness, 9.0 on the Richter scale and, insofar as I was able to see in an abyss, I was alone. More alone than anyone in the world. In saner moments, I told myself that all this suffering stemmed from the fact that I was some strange dreamer, a fool in a world of recurring nightmares, clinging to the idea of a simple, graceful, everlasting life. But more often, like dear Adolph sitting in front of his poisonous schnapps, I thought nothing at all: dreams, life, harmony, simplicity were words that no longer meant anything to me. What right did I have to use such words knowing how my father had flouted them? I was in a strange position. Excruciatingly painful. Utterly devastating. I was inside the skin, inside the skeletal monotony of the concentration camp prisoner waiting for the end, and I was inside my father's skin, jealous of his vocation which brought about that end. In me, these two extremes had come together for the worse. Like the jaws of a vise.

Ophélie's lawyer came by. A pretty tubby little woman who seemed to have asthma. Or maybe she panted and wheezed to impress her clients and alarm the opposition. Her cheeks were perfectly pink, her breasts so white they could blind oncoming traffic. She gave me a fiercely professional smile and offhandedly asked me to sign some papers. I did as she asked, not bothering to read them and said to her, "You don't have to give me the silent treatment, it's only fair that everything goes to my future ex-wife. I would be grateful if you would intercede on my behalf, I'd like to stay in the house until I can find a place somewhere far away from here." She promised she would, and gave me a sympathetic smile. On that note we went our separate ways, each happy with the outcome.

I must have done everything mechanically. I don't remember anything. One morning, I found myself at Roissy Airport clutching a boarding pass for Frankfurt, carrying a small rucksack with a change of clothes, papa's military service record and the big notebook I've been carrying around with me since . . . since April 1994, or maybe a little later, since Aïn Deb, when the *thing* entered into me.

As I was going through security, I wondered, why Frankfurt? It was only once I was on the plane that I remembered. According to his military record, Hans Schiller studied Chemical Engineering at the Johann Wolfgang Goethe-Universität, in Frankfurt am Main. The rest I had deduced or discovered from my research. I read that it was in the laboratories of the industrial chemical group IG Farben, with the support of the Johann Wolfgang Goethe-Universität, under the direction of the sinister Nebe, head of Einsatzgruppe B, that they had developed Zyklon B, the poison used in the gas chambers. From the moment I found out, I couldn't help but wonder whether papa, who had just finished his degree at the time, was somehow involved in the research and in the endless arguments that the proposal to gas camp prisoners had triggered among the dignitaries, the intellectuals and the bleeding hearts of the Third Reich. The problem they were fretting over was this: having decided to gas the *Lebensunwertes Leben*—Jews and other *Minderwertige Leute*, the mentally handicapped, the ill, the gypsies, the homosexuals—should the procedure be humane, or were the results all that mattered? The first approach, the humane solution, called for the use of odourless gas, or, better still, prussic acid, which has a sweet smell, something IG Farben produced in industrial quantities for agricultural and domestic purposes, for fumigating grain stores and for domestic rat poison. Those being gassed would feel nothing, would not know they were dying, at a certain point they would simply drop like flies and it would all be over. This would be the most humane way to kill them, *eine der humansten Tötungsarten*. Moreover, it would spare their killers much of the horror of the work. But it turned out that this method posed a serious risk to German soldiers and those who operated the gas chambers, the *Sonderkommado*—camp prisoners who were subjected to the torment of having to remove the bodies of their brothers and take them to the crematoria—since they might venture into the chambers after a batch of killings and be poisoned without realising it. Others—and these were the people who won the argument—were in favour of making the gas highly irritating by the addition of an odorant—*warnstoff*—which would alert them to any residual gas in the chambers or to any leaks when handling gas canisters. The choice, they maintained, was between the soldier and the prisoner, between the safety of the former and the comfort of the latter. The problem having been formulated in such a way that it led naturally, humanely, to favouring their own, they decided this would be the wisest course of action. Those being gassed would suffer terribly, but since the eventual intention was to kill them and burn their bodies, this minor inconvenience hardly mattered and was morally acceptable. To placate more sensitive souls, they decided on a ruse: those taken to the gas chambers would be told that they were going to shower, this way they would be happy and grateful. But this is the sort of ploy you can only use once. Word quickly spread in the camps, everyone knew everything. Eventually, this hollow promise was reserved for those newly arrived: the worthless, the old, the children, the pregnant women, the sick and the handicapped who would be only too happy to believe it.

I read that tests had been carried out on human subjects in Frankfurt and in one of the suburbs which no longer exists. Experiments were carried out on groups of five, groups of ten,

on standardized groups—all men, all women and all children—
and on mixed groups: families—father, mother, son, daughter,
grandmother, even the maid if she was Jewish or a little soft in
the head. The purpose of the experiments being to determine
how much gas was needed in both cases to kill quickly and efficiently. Since lung capacity differed from one subject to another,
it was possible to establish a correlation between the volume of
air inhaled and the time taken before death ensued, taking into
account natural disparities, such as the fact that though a baby
inhales less air than an adult, being considerably weaker, it
takes less gas to kill it. It's the story of Galileo when, before an
audience of stunned prelates, he demonstrated that, whether
light or heavy, bodies free fall at an identical speed which is,
therefore, independent of their mass. An adult is resilient but
inhales considerably more air than a baby, but the baby is physically weaker. In the end, death comes to both at the same time.
These experiments demonstrated that people could be gassed
in groups without regard to sex, age or physical condition.
Whether by bullet, by rope or by gas chamber, they died just the
same. There was no need to separate prisoners into groups,
something of an advantage in a mass extermination. The problem, however, remained a complex one with many variables—
the stress levels of the subject, the dosage, the shape and size
of the gas chambers, the skill of those operating them, etc.
There were fears that, though life and death are abstract con-
cepts, the supernatural and the religious might produce unwel-
come thoughts in the minds of those operating the chambers,
there was talk of the rabbi's curse, of avenging ghosts, of strange
miracles. A production-line process, they concluded, would put
paid to such nonsense by giving each individual worker the
impression that he was performing only the most innocuous task
in the extermination process. Just as in a firing squad, every soldier is free to believe that he fired the blank. A production-line
approach was applied to every stage of the process, from the

rounding up of the Jews, through their arrest and transportation, to the burning of the bodies in the camps. The link does not know it is part of the chain. We are not all equal in the face of death, a breeze may be enough to kill one man, while another, no bigger, no stronger, no more intelligent, may survive an earthquake. It falls to the Machine to equalize our relationship with death. A means therefore had to be found to take into account the principal variables. Calculating devices were created to make the process easier for a workforce that was not especially bright. By turning a dial to the number of people packed into the chamber, and moving a slider to the volume of the chamber in cubic metres, it was possible to read off the quantity of Zyklon B necessary; this quantity was further refined by setting one slider to the temperature of the chamber and another to the initial figure for the quantity of Zyklon B. In warm weather, say 25°C, death could be guaranteed for 95 percent of the subjects in a thirty-minute period. In cold weather, however—below 5°C—the mass of air is stationary, gas disperses poorly and productivity is negatively affected, making it necessary to repeat the procedure or increase the quantity of Zyklon B, either of which represented a waste of the Reich's time and money. A loss of ten minutes and three *Reichsmarks* per subject may seem insignificant, but with some ten million subjects marked out for death, the shortfall would amount to 100 million minutes and 30 million *Reichsmarks*, an unacceptable folly for a country already involved in an otherwise profitable world war.

It was later discovered that this theory was mistaken and held true only in small-scale, controlled laboratory conditions. In practice, things worked differently. Leakage presented a significant problem. Hermetically sealing a tiny cubicle containing two or three weak experimental subjects was a very different matter to sealing a vast hangar filled with two thousand people hardened by incarceration. Productivity, it turned out, was disastrous in periods of warm weather and cold conditions proved to be ideal. This anomaly perturbed a number of scientists, but this mystery was quickly solved just as others emerged—since nothing is ever as it seems on paper. The canisters of Zyklon B, it turned out, did not contain two hundred litres, as stated on the invoices and on the labels printed on each canister; in fact the volume varied so widely that one out of three gassings was compromised. The obvious explanation was leakage, but much of the blame lay with the exaggerated claims which friends of the Reich—IG Farben in particular—made in order to massage the statistics sent to their supervisors. There was a lot of money involved, a lot of back slapping and bribes. The anomaly concerning temperature—a variable which created considerable problems—deserves further explanation. In warm weather, gas expands and rises, the greatest concentration being found at the ceiling of the chamber. That, after all, is one of the intrinsic properties of a gas. The victims quickly realised this and, at the first sign of sickness, they threw themselves to the ground, closed their eyes and slowed their breathing. Thirty minutes later, when the doors to the chamber were opened, the *kapos* were stunned to find the subjects lying on the ground, weakened, but for the most part still alive. It seemed likely that those who died did so as a result of panic, overcrowding and suffocation rather than the effects of the gas. In cold weather, on the other hand, the gas remained concentrated at floor level and productivity was excellent. There were still survivors, mostly infants whose parents had held them on their shoulders for as long as they were able, but such exceptions merely confirmed the rule and the poor mites were usually in such a bad way that they usually died on the way to the *Krema*—the furnace—so it was unnecessary to gas them a second time—a horrifying prospect for those operating the chambers. The shape and size of the chambers also proved to be critical. Although a long, narrow, low-ceilinged chamber produces excellent results, it is difficult to persuade subjects to go inside, they panic when they see what looks like a tomb. Were they to refuse it might result in chaos, something which had been declared a cardinal sin in Germany. This happened in a number of camps, and the authorities were obliged to enlarge the chambers. A large, high-ceilinged chamber reassured the subjects. Who knows why—human nature is unfathomable—since the end result, as even the prisoner knows, is the same. The *Sonderkommando* preferred large chambers. Less work, more bodies, but this was frustrating for those operating the *Kremas*, since the furnaces did not have the capacity to deal with the deliveries. Corpses began to pile up, they rotted, attracting rats and flies and all sorts of vermin, which again resulted in chaos.

Overseeing an operation of this nature is not as easy as it might seem. It is a complex industrial process with all the flaws inherent in such systems: a poorly educated workforce prone to absenteeism, then there were the power failures, stock shortages, disparities between supply and demand at the *Kremas*, which disrupt schedules and break the working rhythm, creating bottlenecks and resulting in workers unable to work. Then there is the necessary micromanagement—as we call it these days because it sounds more complex than management—with all that it entails: unfeasible performance targets imposed like religious tenets, inter-departmental rivalry, the cliques, the clashes of interests, the scrabbling for seniority, the blunders. The extermination camps competed fiercely for everything: the best equipment, the biggest budgets, the top-flight experts; they vied with each other in their savoir faire, their passion, their inventiveness, each trying to please the Führer, each trembling at the thought of disappointing Himmler. But it's impossible to keep track of everything, and when one thing breaks down, there are repercussions all down the production line. In such conditions, it's impossible to allocate blame and, by the time the problem is fixed, half a dozen more have appeared elsewhere. It might be a catastrophic event—a fire, an explosion, a virulent pandemic, an escape, an act of sabotage—with all the attendant disruption: reports to be written up, stress levels to be calmed, disciplinary action to be taken, another purging of the ranks, all of which negatively impacts on the great god of productivity. Experts had to be on site to do real-time problem solving. There was no place in the Machine for incompetence and amateurism—two things which, in the Third Reich, were considered to be greater than the seven deadly sins. It only takes five minutes to round up a firing squad, and a lot less to sign a transfer to the Russian front. An experienced chemical engineer needed to be on hand for the gas chambers, and a combustion expert was needed for the furnaces. Then there were the doctors, the lab assistants, the accountants and quartermasters: the operation involved much more than the gas chambers and the *Kremas*. There was everything else to consider: the various workshops and farms responsible for keeping the Reich supplied with everything it might need. A good-sized camp, after all, comprised three or four hundred thousand prisoners, turnover was high, you needed enough guards to supervise everyone, a dozen service sectors and a systems management team keeping everyone working to full capacity. Ask any CEO, he'll tell you, running a town or a company of that size is no easy task. Murder on this scale is not something that can be achieved by a random serial killer. And coordinating twenty-five extermination camps spread over several countries is a colossal undertaking, one that would cripple many a government today. The logistics of the railway system alone give some idea of the countless tasks which have to be timed to the split second. A railway system is not a toy. Before they could be gassed, these millions of people had to be tracked down, identified, inventoried, captured, grouped, transported and shipped out according to various, sometimes contradictory, criteria, then re-registered, fed, clothed, examined, made to work according to the standards of the Reich, guarded, disciplined and finally destroyed, and all of this had to be done according to a strict timetable and in complete secrecy. Let us not forget: secrecy was the sine qua non of the final solution, the one thing without which it could not function. Secrecy was to the final solution what invisibility is to God—take away the one, make visible the other and the whole system collapses. I read somewhere that at its height, Auschwitz alone cremated more than fifteen thousand people a day. They must have been working flat out. Papa worked in Auschwitz for a while, it must have been tough work, but he'd already spent time at most of the camps in Germany and Poland so his experience would have stood him in good stead.

It was thinking about him, about his incredibly stressful, unrewarding work that prompted me to collate all this information on the gas chambers and the *Kremas*. I wanted to be able to picture his daily routine in the death trade. I also felt that to judge my father I needed to understand his crimes, to set down each stage, to reconstruct everything as accurately as possible. There would still be a chapter to be written about extenuating circumstances but, having given this some thought, I decided that a man engulfed by evil who does not commit suicide, does not resist, does not give himself up and demand justice in the name of his victims but runs away, hides, conspires so his family are oblivious, has no right to compassion, no claim to extenuating circumstances. Children always judge their fathers harshly, but they do so because they love and respect them more than anyone in the world. I also thought—thought first and foremost—of the victims in this vast hell, and it occurred to me that all the meaning in the world had gone up in smoke with them. We live in a new era, an era in which the impossible is the only thing that is possible. With computing, automation and modern methods of manipulating the masses, the Great Miracle is now within our grasp—just look at the horrors visited on so many honourable peoples in the service homilies as pathetic as *Mein Kampf*, and with only the meagre resources of third-world countries: Mao's *Little Red Book*, Qaddafi's *Green Book*, the writings of Kim Il-sung and Khomeini, and those of the "Türkmenbaşy"— Saparmurat Niyazov—and the millions of people destroyed by sects devoid of ideas and of means.

I studied so many other things. One question was never adequately answered—by which I mean in general terms, which might be applied to all the camps: what is the optimum physical condition for camp prisoners—that which best corresponds to the demands for productivity and imperatives of security? When prisoners are sick and weak, they don't work, they are a drain on the assets of the Reich, but when they are healthy, they are dangerous: they think, they rebel, they foment unrest, organise escapes, sabotage equipment, lie to the *Kapos* who are too stupid to fear what they cannot see, they sap the morale of younger soldiers not yet inured to evil. This problem, which is easy to formulate but difficult to solve, was the subject of countless studies and numerous experiments. There are a number of considerations: first, the sick are not always genuinely sick. Research demonstrated that those who claimed to be at death's door often watched countless coreligionists die before they finally succumbed; and many of those who claimed to be in perfect health were actually suicidal and attempting to kill themselves through work. These are the most dangerous prisoners, desperation makes them cunning, bitter, depraved, they are capable of anything, capable of grabbing a machine gun and firing wildly until they have emptied the last round, of setting fire to the barracks, of rushing a guard and slitting his throat or slamming him against the electric fence until their burning bodies fuse in death. The best advice, often repeated, is to flush them out and eliminate them as a warning to others or—if possible, since they represent the workforce—give them hope. There are many ways of going about this, sometimes a friendly gesture is enough to calm their self-destructive fury, often strong-arm tactics are the only solution.

In modern jargon we call this Operations Research Modelling, a particularly complex paradigm involving quantifiable behaviour models that can be studied by doctors, and other factors which cannot, like the impact of long winters on behaviour, the stench that saps the soul and tears it apart, the boundless agonising loneliness, the squabbles between prisoners, the impact of rumours, the arrival of new prisoners which may spark new tensions or bring fresh despair, the prevailing winds, what do I know, morale is like a wisp of smoke, it takes little to send it one way or the other and eventually it fades, dissipates into madness. Only the intuition and experience of old hands in the camps made it possible to overcome these problems. All of the solutions were discovered through trial and error, never in the labs in Berlin where researchers indulged in wild speculation and secret experiments. As with most problems, solutions proved more likely to present themselves in the field than in sterile, artificial reconstructions designed to impress the *Bonzen*, to curry favour, to earn their stripes. Small-scale models are meaningless, they have no bearing on reality, revulsion is not some minor experimental variable, it is at the very heart of the Machine. In the camps, the personnel are constantly dealing with blood and shit, they risk their souls, they struggle, everything depends on keeping up staff morale, on fostering rivalry: you organise parties, competitions, fights, you disseminate false information, tell the guards the camp is about to be liberated, that there are massive new deliveries of potatoes, of bread, of pots and pans, that the camp is to be expanded, the work detail reorganised, that real showers are being installed, that libraries will be opened, that the prisoners will be able to send letters. Why not? In a vacuum you can say anything, there is always someone who will believe it. Then again, you can do the reverse, you can crush the spirits of the guards, deprive them of everything, thrash them, spread fear, work them day and night, beat them hollow. When they have a glimmer of hope, they become animated, they work hard, they become daring, it only takes a single spark. By lying to them, blowing hot and cold at precisely the right moment, it is possible to regulate working conditions, stamp out subversion, break up factions and, in doing so, gain time and maintain—or perhaps even improve—productivity. It is the age-old method used in drilling army conscripts: you march them around for no reason until they are exhausted, force them to muster every five minutes for no reason until they are dazed, work them from dawn till dusk for no reason until they forget even the notion of freedom, organise alerts for no reason until they are constantly unsettled, punish them for no reason until they realise their lives hang by a thread, then one morning you march them out of their barracks for no reason and send them off to die somewhere else. The only difference is that, in the camps, work is death, punishment is death, cruelty is death, kindness is death, time off is death, recreation is death, rations are death, alerts are death and redundancy is summary execution. A man *who dies at a yes or a no.* The safest strategy, obviously, is to weed out old hands before they become inured, before they infect the new recruits. The problem with this approach is that it is the old hands, the veterans, who maintain productivity—new recruits are too terrified to work efficiently. Fear spreads, and in a twinkling fear turns to panic. This too, presents a difficult operational problem, a balance needs to be struck so that the system runs efficiently, constantly, without excessive risk. Let us not forget that the purpose of the camps is extermination, and although everyone knows this, no one says it or even thinks it—neither the prisoners, who need to cling to hope, nor their executioners, who think only of productivity—everyone behaves as though death were simply one particularly harsh punishment in the disciplinary arsenal, it is this which makes their working relationships exceptionally complex.

The running of such camps is anything but easy. When I put myself in papa's shoes, when I consider the incredible difficulties he faced and compare them to the problems of a multinational like ours, even in an adverse economic climate, faced with criticism from newspapers, takeover bids form speculators, disloyalty from clients, edicts from civil servants and union terrorist ploys, I have to laugh. The achievements of the formidable Nazi military-industrial machine are unparalleled, they are without equal.

Was the journey necessary? Technically, no. I already knew what there was to know. What I wanted was to be in this place where my father had been, to talk to him across the years. Who else could tell me what I needed to know, what his career path had been, what his state of mind had been when he meted out death on such a scale? Had he resisted? Did he glory in his power? Why this loathing of the Jew, this all-consuming hatred? What did he think might come of it? When the Third Reich was crumbling, was papa thinking that it was the end of the world or simply the end of a world? What did he feel when the extermination camps were discovered and humanity gave a howl of terror that surely echoed to the ends of the universe? Did he suddenly come to his senses? Did he become affronted? Did he say to himself that humanity had clearly understood nothing, that at the ends of the universe the end of a world is a triviality, it is in the order of things? Chaos is born of chaos and returns to chaos, it is mathematical, it is written in the heavens. Untold civilisations, vast empires, great peoples have vanished, this is not news, the old must die to make way for the new. These questions drive me insane because I know the answer: Papa did not kill himself, did not give himself up, he ran away, he lied, he forgot. He told me nothing.

I got a room in a tiny boutique hotel as bright as a small spring sun. From my window, I could see the university in its lush, magical setting. Manicured lawns, hundred-year-old trees,

hedges clipped and sculpted with lasers, fountains with, I imagine, fat fish fed by an invisible hand with the best of intentions,
or at least with impeccable attention to punctuality, scale and
quantity. In the middle of the campus, on a grassy hill, the
majestic Johann Wolfgang Goethe-Universität sits enthroned. It
is a magnificent building, stately, opulent, in delectable warm
shades of stone. I thought back to my university, the École Cen-
trale in Nantes, a poor relation by comparison. This, clearly, is a
temple to science. The hordes of regimented students walking
in groups or single file already had the austere, preoccupied
look of veteran scientists while also being tousled, smiling,
pleasantly scruffy like all students their age. The professors, old-
fashioned, shambling, essentially innocuous, carrying baskets
or old canvas bags, looked as though they had just arrived from
the country and gone to the wrong place. Germany, I remembered, was in the throes of an environmental crisis, something
that dovetailed neatly with is formidable industrial infrastructure.
Leather and faux-leather satchels were clearly the fashion in
Frankfurt this year. When I was a student in Nantes, it was nylon
rucksacks, and I remember Monsieur Candela, self-obsessed
soxiante-huitard that he was, telling me that in his day, you
turned up for lectures empty-handed and left with a girl on your
arm. Things change.

Until now, I had been able to allow my future father some
extenuating circumstances, to see in him the conscientious
schoolboy, the fun-loving student, the decent, happy-go-lucky
soldier. He is young, he doesn't know, the Final Solution is a
state secret, a confidential matter known only to the Führer
perched in his Eagle's Nest, in the impregnable *Berghof*, and the
starving prisoner in some far-flung part of Eastern Europe, in a
death camp cut off by snowstorms from the rest of the world.
People suspected, they spoke in euphemisms, they had noticed
that there were fewer and fewer Jews and other *Minderwertige*

Leute on the streets, that many shops were closed and derelict, that the *Judenhaus* and the synagogues had been repurposed, but a war is a war, it must first be fought, only afterwards can you calculate the dead and the disappeared, only then do state secrets, like corpses, float to the surface.

I wandered around the university campus. Students spend their lives in cafés and bars, that's where they talk, where they set the world to rights, where they drown their sorrows, it was where I spent most of my four years in Nantes. In Frankfurt I visited every café, every bar, but nowhere did I feel the oppressive, arrogant, feverish atmosphere of Nazi Germany. In the model, European, impossibly liberal Germany of today, everything is immaculate, pristine, warm and young, although the populace seems older than ever. I wanted to be a conjuror, to wave a magic wand, turn back time and shroud everything in black and grey and fog, restore to the streets their cobblestoned past, to the buildings their pre-war decrepitude, to the ladies that bourgeois charm perched somewhere between decorousness and depravity, to the girls that air of Olympian athletes, to the civil servants the starched formality of dangerous automata, to the working-class the demeanour of bankrupt country squires ripe for exploitation and manipulation, to the politicians, the shrill rhetoric of the madman. I couldn't picture the young Hans Schiller, too many other images cluttered my mind, the irreproachable SS officer in his black uniform, the Cheïkh of Aïn Deb I remembered from childhood in his spotless white *burnous*, the image of the German businessman trussed up in his dark suit, the picture of these promising students who seemed prematurely solemn. This youthful Hans I cannot picture deserves my compassion, he is young, he does not know. He fell in with the muscular Hitler Youth, the *Hitlerjugends*, and there lost what little adolescent wisdom had survived from childhood. I did much the same thing in the FLN youth, the *FLNjugends*, it was not as extreme, just the crackpot rantings of rank amateurs, but I know the symptoms, the dull roar in your head, the spit-flecked slogans in your mouth, the murderous twitch in your hands. His years at university did nothing to improve Hans, his character by now was mapped out, and the spirit of the times was of relentless propaganda, iron vigilance and, shortly afterwards, of Blitzkrieg. It's easy to understand how difficult it must have been to think for yourself. From here to his induction into the research team working on Zyklon B is a matter of simple probability. He was in the right place at the right time, they needed men in white coats to hold the test tubes, monitor the distillate, take notes. Hans, the newly qualified chemical engineer, surely thinking he had been recognized, chosen, honoured, patted himself on the back. He probably genuinely believed that the gas they were working on would be used, as he had been told, to eradicate lice in the camps. What camps? he might have asked. The *Arbeitslager*—the labour camps of the glorious Reich! someone would have snapped, as though talking about a campaign to end poverty and degradation. The real question, What the hell is going on? would have come one day, at dusk, at dawn, between two pale pools of light, in some remote Frankfurt suburb in an atmosphere you could cut with a knife, as he witnessed his first live experiment—the gassing of a Jewish family too bewildered to protest or of a group of tramps too drunk to realise what was happening; and with that first question a flood of others would naturally have come: What am I doing here? Is this really happening? Why? I'd like to think he objected, but caught up as he was in some vast secret Reich, he realised there was no way out. The first step is the only one that matters, and he had already taken several. The rest follows, you brood over your own pain, you lick your wounds, you keep going, you keep your opinions to yourself, you forget them, and every day forgetting becomes a little easier, you parrot the common view and every day you believe it a little more fervently; you see cowards, braggarts, killing willingly, zealously, and this persuades you that you are on the right path, the only path. Papa quickly penetrated the inner sanctum of his horror, something which must have required some special trait. An incurable innocence? A healthy dose of cowardice? A little fervour? Perhaps a lot. Maybe a heart-felt rage at the Jews and other *Minderwertige Leute.*

My God, who will tell me who my father is?

I left Frankfurt am Main just as I had arrived, no different from when I came back from Uelzen and from the godforsaken hole near Strasbourg where my friend, my partner Adolph—*his father's son*—lived. I had to keep going. To follow this path to its conclusion. To the end.

16 AUGUST 1995

I f anything is truly futile, it is this: I wrote to the Algerian minister for Foreign Affairs. I know he will never actually get the letter, it will be intercepted and shredded long before it reaches him, or forwarded to the secret police who will use it as they see fit, just as the accompanying note "for whatever purpose it may serve" suggests. But I thought it needed to be done so I did it. When the time comes, I'll consult a lawyer about how to pursue the matter. And in that too, I'll go to the end.

Minister,

On 24 April 1994, at about 11 P.M., my parents, together with thirty-six neighbours, men, women and children, were savagely murdered in the village of Aïn Deb, in the province of Sétif by an unidentified armed group. According to the French news reports, citing those from Algerian television, this unidentified group is unquestionably a group of Islamist terrorists known to the Algerian police force. I expect that you are familiar with the tragedy in question—the matter has certainly been raised with you. Foreign observers and human rights organisation have undoubtedly discussed the incident with you, they may even have called for explanations.

On the list of victims drawn up by the Ministry of the Interior, and sent by your offices to the Algerian embassy in Paris, my father and mother are listed under names that do not correspond to those in the official records. My mother is listed by her maiden name, Aïcha Majdali, my father by a pseudonym, Hassan Hans, known as Si Mourad. I enclose herewith, copies of the official Identity Cards on which, as you will see, my father's name is given as Hans Schiller and my mother as Aïcha Schiller, née Majdali, both Algerian citizens. It would seem to me to be entirely usual that the citizens of a country should be born and die under their official names, and that it is by these names that all official information pertaining to them should be published. In this, I do not think that Algerian law differs markedly from the laws in force elsewhere in the world.

Therefore, I would be indebted to you if you would instruct the appropriate department to amend the list of victims to reflect my parents' actual names, and forward an official copy to me. Failing which, I will be forced to consider my parents as missing and take all necessary measures to locate them, specifically to lodge a legal action with all relevant Algerian, French and German authorities, and with the International Court of Justice. You will understand that I am within my rights to wonder whether the Algerian government is involved in their murder, and that the official list is proof of that involvement, or at least evidence that it has something to hide concerning my parents. Should you decide that correcting the list is impossible, I would be grateful if you could inform me of your reasons. I can understand that force of circumstance may prevail.

I would like to take this opportunity to ask what progress has been made in the search to find and arrest the perpetrators of this heinous crime and bring them to justice. Fifteen months have now elapsed, and, to date, no information on the progress of the investigation has been offered to the public or to the relatives of the victims. If need be, I am prepared to take legal action to compel your answer and to prove that you are involved in an attempt to suppress the truth.

Yours most sincerely.

It's too late. I've already posted the letter, but when I reread it now, I feel ashamed—it's conciliatory. Because I was writing to a minister, I stupidly adopted the attitude of the petitioner—unassuming, patient, a good citizen aware that the *Bonzen* have so many demands on their time, so many requests, so many official commitments. I find it humiliating that victims are always forced to ask, to plead, to wait. It's intolerable.

When the time comes to send a reminder, I'll express myself as a victim should: demand, insist, refuse to tolerate evasion, preempt equivocation. These people are there to serve us, not the reverse.

15 DECEMBER 1996

It's a miracle I made it to Aïn Deb. My God this has been some adventure. As soon as we came down the steps of the plane at Houari Boumédienne International Airport, Algiers, all the passengers—men, women and children—were rounded up herded into the middle of the runway where we waited for more than an hour as driving rain and freezing wind whipped at us. The men were coughing, some of the older, weaker ones collapsed, the babies were crying, their mothers pleading with them to be quiet, desperately trying to comfort them. There was a lot of whispering. We were soaked to the skin. It's one thing to read about it, to hear about it, you have to picture two hundred people with all their luggage, utterly terrified, standing on the tarmac in weather like this watched over by a mob of guards invisible in their oilskins. An hour later, a black car pulled up carrying four cops in dark green raincoats and dark glasses. Doors slamming, bang, bang, bang, bang, they all got out. Special agents. Something was obviously about to happen, these guys were completely terrifying. The leader put up his collar, pushed his sunglasses back off his forehead and began to circle us silently, slowly, very slowly, staring intently at each of us in turn, though we had no idea why. He'd say to someone, "You, stand over there . . . and you . . . and you . . . You, step forward . . . and you . . . you go over and stand with them . . . You there, stop trying to hide, get out here." He glowered at the women too, to one he said, "Take off your glasses!" to another woman, "Pull up your hood!" to an old man who'd fallen down, he barked, "Get up!" Just his voice had me shitting bricks; it was flat, unemotional, colder than you could possibly imagine. Obviously no one had ever dared to disobey this guy—he could be at home in bed or sitting behind a desk and all over the country people would meekly obey him. When I think that Com'Dad has to argue his case, then take it before a judge, I realise that there's something not right with the system in Algeria. Or maybe the system in France. I was the sixteenth to be pulled out of the line. He looked at me, never blinking and said dismissively: "You, over there with the rest of them." After me, he picked out five more. Mostly young guys. The rest of the passengers were led to a stunted little building with a huge sign on the front saying in three languages: *Hall d'Arrivée. Bienvenue en Algérie. Arrivals Hall. Welcome to Algeria.* And something in Arabic, which I can't read or write. Our fellow travellers had already forgotten our shared nightmare—not one of them turned to say goodbye or to pity us, they were smiling, pushing and jostling to get away as quickly as possible. They were lucky. Some time later, when the water was up to our ankles, a covered military truck screeched to a halt in front of us. The head guy gave some order and the special agents told us to hand over our passports, our tickets, our hand luggage and get into the truck. I couldn't believe it, I was shaking I was so scared, it looked like we were going to be deported. Back in France I'd never been scared of the cops, actually I got a buzz out of winding them up, watching them try to work out how to play things. Now, I was paralysed, I couldn't think, it felt like I would never move again even if they suddenly said it was a joke and we were all on candid camera. Then the truck started up and zoomed towards this place that looked like it was an old cargo hold. Huge rusting hangars separated by paths a hundred metres wide, stuff lying around everywhere, loose concrete slabs, an armoured car parked under a water tower and everywhere you looked sandbagged army posts, each manned by two soldiers hugging a machine gun. Not another living soul. Nobody seemed to breathe, all you could hear was the howl of the wind, the hammering of the rain, a shriek of rusted metal that set your teeth on edge. Just the feel of the place had me squirming. The driver turned the truck into one of the hangars and slammed on the brakes, which squealed like scalded cats. He kept his foot to the floor, revving the engine hard for a long time, then cut the ignition. The hangar almost exploded with the sudden terrible silence that dropped on it like a bomb. A silence like that can turn your bowels to water. I'd never have believed that silence sound could be so deafening. It's insane, it's like saying someone is alive and dead at the same time. And that's what we were, more dead than alive. Some of them were hacking like they were about to cough up their lungs, others were grey and pasty, my eyes were watery with acid tears. I wondered for a minute if the driver was trying to exterminate us with the exhaust fumes, but since he was in the hangar with us, I figured he probably wasn't, he was just getting the oil out of his engine. I mean, no one would be stupid enough to gas themselves, flammable gasses stink so badly you can smell them a mile off, it's not like roses. A *Sonderkommando* who forgets to get out of the gas chamber in time doesn't last too long. The hangar was so big and so ramshackle that it would have taken thirty trucks a whole week to eliminate us, as Rachel would put it. By then we'd have died of starvation. Or madness. I thought about poor Rachel, this was how he died, his lungs dried up, his heart bruised, his body broken. Alone in his garage. More alone than anyone in the world. After that, everything happened quickly. We were ordered to get out, the truck drove off and the door of the hangar slammed shut with the boom of an atomic bomb. They left us in the dark without a word, without a look. At first everyone panicked, but we could hear nothing except the wind shaking the hangar and the rain gushing in waterfalls from the roof, but then we calmed down and huddled together in a corner to keep warm. A couple of people started smoking furiously like this was their first cigarette of the day, or their last. An hour later we were half dead from cold, from hunger, from thirst. And this was just the beginning.

I got talking to Slim, the guy huddled next to me in this hell, he was a university student home to spend Christmas holidays in the *bled* with his family. I asked if he knew what was going on, but he had no idea. He said he flew Paris to Algiers all the time, but this was the first time they'd pulled him out of the line up. "Maybe I'm starting to look like a terrorist," he laughed. He was an optimist. We talked about this and that. He was studying computer science at Jussieu and lived in some posh house in the sixteenth arrondissement with his uncle who's a professor at Pitié-Salpêtrière hospital. Poor little rich kid. But Slim said it wasn't like that at all, he said he had to live off some measly grant, he said all he got from his uncle was room and board, his travel card and a bit of pocket money. Oh, and on weekends his uncle would lend him his Mercedes 300 convertible with a full tank of petrol and enough money to cover his expenses. Slim bitched that he'd even had to work as a management trainee in a merchant bank run by some friend of his uncle to pay for his skiing holiday in Switzerland. Then he bitched about France, the cold, the discrimination, the crime rate, the cost of living, the filthy streets, the pig-headed police, the civil servants and on and on, the *préfecture* refusing to give him a ten-year resident permit for no good reason. Slim was a pain in the arse. He told me as soon as he finished his degree he was going to move to London and set up a department of international studies with his cousins so they could make some money out of Africa. I listened, I nodded, I understood, but I can't help it, I've never been able to stomach spoiled brats. I said to him aunt Sakina was always saying to me: "Don't be so ungrateful." But Slim said it's not him, it's France that's ungrateful. Slim is a royal pain in the arse. "There goes someone who thinks his shit doesn't stink," as Monsieur Vincent used to say whenever some guy showed up with a Ferrari, tossed the keys at him, stared at the ceiling and said, "Check her over for me!" With guys like that, small-time crooks bigging it up like gangsters, we'd push the car into a corner of the workshop and take our own sweet time racking up a bill fit for a king. Slim and I talked about this and that, talked about meeting up again in Algiers and in Paris. Neither of us figured we were going to be shut up in this hangar forever. When you don't know what's going on, it's best to be optimistic.

An hour later, the special agents came back. They lined us all up in front and the head guy asked each of us a series of questions. When it came to my turn, he asked if my name was really Malek Ulrich Schiller, if I'd got my passport through the legal channels, if I really was going to Aïn Deb to see my family, if I was planning anything illegal and if I harboured any ill intentions. He was a bit thrown by my name, he said, "Your father is German, but you're Algerian?" I explained that my father was a scientist, a Muslim, a hero, a veteran Mujahid, a respected cheïkh and a *chahid*. He pointed to his left and said, "Go stand over there." A minute later my new best friend Slim joined me. An hour later, there were two groups, one on the right, one on the left. We eyed each other tearfully, resentfully, everyone thinking, it's their fault we're in this mess. The selection process finished, the group on the right were loaded back onto the truck and driven off. Where to, I don't know. A cop came over to our group and said, "Follow me." We trailed after him like sheep. He led us to the building marked *Arrivals Hall, Welcome to Algeria*. He said, "Now fuck off." We didn't need to be told twice. Still shaking, we went through the necessary formalities: immigration, customs, baggage check, body search, brief routine interrogation, sundry declarations, com-

pulsory foreign exchange, payment of taxes and found ourselves outside, half dead from exhaustion, hunger, thirst, cold,
humiliation, soaked to the skin but free and ecstatic to be free.
I felt like I'd just done a thirty-year stretch. The sunlight hurt
my eyes and aunt Sakina's suitcase was ripping my arm out of
its socket. For a long time I wondered what had happened to
the other group. I can't bring myself to believe that the cops
tortured them, killed them, deported them. I'd rather believe
they just locked them up and that their parents aren't worried.
Some day, when the war is over, when the camps are liberated,
we'll find out.

Slim phoned his parents and got them to come and pick
him up. "They were convinced I'd been turned back at the
border or murdered or something—it was complete panic, the
old man was already on the phone to Paris," he said, laughing.
Slim is a spoiled royal pain in the arse. While we waited, we
watched the comings and goings in the airport. The whole
place was deathly silent. The people looked normal but maybe
they were being extra careful. At one point we saw some cop
dragging away a gang of young guys handcuffed together in
pairs. They'd obviously thought they could just up and leave
the country. They've had it now. Trying to leave is an insult.
They're bound to be gassed. We were trying to get into the
country and we'd been given the third degree. Later, I saw the
special agents, who'd been sitting in the cafeteria, suddenly get
to their feet, button their raincoats, slip on their dark glasses
and march off quickly. They walked straight past us, but we
ducked out of sight just in time. Compared to Algiers airport,
our estate is like an old-folks home, everyone hanging out,
bored senseless. Or it used to be—because since the new imam
and his emir showed up, the Fourth Reich is well under way.
By the time I left for Algeria, it was all set, the propaganda
machine was up and running, strict security was being
enforced and you could smell Blitzkrieg in the air. I wonder

what it will be like by the time I get back, whether my family, my neighbours, my mates will still be there. I miss them already. I can't imagine a future without my mates, without Momo, Raymou, Togo-au-Lait, Idir-Quoi, Cinq-Pouces, Manchot and Bidochon, the coffee jockey who can't even make a decent cup of coffee, all sons of dirt-poor, honest working men. Slim, the royal pain in the arse, told me about his life in Paris, his mates, his girlfriends, and he told me about what he did in Algeria during the holidays, days spent playing video games, big family meals, little parties at the house, his sisters inviting their friends over pretending they needed to revise. I didn't know what the fuck he was talking about. I told him about life on the estate and he looked at me like I was from another planet. Just then, his father showed up, frantic but happy, he's some important professor at Algiers hospital, he used to work in some hospital in Paris. They gave me a lift, dropped me at the bus station. Slim, the royal pain in the arse, winked at me and said, "Come by the house when you get back from that godforsaken hole you're going to, we can do some revision."

Rachel was a bit of spoiled pain in the arse himself. I mean, he didn't have to spend a fortune taking a taxi to Aïn Deb. They have got buses in Algeria and for a couple of *dinar* they'll drive you, your family and all your belongings to the ends of the earth and back. Outside the bus station—a patch of waste ground with barbed wire fences where a hundred rusty ramshackle buses waged all out war to get in, fight over passengers and get the fuck out—was a guy like a scarecrow whose job was to give directions. I told him my story. For fifty *dinar* he told me what I needed to do, all the while giving directions to a bunch of other lost souls, "Yeah, yeah, that's right, take bus number 12 to Sétif . . . You, you need to take the number 8 to Oran . . . and you . . . uh . . . 36, that'll take you to Sidi-Bel-Abbes . . . What? Oh yeah, so when you get to Sétif, take the bus for Bordj Kédir . . . and you . . . give me a minute . . . you can take the bus to Tiaret or the one to Mascara, doesn't matter . . . You need to take the Ouargla bus and from there you take the caravan that goes to El Goléa . . . and you . . . you need to hitchhike the rest of the way to—where was it again?" I repeated the name pronouncing it carefully. "Aïn what . . . ?" He said as he hurried over to pick a fight with another scarecrow who was cutting in on his turf. "Aïn Deb? Yeah, yeah . . . it's like I said." And he left me standing there in the mud and the chaos.

It was all exactly the way Rachel had described it in his diary. The military convoys, the roadblocks, the police, the deserted roads, the stupefying silence, the bus driver, foot to the floor, not looking left or right, the passengers so scared they were throwing up. The only difference was that it was bucketing down and wind whipped at us on the near side. At every bend, the wheels of the bus hung over the cliff. If the terrorists don't kill us, the bus will. Or the cold. We stopped in a tiny village that looked like it had died out with the last dinosaur. Not a man or a ghost, nothing but shapeless figures muffled up so you could hardly see their faces. The guy in the café served us scalding hot coffee, took our money and disappeared. I had to change busses in Sétif, but things there were more efficient than they'd been in Algiers. In Sétif, the self-appointed guide only charged me five *dinar* to tell me, "all the blue mini-busses go to Bordj Kédir, you can't miss it." In Bordj Kédir I managed to find a taxi driver who was prepared to take me closer to Aïn Deb for a reasonable price. His Peugeot 403 looked like nothing I'd ever seen. "There's something strange going on out in Aïn Deb," he told me, "people coming and going all the time . . . it's weird." "What people?" I asked, "What are they looking for?" He stared at me but said nothing. Maybe he didn't trust me, maybe he didn't understand me, I was talking to him in my best pidgin French with a thick sink-estate Arabic accent. I have to say I didn't really understand him. I assumed that he was talking about terrorists, because he was looking around him all the time like he was expecting an ambush. He dropped me off at a crossroads of two flooded dirt tracks you could barely see in the darkness. To the left, the path climbed steeply, to the right, it ran downhill. "It's that way . . . about three kilometres." He said, at least that's what I understood from him pointing to the left and waving three fingers in my face. "Kilometre" is international, it didn't need translating. He disappeared back into the darkness, his headlights turned off. I took a deep breath and slogged uphill through the driving rain, but at the least the wind was now whipping at my arse.

Anyway, long story short, I arrived in Aïn Deb half dead from exhaustion, hunger, and thirst, soaked to the skin, both arms pulled from their sockets by aunt Sakina's suitcase. And to top it all I'd caught a dose of flu. If it was like this in the camps, I'd volunteer to be gassed straight off, I thought, as the night got blacker and up there, on the hill, where Rachel had once stood, lost, the wind blew harder. It nearly sent me toppling into the abyss, but, with my big emigrant's suitcase to weigh me down, I only flailed a bit.

Then, suddenly, I wondered what kind of welcome I would get. I hadn't written, I hadn't phoned. I hadn't even thought about it, the trip was spur of the moment, because of the money Ophélie had sent me. Who cares, I thought, now that papa and maman and Rachel were all dead, I had no ties to Aïn Deb. I was a stranger turning up unexpectedly. But I was also a son of the village, following in my brother's footsteps, in search of my father, my mother, our truth.

You could barely see the village from the hill. I waited for the next flash of lightning to get my bearings. I bounded down the hill like a sky-diver. At some point, as a flash of lightning lit up the sky, I spotted smoke rising from chimneys. I had finally arrived.

When you grow up on the estate, you learn to improvise. Dragging my suitcase, I went and knocked on Mohamed's door. He was the son of the local shoemaker, we were friends back when I was a kid. I remembered people used to call him Mimed and I don't remember seeing him going barefoot back in the day. I figured this was the best thing to do—I didn't want to panic the whole village. The memory of the massacre must still haunt them. As I crept through the village I prayed to God that Mimed was still alive. At this hour—it was after 8 P.M.—the good people would have recited *Isha'a*, the last prayer, and would be sleeping the sleep of the just.

I'll spare you the details, but fuckwit that I am, I scratched at the door instead of knocking properly and that set off all kinds of furtive goings-on and terrified whispers inside, then I nearly sent them into a panic because, instead of introducing myself properly, I whispered: "Mimed, open up, it's, Malrich . . . " Malrich is what they call me in France, it doesn't mean anything to anyone here in the *bled*, they probably thought it was a secret password or something. But everything worked itself out in the end. I introduced myself properly: "It's Malek, Hassan and Aïcha's son, Rachel's brother, open the door for God's sake." Mohamed didn't recognise me, and I didn't recognise him. It took some time and some memory jogging before we could say, "It's you, Malek, Cheïkh Hassan's son, I can't believe it! It's you, Mimed, Tayeb the shoemaker's son, I can't believe it!" He was expecting an old man and here I was, this young guy; I was expecting a young man and what I found was an old man with a swarm of kids bawling and clinging to his ankles. The poor things were pissing themselves they were so scared. He kissed me on both cheecks and brought me inside. The kids magically disappeared, I could hear them on the other side of the curtain. His wife, an old woman who was still young and healthy, gave me some leftover couscous, some dates and some milk, then she disappeared for a second and came back with a rug, a blanket and a pillow and made a bed up for me in front of the fire. I ate like an animal. Through a gap in the curtain, the kids were staring at me. Poor things never seen a stranger, they didn't know such things existed. Mohamed threw a white *burnous* over my shoulders then stoked the fire. Gradually, I came back to life a bit. Since it was really late for them—9 o'clock—and since I was dead on my feet, they said good night and went back to their room. I blew out the oil lamp and got under the blanket which smelled wonderfully of mountain sheep and straw. The fire sputtered in the grate, throwing off sparks. It was beautiful. Beside the fireplace, in an old scorched basket by the fire was a cat with her litter. I think she smiled at me, her eyes shining in the darkness. It really was beautiful.

Outside, the wind howled as hard as it could, rain came in flurries and the village dogs, smelling an unfamiliar scent, my scent, were barking as loudly as they could. I knew, I remembered: if they were pups of the dogs we used to have, they wouldn't stop until dawn, not until the goats were let out and bounded down into the valley, to the roaring torrent of the wadi. I felt suddenly happy. Everything seemed innocent, so incredibly permanent that you forget everything, forget your own troubles and the troubles of the world.

I slept like a baby that night. It had been a long time.

I t had been a terrible day. I'd done just what Rachel had done, gone from house to house, drunk coffee after coffee, babbled as best I could and in the end—partly because I felt shattered and needed to get the hell out and partly because mourning does not wait on twilight, Mimed took me to the cemetery. The sun, which had risen early was sinking now, framed by big black clouds but still visible, the wind had died away. The air stinging my lungs was bitterly cold.

This, then, was the martyrs' section where my parents were buried. The grass had grown over it, the whitewash on the stones had faded and they were covered in mud. Now the martyrs were like the rest of the dead, there was nothing to distinguish them from the others, they had joined the rest of the cemetery where the people who died of natural causes were buried, or maybe, more rightly, those who'd died of natural causes had come to join the victims to shoulder some of their pain. Soon they would be united in the same dust. You couldn't see the small monument erected by the authorities any more, all the dead were now subject to the same power, to time which obliterates everything.

Mimed stood off to one side and left me to myself. He bowed his head and prayed while standing in front of my parent's grave. I tried to meditate, to remember happy times from my childhood with papa and maman. I couldn't seem to do it, but figured I'd soon get the hang of this meditation thing, Rachel got so good at it he went round philosophising like a council of imams. Suddenly I felt a stabbing pain, a spasm ripping through my guts. What had been vague, something I'd known only secondhand from reading Rachel's diary, something I'd kept private, suppressed, carefully contained, was now here before my eyes: my parents' graves, the graves of papa, of maman, of our neighbours, the graves of childhood friends, of babies I had not seen born or grow up, all of them butchered like dogs by God knows who. My head exploded, I started to sob, to scream, I couldn't think straight, I fell on my knees and started to beat my head against the ground. It was all so unfair, so strange, so many things had been hushed up, and everywhere I could smell the stink of injustice, twisting the knife in the wound. I didn't know what to do. Then suddenly, a sort of madness took me, I wanted smash things, I was filled with hate—I hated myself, I hated the whole world, hated Rachel and this country and these people. I hated the way things were. I hated the people of Aïn Deb for living in silence, for tending that silence like a sacred flame, like a barrier protecting them from themselves. I despised them for treating truth, treating life as things that could be hidden, hushed up, for bringing children into a life of lies, of pretence, of ignorance and amnesia. I am paying the price. Papa never told us anything, and when his turn came, Rachel never told me anything, the authorities tell us nothing, they have broken our spirit. We are helpless, pitiful, weak, ready to make any concession, agree to any cover-up, collude in any cowardice. We're dead men, we're sheep, we're concentration-camp prisoners. I hated my father for making us pariahs. I hated God through whose will things were this way, God who, almighty, invisible, serene, extends across the universe, who doesn't hear our cries, doesn't answer our prayers. Well, fuck Him, His truth is not our truth, and our truth is not His. He is not one of us. That's why I want this diary to be read by people all over the world, people like me, like us. I've nothing to hide, I don't want to hide anything, I want people to see me for what I am, to know who I am and where I come from.

I struggled to my feet, raied my arms and shouted: "My name is Malrich, I am the son of the SS officer Hans Schiller, a man guilty of genocide. I am carrying the weight of the greatest tragedy the world has ever known, I am its repository, and I'm ashamed, I'm afraid and I want to die! I'm begging for your help, because no one told me anything, all of this has been visited on me and I don't know why. My brother killed himself, my parents and their neighbours were murdered and I don't know why or by whom, I'm alone, more alone than anyone in the world."

It was then that I felt rage, black rage, grip my insides, I had no right to feel sorry for myself, the only truth is *Nakam*—revenge. I hated the Islamists, those Nazi bastards, I wanted to kill every last one of them, to kill their wives, their children, their grandchildren, their parents, to bulldoze their houses, their mosques, their bunkers, break up their sleeper cells, hound them into the next world and crush them before God Himself, the same God they claim to represent. I wanted fireworks like on Bastille Day, to celebrate their deaths our rebirth. Why are they like this, God? Why have You made them like this? Who can save them? Who will save their wives, their children? Who will save us from them?

I was trembling, I collapsed on the ground and rolled in the mud. I wanted to die. "I want to die," I howled as loud as I could.

Mohamed came over, put his arm around my shoulder and led me back to the village like you'd lead a blind man. He didn't speak French, so he thought I had been lashing out at Allah. Over and over he said in a reproachful tone, "It is *mektoub*, Malek, it is fate, we must accept it." At that moment I wanted to kill him too. I pushed him away and said, "*Mektoub, mektoub* . . . So Allah made you this way, so spineless and weak that when people come to slit your throats like sheep you do nothing?" Even as I'd said it, I felt ashamed. That whole day in the airport, special agents had treated us like dogs, like camp prisoners, we'd been terrified, starving, numb with cold, soaked to the skin, they'd taken our suitcases, our papers, our identities, gassed us with exhaust fumes and left us in the dark, in the filthy hangar, without a word, without a look, and not one of us had done a thing, we hadn't asked questions, hadn't demanded that our rights be read to us before we let them take us away. We were all thinking, This is how things are, there's nothing we can do. And we all watched, silent, relieved, when the others were loaded back onto the truck and driven off into the unknown. "It's not *mektoub*, Mimed," I said, gasping for breath. "It's us, we're the problem."

I needed to be alone. Alone forever.

I went back to my parents' house. My house now—I am the last of the Schillers. It smelled of mould and neglect. I aired the rooms and lit a fire in the fireplace. Then I changed my clothes, put on my white *burnous*, sat in maman's chair and wrote down the first thing that came into my head.

I needed to be happy, to be hopeful for an hour or two to recharge my batteries or I'd go mad. I wrote stuff down as it came to me, little things, everyday things. I wrote that aunt Sakina and uncle Ali would be happier here in Aïn Deb. The air is fresh, the silence is peaceful. Living on the tenth floor of a tower block on the estate, they never go out, except when aunt Sakina goes shopping with Maïmouna, the old woman who lives down the hall. They always go together, they always buy the same things, pasta, rice, tinned tomatoes and a nice white baguette. In Aïn Deb they'd have the whole countryside, neighbours to look out for them, they wouldn't have to deal with all the noise, the hassle of living in a city. They could get a couple of chickens, a few goats and the rest would come naturally. The years would go by, they'd get used to things, adapt to the seasons and one day they'd die and it would not be a tragedy but they would not go unmourned. And the cemetery is just down the road, they would be buried with their family, with their people, and go into the next life with them.

I remembered my mates and I thought, now that it was my turn I'd tell them everything. I'd tell them all the things I'd been hiding. They've lived in silence and ignorance long enough. Maybe it's too late, maybe they'll be hurt when they find out, but maybe it will give them hope, the sort of hope that gives you wings and the urge to fly. This was what I need-ed, hope, to live and to be happy to wait for tomorrow.

I thought about the estate, and I knew now that we *could* change it. It would be easy—all we had to do was talk to each other and tell the children everything. The rest would come naturally. Despair would scuttle away having nothing left to cling to. The authorities would have to listen to us, they would see in our eyes what we knew, what we wanted: truth and respect. The jihadists wouldn't dare come near us, they'd run away—heads down, tails between their legs, beards at half-mast. The devil would take them home and devour them. And that would be that. We'd turn the page and throw the party to end all parties.

I thought about Rachel and I promised myself I'd visit his grave and tell him everything. Tell him that I knew everything, and that, thanks to our diaries, the whole world will know who we are, what we suffered, that we will no longer need to to hide, to be ashamed, to lie.

That night, I didn't sleep, I spent the whole night talking to my parents like I used to do years ago, talking to Rachel, the way we never did, talking to my mates, the way we soon would. It was like I was happy already.

Note: The way the following chapters are laid out and the excerpts from Rachel's diary were suggested to me by Madame Dominique G.H.

Rachel visited Istanbul and Cairo in March 1996, after the long trek that started in Frankfurt in June 1995 and took him through Germany, Austria and Poland, ending in Auschwitz in February 1996. With one exception, Rachel followed a logical, necessary route, he retraced papa's career as it appears in his military record: it begins in Frankfurt, goes on to various camps in Germany and Austria and ends in Poland, not Auschwitz, but at Lublin-Majdanek. There are other postings mentioned in his military record—in France and in Belgium—but Rachel assumed they had nothing to do with the Holocaust. They were brief, probably scientific, stints in Paris, Rocroi, Ghent and elsewhere, places where the Reich didn't have concentration camps. Papa was a chemical engineer so he might easily have been sent to a factory, or a training centre or one of the laboratories run by the Reich. The one thing I don't understand is why Rachel made Auschwitz the last stop on his journey, when papa had been there mid-way through his career. Was it because to most people Auschwitz is synonymous with the extermination of the Jews? I don't think so. Rachel had done his research, he knew the horrors in Auschwitz were no different to any other camps, and besides—as he says in his diary—prisoners were regularly shunted from one camp to another, what they didn't suffer in one, they suffered in another. Whatever his reasons, it's obvious that his trip to Auschwitz, more than any of a the others, utterly devastated him. I think it was there, at a very specific moment, that he decided to kill himself—to gas himself—as soon as he got back to Paris. Maybe he'd thought about it before, maybe he'd thought about it from the very beginning back in Aïn Deb, maybe it happened in Uelzen or in Frankfurt, or later in Buchenwald, in Dachau, or during the weeks and months he spent alone in his house after he lost his job, after Ophélie left. Maybe Auschwitz was only a catalyst, a trigger. But maybe, in a very specific way, the scene at Auschwitz he describes at length was what finally decided him.

According to papa's military record, he was at Lublin-Majdanek when the Nazis were defeated. Soviet troops had marched into Poland and were advancing towards Berlin like a steamroller. After that, there's no mention of him. Did he and his friends go back to Germany to make a last stand? Did they hide out in Austria, go to ground in Poland? Rachel doesn't know. Nazi troops were deserting in such numbers and the chaos was so great that one guess is as good as another. The only thing we know for sure is that at some point—in Poland or in Germany—papa made contact with Unit 92 and, with their help, made it to Turkey and from there to Egypt.

I've taken some liberties in the way I've organised the rest of the chapters, and in the pieces I've chosen to include from Rachel's diary. I've moved the section about Istanbul and Cairo to the next chapter, and out of all the stuff he wrote about his long journey through the camps of Germany and Poland, I've only kept the piece on Auschwitz, which is in a later chapter. If I'd included everything Rachel wrote, our diaries would have been too long, too terrible to read. Some day, I'll put everything in one book, but I doubt there are many people who could bear to read it to the end.

In his journey to the heart of darkness, Rachel wrote hundreds of pages filled with incredibly technical details about the camps and the appalling, unimaginable stories he heard along the way—some from the guides who showed him round the camps, some from former prisoners who had come to make pilgrimage. Meeting survivors was incredibly painful for him. He wrote pages and pages about it, harrowing and heart-breaking. Sometimes he'd pretend to be a researcher, or a relative of someone who'd been in the camps. He'd persuade them to talk, press them for the most precise, the most intimate details of what they had suffered. He collated the names too, although he already knew everything, he had researched every detail, he had index cards about everything, though I have to say most of them are illegible. The notes he made from the books he read are filled with formulas and symbols, diagrams and sketches and quotes about how the camp prisoners were fed, how the laundry worked, what medical services existed, about the sectors where the clothes were sorted, the laboratories where the experiments were done, about the workings of the famous selection *Kommissionen*, about the black market that operated in the camps, about the appalling behaviour of the SS officers, constantly on the lookout for someone with a stash of jewellery, for a pretty girl like Nadia, for a bottle of booze or a nice fur coat or a bare-knuckle fight they could cheer on: he wrote about the military ceremonies, the civil and religious commemorations, the inspections when the *Bonzen* came round, the brothels for the *Kapos*, the brothels reserved for the officers. He knew all the books by heart, but he needed to hear it from the mouths of those who had lived in the camps, who forgot that there existed a world outside, a world where people lived and danced and read books, where they learned and loved and bought flowers, raised children and thanked God for His blessings. It was uncomfortable, Rachel says, but he was tactful, asked questions only if he felt someone needed to talk, said nothing and stared straight ahead when a man began to choke on his sobs. He'd ask, in an offhand way, whether they remembered their guards—names, ranks, whether some had any particular vices, whether they were more cruel than the rules dictated, whether some behaved humanely. But he always came back to the gas chambers, to the *Sonderkommando*, the *Einsatzgruppen*, the soldiers who took the prisoners whose turn it was to "take a shower," to that self-effacing man—the chemical engineer who prepared the Zyklon B—and asked if they remembered his name. He felt unspeakably guilty, constantly thinking, this man knew my father, he has never forgotten him, he will never forget him, I have to tell him, this is his truth as much as it is mine: Sir, I need to tell you, I am Hans Schiller's son. I don't think he ever told anyone—or if he did he doesn't mention it in his diary. It would have been a terrible thing to do, it would simply have been adding to their suffering.

After he left Dachau, Rachel promised himself that some day he'd go to Jerusalem to visit the Holocaust memorial of Yad Vashem. He wrote: "The victims are in the camps, their dust, their ashes mingled with German soil and Polish soil for all eternity—it is here that I need to ask for forgiveness, here in front of the gas chambers, in front of the *Krema*, where my father took their lives. But at Yad Vashem I can put a name to every victim. It is important to say aloud the names of those who, to my father, were nothing more than a yellow star and a number branded on their flesh."

He never went to Jerusalem, to Yad Vashem. If I have the money some day, I'll make the journey for him. And for me. I'll read the names aloud, and, after every one, I'll ask their forgiveness in my father's name.

I thought about my parents, whose names had been stripped from them, who were buried under names that were politically convenient. Did it matter? I don't know. Rachel seemed to think it was important, to me it seems secondary. The name on maman's grave is her maiden name, Aïcha Majdali, as if she died unmarried, childless, an unclean woman nobody wanted. My father's grave reads, "Hassan Hans known as Si Mourad," no surname, only his first name and the name he used in the *maquis*, like he was a bastard who never knew his father. I don't know what to think, that's how the story was written. To everyone in Aïn Deb, "Hassan Hans, known as Si Mourad," is the name of the cheïkh, the mujahid, the man with the big heart, the *chahid*, and to them, Aïcha is the daughter of her father, the honored Cheïkh Majdali. I think they would have felt intimidated, awkward before a grave marked *Hans Schiller*, the way people are when they're faced with something they don't understand. Questions still go round and round in my head: did the Algerian authorities know about papa's past? They had to know back when he was in the *maquis*, and even after independence, but that was a long time ago. I'm sure the young *Bonzen* these days don't know shit, they were brought up in a culture of lies, taught the discipline of forgetting. In a system like this there are only certainties, and if you don't have any, then vague outdated regulations will do just as well. To them, Aïn Deb is the German's village, and the German is Hassan Hans known as Si Mourad. What about the people of Aïn Deb? Did they know about papa's past? Did they hide it? Papa lived with them for more than thirty years, did he never tell them anything, did they never ask questions, did they have some sort of unspoken agreement never to mention it? These are good people to whom hospitality is a sacred duty. When a man knocks at your door, you ask for nothing but put yourself at his service, and if he wants to settle there, you marry him off to the most eligible girl and treat him as one of your own. Have people in Aïn Deb even heard of the Nazi extermination of the Jews? Or are they completely ignorant, like I was, knowing only whatever the imam sees fit to tell them? And what about him, that parrot up there in his minaret, how much does he know? I'm guessing that the Algerian government doesn't teach this stuff in schools, the kids might get upset, they might feel sorry for the Jews, they might start to realise some other truths. I'm guessing they teach kids to hate the Jews, to keep their minds closed. I remember back when I was in the FLN Youth—the *FLNJugends* Rachel calls them—they talked about the Jews all the time, the instructors could hardly open their mouths without saying *Lihoudi*—dirty Jew—then spit on the ground and recite the ritual for cleansing the mouth: "May Allah curse him and wipe him from the face of the earth." But I suppose things have changed, these days it's all sugar coated. Algeria is a member of the UN, so they probably have to abide by certain rules even if they don't agree with them—something *Bonzen* are pretty good at. They keep the country locked up like a vault, and it's always the same reason: the poorer, the angrier and the more racist you keep the people, the easier they are to manage. Rachel wrote: "You can't commit atrocities with enlightened people, you need hatred, blindness and a knee-jerk xenophobia. In the beginning, all states are shaped by madmen and murderers. They kill the good people, drive out the heroes, lock up the people and proclaim themselves liberators." In the end, I think maybe no one knows. Some day, when peace comes, I'll come back to Aïn Deb with aunt Sakina and I'll tell the true story of Hans Schiller to Mohamed, the shoemaker's son, and get him to tell everyone else in the village. He can explain it better than I could. If I told them, they'd go mad, they wouldn't believe me, they'd argue, they'd curse me, but truth is truth, it has to be told. At least in the minds of the children it will take root.

Rachel didn't really need to go to Istanbul or Cairo, he knew everything there was to know about the ratlines Nazi officers used to disappear, to escape justice. In Istanbul Rachel never even left his hotel room, he spent the whole day lying on his bed or daydreaming in front of the window, scribbling in his notebooks and the next morning he was off to Cairo to try and find out how papa ended up getting involved with Nasser's secret services, the *Mukhabarat*, after the coup d'état against King Farouk, and how he ended up being sent to Algeria to train the *maquis*, or whatever it was he was sent to do.

But he had no hope of finding out—secret services are secret, and everything they do is secret. There was one thing he did in Cairo that I found weird, something that showed me just how mad he was by then. There was only one reason for his trip to Turkey and Cairo in my mind, he was trying to kill time, he needed a break after his descent into the abyss, and he was trying to keep busy until the time came to die. He had already chosen the precise time: 11 P.M., on 24 April 1996. The massacre in Aïn Deb had taken place on 24 April 1994 at about 11 P.M. That was the moment when papa and maman and our neighbours became victims, but it was also the moment when SS officer Hans Schiller, exterminator and imposter, died, taking his secrets with him to the grave. For Rachel, justice was never done. It was a burden he carried with him to the end, a burden I carry now.

RACHEL'S DIARY

ISTANBUL, 9 MARCH 1996

No one riles me more than a Turkish man. Self-important, steeped in the idea of himself as a rebel, he constantly feels the need to prove himself. You only have to look at the way he walks, like he's about to head butt a wall and bring it crashing down or grapple with a rutting ram. I get pissed off by people who feel they have to live up to national stereotypes. The Italian who's permanently cheery and insists on trying to help you when you haven't asked for anything, the Spaniard who gets belligerently protective when you ask after his sister, the Pole who feels he has to knock back another six vodkas when everyone else has stopped, the Arab who gets his hackles up and draws his sabre when all you've done is congratulate him on his celebrated restraint, not to mention the Englishman who keeps a stiff upper lip when you tell him his clothes are on fire. The Algerians piss me off—and I'm half Algerian—they claim they're the most hospitable people in the world when they've turned their country into the most inhospitable place on earth and made their government the most repulsive under Satan's sun. As for the French—don't even go there. We're all of these things and more besides. It's the Universalist in us. In other countries when people bad-mouth the French, they know what they're talking about. The Frenchmen who've gone before us have given them all the evidence they need to calculate the extent of our arrogance. Someone should write up a guide to national stereotypes and hand it out with travel guides, that way the unwary traveller would know where not to go and what not to say. Of course, they're simply stereotypes, all these people could shake them off and live happily ever after. No stereotype, no song and dance, everyone just gets on with his life—that's something it might be worth teaching people.

Anyway, from the minute my plane landed to the minute I got to my hotel on the Bosphorous, in a steep alley in the shadow of the Blue Mosque, every *Mamamouchi* I met has blanked me. I didn't hear a single "*Merhaba, Salam*," still less a "*Günaydın*" or "*iyi günler*" or the "*Güle güle*" that they're always saying to each other. I suppose my cadaverous appearance and my hollow eyes made them feel afraid and disgusted. I was a walking corpse, a dead man who had seen too much. At the airport, the security guard looked at me like I was a drug dealer, one taxi driver refused to take me because he said I was dangerously ill and at the hotel, the receptionist took so long to answer me I thought he was going to grab me by the throat and send for the *başıbozuk.*

But that's not what this was really about. I looked at them contemptuously. To me Turkey is a country which, though technically neutral, colluded in the Holocaust. They signed a pact of friendship with the Third Reich, they had a close relationship with the Axis powers and they offered Nazi officers an escape route. They have a genocide of their own, one which is all the more terrible since they have the gall not to admit to it. Why don't they follow the example of the Germans whose crime is the most heinous ever committed? But who am I to cast the first stone, sitting here driving myself mad, wondering why my father never confessed his crimes?

I used to love Turkey, the country is beautiful, the air is fresh and clean. The multinational I used to work for has an assembly plant here in partnership with some big Turkish conglomerate. I used to come here all the time. There's not much I don't know about Turkish food, or the underhand deals they're so fond of, perched as they are between two stools—two divans, I should say—between West and East, and being so secretive they end up winning on all counts. I never could stand the way they were secular in the morning and mysterious at night, when we were always completely cut-and-dry, utterly transparent. Tomorrow, I'm taking the plane to Cairo. The air might not be as fresh, but, from what I've seen from my numerous business trips there, the people have both feet in the same camp.

From my hotel window, I sat staring out on this mystifying world, nodding as I watched. At one point, I'm not sure why, I watched a young European guy discreetly following an old Turk wearing a frayed *saroual* but solid as an ox, as they disappeared into a dark alley. In that moment, I slipped into my father's skin. This is the way I've learned to understand him better, I steal into his thoughts, walk in his footsteps, following the terrible road he travelled. I am Jekyll and Hyde. I can picture myself as my father—after a hard ride across Poland, Slovakia, Hungary, Romania, with the Balkans in flames all around me, travelling by night, sleeping by day, cutting through field and forest, careful to avoid the towns—finally arriving in Bulgaria to find myself surrounded by Bolsheviks. From here, I steal into Istanbul where Turkish traffickers are waiting to help me. There have been rumours going round for months, rumours that reached the camps just as we began the process of liquidation and closure—a process marked in Auschwitz by the terrible "Night of the Gypsies" when 2,897 Romany gypsies were exterminated, and in every camp by the massacre of the *Sonderkommando*. According to the rumours, secret negotiations were taking place between the Headquarters of the Reich Security Office on behalf of the *Wehrmacht*, the Waffen SS and the Gestapo, and the Turkish secret services, negotiations establishing escape routes allowing German officers to use Turkey as a hub—at least for as long as Europe is in turmoil. It is the only possible escape route, every European country is occupied by one power or another and the hunt for collaborators and war criminals is in full spate. A lot of money had been transferred into Turkish bank accounts in Switzerland to save the German military elite. Later, in 1947, when ODESSA is up and running, there will be other escape routes—through Switzerland, Italy and Austria, the chaotic plans of the early postwar days over, a new era will dawn, an era ruled by business interests, horse-trading involving millions of dollars, buried treasures, priceless paintings, rare documents, mythical objects worth their weight in diamonds, top-secret files. There will be classified negotiations with governments, secret organisations, high-ranking emissaries, clandestine wars will be fought, old ideologies explosively rekindled. The concentration camp prisoner and his tragic tale will be forgotten, as though the next world war were already being fought. Demand will outstrip supply, everyone will want their very own German—an expert in missiles, solid fuels, chemical and atomic weapons, an expert in medicine and military engineering, in military-industrial systems, in ciphers and codebreaking, in propaganda, in art, in dealing with minorities. There will be no country who is not prepared to do a deal with ODESSA. I can imagine myself, a clandestine European in search of some adventure too shameful to mention, slipping through the streets of the medina, holing up in some insalubrious *caravanserai* and waiting, just as I am doing now in this hotel, spending my days staring furtively through a rickety oriel window and nodding. I can imagine myself startled by the slightest noise, listening to the BBC as it triumphantly announces the end of the world—the end of our world, reporting one after another as our cities are bombed, as Allied and Russian troops squabble over the Reich, over our beloved Berlin, as senior party members are arrested, the reports of the Führer's suicide, of the mass surrender of whole divisions of our magnificent army, of starving people scrabbling through ruined streets. I think of Uelzen and I can hear my elderly parents moaning beneath the rubble. I can imagine myself, desperate, holding my head in my hands, hesitating between suicide, between fight and flight.

Then, at dawn one morning, someone comes to tell me the coast is clear. I have to hurry. I must be careful not to speak German. They dress me as a Turk, give me false papers, perhaps a message from my distant benefactor, the famous Jean 92, and send me off in a relic dating from the First World War. Are there other SS officers in the truck? Why not? After all, there are thousands of us trying to save our skins. Despite screams and threats, I refuse to hand over the knapsack that contains what no officer of the Reich should ever be without: my military record and my medals. After all, the war is not over—there are other ways to fight: resistance, sabotage. In planning for victory, one must necessarily plan for defeat, too—perhaps the German High Command has plans to set up for this eventuality. After all France—hardly the greatest military strategist in the world—after its defeat regrouped in London, in Algiers, and went on fighting. The trek across Turkey is long and difficult, there are constant alerts, then one day someone whispers that the border is just across the horizon and a Syrian guard is waiting for me there. Egypt is still a long way off, but I have already made it to the East, to the sun, the deserts, the caravans, the chaos, the motley colours. No one will go looking for a needle in a haystack here. When everyone wears a *djelleba* and a *keffiyeh*, everyone is anonymous. Egypt, of course, is still occupied by the British, but there is so much turmoil, so much confusion, that hope is possible, anything is possible—a man could easily disappear and reappear again. King Farouk has clearly had his day and no one knows what will come after him—rumours and speculation are rife but they corroborate and conflict until no one knows what the truth is. Spies from all over the world are already in Egypt posing as smiling diplomats, harried archaeologists, greedy businessmen, devotees of Islam, sheep-like tourists, with one eye on the derricks and the Suez Canal and one on the other spies. This is the Middle East where, since the dawn of time, nothing has ever been straightforward. Having studied the possible routes to Egypt, I assume my father travelled over land. The sea route was shorter, but infinitely more dangerous. American and British marines everywhere were on constant alert, the war was over but the embers were still smouldering. Warships patrolled the Mediterranean, inspecting, checking, seizing cargo, the shipping lanes were teeming with smugglers trafficking opium, American cigarettes, alcohol, weapons, secret documents, forged papers, works of art, this was the hub of piracy and of a slave trade that affected even the faithful from Europe and North Africa making pilgrimage to Mecca, to Nadjaf, Qom, Karbala, Jerusalem. The British, furious with the Jews, were determined to stop them emigrating to Palestine where they wanted to establish a state encompassing Galilee and the desert of Negev—the State of Israel, something which would have incensed the Arabs already waging war on anything that moved, threatening, dreaming of independence, toying with communism, socialism, Pan-Arabism, fundamentalism, even going so far as to flirt with that ridiculous Judaeo-Christian concept, democracy. They would never agree on anything, being too divided, too rich for their dreams, too poor to make them reality, it was this which would push them into the arms of Moscow. As is often the case, the longest road is the least dangerous. I decided that my father and his guides had probably travelled via Adana, Dörtyol and Hassa in eastern Turkey, crossed the Syrian border at Afrin and from there travelled via Alep and Damascus to Mafraq in Jordan, and from there through Amman and Ramm in the south of the kingdom. All that remained, then, was to cross the Akaba Gulf to Sinai and travel by camel to Suez and on to their final destination, Cairo. A journey of thousands of miles beneath an ancient, implacable sun.

Exhausted, I surfaced from this endless, monotonous journey through the deserts of the Middle East. I took a shower, collapsed on the bed and fell asleep.

RACHEL'S TRIP TO CAIRO

10-13 APRIL 1996

I used to come to Cairo all the time when I was working for the multinational. I loved it, I was always impatient to be back in the sun, in this dreamlike city, eager to melt into the vibrant crowds, to let myself be swept up in the intoxicating atmosphere you only find in the south, in a world turned upside down like Egypt, a mass of contradictions, clinging to the past but far removed from its three-thousand-year-old history, open to all the world but only through the narrow chink of tourism, peaceful only in its monuments to the dead. This is why we come, we are drawn to the exotic, we leave conformity at home. Egypt is a miracle whose existence depends entirely on the Nile delta, the meagre market gardens, the *fellahs* who look as though they have stepped from a bas-relief. But agriculture requires irrigation and I was working for a company selling pumps and sluices, turnkey solutions, cash up front, US dollars only. This was the way we looked at things—it was the only way to look at things—a market needs suppliers. We were suppliers, and we knew everything there was to know about their needs, their weaknesses, their endless tales of woe. We called it *market analysis*, an essential part of a *global marketing strategy*. The minute we got a green light from head office, we descended on the country like locusts in some biblical plague. By the time they had a chance to look up and say "Allahu Akbar," we had the whole country kitted out with pumps and sluices and deep in debt for the rest of its days. No longer would the waters of this legendary Nile flow serenely to the sea as they had done for thousands of years to the haunting cries of helmsmen in their *dhows*, the absurd croaking of the gulls and—at auspicious moments—the happy gurgling of a chubby baby kicking in his basket of bulrushes carried by the sacred waters. We had dammed the Nile, diverted it, churned it, filtered it, canalized it, pumped it, fertilised it, cycled and recycled the water and only then, pumped it back—filthy and reeking—so that the ancient, troubled Nile might flow onwards to the sea. No longer would people wait for the Nile to flood as a sign from the gods, something to be celebrated like New Year. All this we did for thirty pieces of silver and a five percent *baksheesh*: we changed the course of a history as old as the world. They need to update their hieroglyphics.

When business was done, we'd dive into the crowds and commune with our human brethren in the medina. The moment we stepped out of our air-conditioned offices, we were off in search of neighbourhoods so poor they could only exist in the imagination of the destitute south, places that endure only by some miracle, breathe only by the grace of God. We would seek out the most tortuous streets, the narrowest alleys, the riotous confusion, the flood of colours, sounds and smells, the bewildered smiles of the destitute—*Al-Masakeen*—the relentless patter of the merchants in the *souk,* whose age-old spiel can still dupe an international conman, the lyrical flights of the beggars, the teeming packs of children, the *Bounayes*, the *walads,* the affected indignation of the thieves, the *sirakinn*, the bleating of fat *chaouchs* pleading poverty, like ticks feeding on the misery of others, the cursing of the carters, the pleas of the beggars, the *toulabs,* so piteous that no one ever hears them, the dreamlike pronouncement of the scribes, their ears so full of secrets they would make a saint blush, but more than this, watchful as hawks, we were seeking a glimpse of an Egyptian woman wearing a close-fitting tunic, a headscarf framed by coloured pompoms. If their husbands were nearby, keeping an eye on them, it was all for nothing, they have no control over their wives for all their furious glares, the whistle of their canes, their wives have lots of tricks to give these latent murderers the slip. Then, finally, we'd find a woman who looked as though she has stepped from some furtive dream, a devil in the flesh, hips swaying, arms outspread, full breasts, a mischievous smile, a pair of bewitching eyes. This was what we have been looking for: the living gaze of the Sphinx that sees beyond the Beyond. It is as mysterious, as enchanting as everyday immortality, her eyes flash like lightning, more terrifying than the curse of a pharaoh, were he Tutankhamen himself. What we saw in these women was the reincarnation of Cleopatra, a *Malikah* worthy of the Caliphs, a *houri* beloved of Allah, a princess from the *Thousand and One Nights*, a siren conjured from the troubling world of the *djinn*. We were all widely travelled, we had all seen the world, but we all agreed that there was nothing on earth more thrilling than the dazzling, kohl-rimmed eyes of an Egyptian woman, glittering with the most ancient mystery in all the world.

Having made our pilgrimage, and with a little ebony scarab or a terracotta sarcophagus for Ophélie packed into my suitcase, we would go our separate ways to different countries, petrified at the prospect of having to face the ruthless realities of the modern world.

But these are memories of a past life, a carefree life. Now I am mired in the past, plunged into a hideous war, crushed by horror, tormented by my own father. Egypt will never again be a dreamlike country, a picture postcard. This was where my father came, his crimes packed up in his suitcase and, from what I can tell, he had a wonderful life, he became a new man here and found a position in the Egyptian secret service. What I need to understand is how, arriving from a hell of your own making, from the bleak horror of life in the camps, does this man adjust to a shimmering world of sweltering sun, gentle humility, affably shambolic poverty, where a *hookah* and a glass of mint tea are always to hand, a belly dancer's navel is always at eye level, where your bed is always open to the stars? What does he think, this man? What regrets haunt him? What pleasures can help him forget the pain he so lavishly meted out in the cruel, sinister world of his former life, an absurd, insane, incessant mechanical ballet where every day was reduced to nothingness, to listening to agonised howls bleed through the walls, to watching the columns of black smoke rising into the heavens? I know this man is unscrupulous enough to forgive himself everything, but surely no pity, no compassion, no mercy can absolve such vile, unspeakable things? Or maybe this man is not a man, nor even the shadow of a man, perhaps he is the devil incarnate. *My God, who will tell me who my father is?*

You quickly realise that the old Egypt, the cheerful, cosmopolitan, raucous, romantic Egypt of Naguib Mahfouz, does not exist anymore. Modern Egypt—*Misr*—is dominated by twin giants as formidable as the great pyramids: religion and the police—leaving not one square inch where a free man may set foot. If he's not taken to task by the police—the *chorti*—he will be by the fanatic, the *Irhabi.* In Egypt, the police force of the Raïs and the religion of Allah conspire to make life a living hell for every single person. Death and dishonour are the twin tracks of this miserable fate. It is hard to believe that in a country subjugated by faith and fear, things would change so quickly. The last time I was in Cairo, two years ago, when we delivered our most powerful pump, the H56—H for horizontal, 56 the diameter of the outflow in inches—from what I saw then (constantly chaperoned by official guides and escorted by patrols of helpful *chortis)* intimidation was so gentle, so graceful you might almost have been tempted to convert to Islam and proclaim your joy. We knew at the time that the guides had been taught to misinform us, but even so the noose has clearly been tightened since then. The people who roam the streets now are not men, they are victims seeking some refuge from the police station and the mosque. Egypt has become intolerable, it is no longer a country for men, or even saints, and all the picture postcards in the world cannot change that. I pity any Egyptian who is not a policeman or a fanatic.

I felt anxious as I walked around the city. I was constantly watching my step. Not a gesture, not a look, not a thought was out of place. I wandered past the Ministry of Interior Affairs, the headquarters of the *Mukhabarat* where my father in his time had been a frequent visitor; this was where they had made his fake papers for him, this was where they had required certain favours in exchange for the hospitality afforded him by King Farouk and later by Nasser. What could they have asked him to do but infiltrate European circles in Cairo, decode secret Nazi documents bought on the black market, develop some sort of chemical weapon and later train Algerian revolutionaries in some anonymous building in the city? I quickly realised I had been spotted—the *chaouchs* were making a pincer movement, indestructible old bangers would suddenly break down nearby, *choufs* would diligently pretend to read their newspapers as they watched. I slipped away just in time. Many things have changed here since 1945—the curtains that hang in the windows, the official cars, the suits worn by the civil servants, the complaints of the orderlies, the sound of the sirens—what has not changed is the atmosphere. Hans Schiller, SS officer, would have felt at home here. Then I remembered that the war never really ended in Egypt—if the Egyptians weren't starting a war, someone else was—wars against the Mamelukes, the Turks, the king, against the British and the French, the war against American imperialism, the wars with Israel, the wars against Islamic terrorists, against the Copts, against the *kaffirs,* the war against the Great Satan and, worst of all, the war they waged against their own people. Having waged all these wars, there was only one thing for the country to do—make peace with itself, return to the happiness of yesteryear, to the Great Egypt, serene, eternal.

I doubled back, went and joined the tourists. They don't know anything, don't suspect anything, they don't care about history, about anything, they're here for the sun and the Kodak moments. Being with them is relaxing, even if they look impossibly pretentious posing for photographs next to the Great Pyramid as though it were an old friend. The pyramid is ageless. How many years have they lived, how many years do they have left before they're six feet under? Why, when they leave their own country, do tourists suddenly forget they are human, mortal? Thinking about Kodak moments, I remembered the photo in my pocket, the photograph of papa next to the Pyramid of Cheops that I'd found it in his suitcase in our house in Aïn Deb that vast and lonely night. Suddenly I was seized by that same frenzy, searching for the roots of evil, staring at the photo of papa dressed like a gentleman from the *Belle Époque* posing with two English ladies next to the pyramid. In those days, you needed to be rich and somewhat reckless to be a tourist, travel was the hobby of the idle rich accustomed to cruises, to vacations. I don't know when the photo was taken, probably while Farouk was still on the throne—between 1945, when papa arrived in Egypt, and 1952, when Farouk was toppled in favour of General Mohamed Naguib. Probably the summer of 1946 or '47. A year later, tensions in the Middle East were running so high after the Palestinian war that it put an end to tourism in Egypt for years. The ladies in the picture, their extravagant outfits, seem suited to the period of the monarchy. I can't imagine papa dressing up in a white suit and pith helmet in the time of the colonels. Nasser considered revolutionary austerity a great virtue and imposed it on everyone. I can picture life during the monarchy, the sumptuous embassy banquets, the palatial boats, the great mansions of the pashas and the viziers, the horse rides through the vast demesnes of the *Effendi*, the cultural visits to the great museum in Cairo, the elegant cruises down the Nile stopping at archaeological sites from Karnak to Aswan, the solitary trips gentlemen made to the *hammams,* the secret harems, the opium dens. No one evokes this atmosphere, placid and refined, cynical and strained, as powerfully as Agatha Christie, the queen of civilised crime. Papa would have effortlessly fitted into this life, he was educated, spoke several languages and, unlike many German officers, he was extremely cultured, he was handsome, well-dressed and, above all, he had extensive experience with death, something which gives the cynical machinations required of polite society a tragic, pitiless, fascinating depth. He would have effortlessly dazzled the ladies and their powerful patrons—something of an advantage for a spy in the service of the king—or any other power. I'm thinking of the Soviet spies who undoubtedly discovered papa's Nazi background and made him an offer he couldn't refuse. Israel, after all, was nearby, it would be easy to ship him a trunk full of Jewish ashes and daub a yellow star on the door of Hans Schiller, SS officer.

Since I have decided to slip into papa's thoughts, retrace his footsteps, I think it's only right that I should live it up here too. We'll see what happens. I don't have much money, but Egypt is dirt poor and, in the *souk,* the few dollars I do have will buy me a lot of the insipid pleasures tourists crave. I went back to the tour group and—whipped into a whirl of excitement and enthusiasm by our guide—we sped through Cairo by day and Cairo by night, raced through the museum, ignored local customs, raided the *souks*, pissed in the Nile, strolled the great boulevards, sat chattering noisily at a table outside one of the mythic cafés that once made Cairo famous, back in the days of Egyptian cinema, of great divas and fabulous international archaeological expeditions. The lustre had faded somewhat, but we made the best of it, we embraced poverty though we were only slumming it, drank syrupy mint tea rather than champagne, took ramshackle buses rather than *barouches* and limousines, walked in the sweltering sun rather than in the shade of parasols, and prattled endlessly about the Cyclopean mysteries of the pharaohs. Then we headed for Giza where, like every other tourist, I decided I'd like to have my photo taken next to the Great Pyramid. But the photograph I wanted had to be special, I wanted to be surrounded by a bevy of elderly English ladies. I looked around and found a group of plump, rosy-cheeked English women, their arms bare, and among them—miracle of miracles—one who was lean and angular as flint, wrapped in a prickly shawl, a dead ringer for the formidable Victoria. Now all I needed to was to secure their cooperation. The old dears were only too happy to oblige. I borrowed a pith helmet from a Dutch tourist, hired one of the professional photographers, positioned the ladies as in the original picture, gave them a sidelong smile and shouted, "*Maestro!* Do your worst!" Five minutes later I had a print, a perfect copy of the original—if you ignore the fact that I looked gaunt as a camp prisoner. On the back of the photograph, I wrote: *"Helmut Schiller, son of Hans Schiller, Giza, 11 April 1996."* Half a century separates the two photographs; that and six million dead gone up in smoke.

In the end, I felt pleased with myself. I had stopped at nothing in my search for the truth. There's nothing now for me to do in Cairo. Or anywhere else. I'm going back to Paris, I have an appointment to keep. From here, it can only lead to the end. My parents died on 14 April 1994, that was the day Hans Schiller finally eluded the justice of men. But for the man that I am to go on believing in the little time he has left, it is essential that there be some particle of good in us. I am not thinking about the God Particle, that doesn't interest me. If God has failed here on earth, how can he expect to succeed in heaven? I will see to it that justice is done, I am better placed than He.

N eedless to say, getting out of Algeria was a fucking nightmare. Boarding the plane seemed to take forever, the paperwork, the *Ausweis,* the security checks, the waiting, the petty bureaucracy, it's like the *Bonzen* in Algeria like nothing better than torturing people. They're like the Gestapo. I was a bundle of nerves, I was terrified that I'd be dragged off somewhere. At one point, just as we were going through the last security check, an officer in a blue jacket came over to us and said: "You, you and you . . . come with me." I thought I'd had it, but it was nothing—he just needed four young guys to help him shift a crate from a truck and carry it down to the basement. I still can hardly believe he said thanks and gave us each a cigarette. Only after the plane had taken off and we had reached the point of no return did I breathe again. I fell asleep straight away. I needed to build up my strength so I could face the estate. I had a sick feeling. I expected the place to be completely different and, on our way back from Orly airport—where they gave me a hero's welcome—my mates told me more than enough to convince me that the place would be unrecognizable. Between what you expect and what you find there's a lot of relativity. The estate looked exactly the same as it ever had, what had changed was the atmosphere; I had felt as though I'd been away for ages, but when I looked up at the tower blocks, it was like I'd never been away. Time, to those waiting on the platform, passes at a different rate relative to those on the train. I felt weird. I had no experience of long journeys, of the dislocation caused by relativity. A week can be a long time and a short time. In Algeria, every second seemed so heavy with meaning that it felt like I'd spent a year there. Back in France, staring up at the tower blocks, it feels as though I've only been gone a couple of hours. My mates feel like they've lived through a whole century, but to me they seem exactly the same as when I left.

By the time I'd taken a quick tour of the estate, popped up to say hello to aunt Sakina and uncle Ali and headed down to meet my mates at the station cafeteria, everything was fine, we were back in sync, I was choked like them by the stifling atmosphere of the estate, in tune the mood of all-conquering Islam. I needed to think, to look at things objectively, if that was possible. As it turned out, nothing much had changed, it was same old same old. People were a little more panicky since the new emir Flicha and Cyclops the imam showed up. There was a lot more violence but the estate hadn't degenerated into civil war; there were casualties but nothing fatal and, although there had been a shitload of death threats, nothing had actually happened. For the shopkeepers, the *jihad* tax had taken a big hike but the protection rackets were gone. The non-Muslims were completely fazed, they said they couldn't afford to pay, they were threatening to move out, march on the Office of Taxation, stage a sit-in at the police station. A lot of boys had dropped out of school and started going to the mosque, a lot of the girls had started wearing the *hijab*, some of them had stopped going out and some of the older men, tired of constantly being lectured, had started wearing a scarf or a *keffiyeh* and sermonising themselves. The few regulars who still hung out in the local bars had started carrying prayer beads. The drug dealers in the south tower blocks have disappeared, but there's no reason to think they're dead, they've moved on or gone into hiding, they'll be back. All in all, the social order has changed without breaking down. Thirty families moved out in the first week, but this was compensated by thirty new families arriving, a bunch from North Africa, one from Mali, a Pakistani family, one from Somalia, a family from Cape Verde and another from Romania. The population has remained pretty stable, but the ethnic and religious mix is narrower. A crew of new *K a p o s*—real hard bastards—has taken over from the old ones who were demobbed for being too lenient, for fraternising with the enemy. "What about Com'Dad?" I asked. No one can understand what he's up to, he's keeping up a Level 4 surveillance and waiting to see what happens. He still does his daily rounds, but twice as fast as he used to. "What about the people on the estate?" "What about them? They're waiting to see what happens."

It didn't seem like much, but it knocked me for six. How were we ever going to stop this thing? Back in Aïn Deb, it had all seemed so simple: I'd imagined the estate extricating itself from this nightmare in no time, I thought all we needed was for people to talk to each other, tell their kids everything. Fuckwit that I am, I'd imagined climbing up on the roof of a car and talking about brotherhood, about truth, about the future. But it was the new imam, Cyclops, who did the talking. The One-Eyed fucker had heard from his spies that my parents had been murdered by jihadists and that I'd gone back to the *bled* to visit their graves. His messenger said the imam sent me his blessings and wanted to meet with me to explain what had really happened. It was a no brainer, I said I'd meet him and hear him out. If he was going to offer me the chance to kill him in place of his Algerian mates, I wasn't going to pass up the opportunity. Given there was nothing else I could do, revenge was a good plan B. Fuck, it was my duty!

I went to Rachel's old neighbourhood to look at the house. My mates had told me someone had bought it. It hurts, seeing strangers living in his house. I kept my hands behind my back and strolled around like I was just out for a walk. I had no reason to be round here anymore. In Rachel's house the lights were all on. There were new curtains in the windows, a dog barking, the TV turned up full blast, an electric drill whining, a hammer banging away, children laughing. The garage was wide open, full of boxes and furniture. The new family was busy moving in, wiping away every trace of us, stamping their own mark on the place. It hurts to see yourself wiped away like that. Do they know that some guy committed suicide in the house? I doubt it, estate agents don't get paid to tell their clients the truth. If they're hammering and drilling away like that, they must be happy, which means they don't know. They'll find out once they've settled in, when the neighbours pop round to bring them up to speed. Then they'll find out that the parents of the guy who used to live there had their throats cut in Algeria. That should shake them up. I hope they take it well. Rachel was a great guy, a good citizen, he never let anyone down, his ghost wouldn't hurt a fly. But I can see how it might spook them. Rachel's house—like our house back in Aïn Deb—is haunted by a terrible secret, by the greatest crime in history, and in the end that sort of shit seeps through the walls, gnaws at your guts, it does your head in, drives you mad. It killed Rachel, and it will kill anyone who gets too close. All the time I lived in that house, I was constantly worrying, crying, trembling, panicking, and the more I tried to block it out, the more clearly I could see the ghosts on the horizon, marching towards me, staring at me with their hollow eyes. Every time I ran off into the night, I could hear their cries following me, only to disappear when the sun came up and the tears dried on my face.

I went to the cemetery like I promised back in Aïn Deb. I sat on Rachel's grave and talked to him for a long time. I knew he could hear me. "Hey, bro" I said. "You know what? I just got back from Aïn Deb. It was all thanks to Ophélie, really, she gave me the cash for the trip. She told me: 'Rachel would be happy to see you taking an interest in your family.' See? I'm not a complete fuckup, and I'm getting better fast. Everything back in the *bled* is fine, apart from the weather, but it's winter so I suppose it's normal that it's freezing and pissing down all the time. The people are really cool. They took care of me, especially Mimed, the shoemaker's son. You probably don't know him, he wasn't even born when you left for France. Actually, you might remember him—that time you came back to bring me to France, he was bawling his eyes out because I was leaving and he blamed you, he was screaming at you. He's a good looking guy these days with lots of happy kids. I didn't tell them you killed yourself, they were so excited to hear about you, I just couldn't bring myself to tell them. I did what you did, I went to papa and maman's graves. It was nice: their last resting place is so peaceful. Your cemetery is nice too, it's beautiful, it's quiet, full of flowers with people coming and going, birds singing, couples whispering to each other. You're lucky . . . And I wanted to tell you, I read your diary. Com'Dad gave it to me after you . . . after the investigation. He said, 'Your brother was a great guy.' It's not like he was telling me anything new, I've always known that. All that stuff about papa's past, it's awful. We'd have been better off not knowing, you'd still be here, still be with Ophélie, things would be fine. At first I thought you were too hard on papa, but thinking about it, I realised you were right. What I read in your diary and what I found out from the books you left sent shivers down my spine. I aged, like, twenty years. I mean, could something like that happen again? I tell myself it couldn't but when I see what the jihadists are doing on the estate and everywhere else, I think they'd outdo the Nazis if they ever came to power. They're too full of hate and pride to just gas everyone. I've been trying to think how we can stop them, the people on the estate don't say anything and the cops are keeping an eye, but from a safe distance. My mates and me, we stand up to them as best we can, but we're just kids, people are more afraid of us than they are of the Islamists. And I wanted to tell you that I'm going to try to publish your diary and mine, I hope you think it's the right thing to do, I hope I can find a publisher. Like that poet Primo Levi said, you have to tell kids everything. Me and the guys are thinking of setting up a club to teach them all the stuff people have been hiding from them, they need to know, they're the ones who'll take after their parents, the good and the bad. If you're okay with the idea, I'd like to ask your old teacher, Madame Dominique G.H. to go over it, make it into a proper book. She won't say no, she had a lot of time for you. Anyway, that's what I wanted to say, bro. Momo and the guys say hello, and aunt Sakina sends her love. I suppose you know poor uncle Ali is a bit gone in the head these days. I love you, I owe you a lot. I'll come back and visit. Get some rest."

Never in our lives had we been so close.

Then I went to visit the imam in his basement. They've turned it into a bunker, steel-plated door, bars on the window and there's a wall of *Kapos* standing guard outside. They body-searched me and brought me to the imam like a prisoner of war. So there he was in the flesh, the one-eyed fucker, he was fifty-something, his hair was completely white, he was wearing a green *gandurah*, a black jacket, he had a beard that comes down to his belly button and one piercing eye. He was sitting cross-legged on the floor with his back against the wall. In front of him, on a low table, were the tools of his trade, the Qur'an, a pile of blank fatwas, a seal, a phone and fax machine. Flicha, the new emir, was next to him, a young guy with a beard, built like a brick shithouse, carrying a gun under his jacket, the butt deliberately sticking out to make sure any visitors didn't try anything. The imam said: "Come here, my son, come here. Sit opposite me. I believe you know Mujahid Si Omar—the ignorant young thugs on the estate call him Flicha.

Talk to me, tell me about yourself, tell me what you thought of our beloved Algeria, an Islamic country suffering under the yoke of a heathen government."

I said, "What do you want?"

"Your happiness, my son, your happiness and that of our faith. When I heard that your parents had been savagely murdered, it grieved me, truly. I immediately got in touch with our brothers in Algeria, who are fighting for Allah, for His religion."

"I didn't ask you for anything."

"I did it for Allah, and for truth, that is my duty as a Muslim, as an imam. I need to tell you that your parents were murdered by the Algerian government, not by the holy warriors of Allah. It is their way, to kill people and put the blame on us."

"Them, you, what's the difference?"

"There is a great difference. Had this been done by our soldiers, I would have told you so regardless of how you might feel, we proclaim our *jihad* before the world. They are the guilty ones, you must avenge your parents, Allah provides for *Qisas*—for exact and equivalent retribution."

"I don't need you, I don't need anybody."

"Pride is a virtue, but now you need Islam to strengthen your heart and your hand."

"I don't need anything."

"What you says is blasphemous, but you will think better of it and join us, we can give you solace, we can help you and your adoptive parents financially, and we can find some useful work for your friends who hang around all day in defiance of the law."

"I don't think you heard me, imam, I don't need you!"

"Grief and anger have clouded your mind, but go . . . Si Omar is here, he will watch over you, guide you . . . "

"Is that a threat?"

"Only Allah can punish, my son, we are but his instruments."

I was about to get up and leave, but I changed my mind.

"Tell me, imam, if you had power over the earth, where would you begin the genocide?"

"What do you mean by that question?"

"There have been a lot of genocides throughout history, what would our genocide be?"

"You have been reading evil sinful books. We have our own books, as you shall see, they will tell you that the only genocides have been waged against Muslim peoples."

"All the more reason . . . Who would we kill to even the score?"

"Islam brings peace, my son, not war. When we come to power, people will be happy to convert to Islam."

"And those who refuse?"

"Those who reject Allah, Allah will reject, there is no place for such a man on His earth or in His paradise."

"We'll kill them?"

"Allah will decide their fate."

"But he rejects them!"

"He will punish them without mercy."

"Will he command us to kill every last one of them?"

"We will do as he commands us."

"You see, that's my problem: how do you go about killing six million *kaffirs* quickly, before they wake up and fight back?"

"You're talking foolishness, my son."

"You're the imam. As a believer I have the right to ask you any question I like."

"Indeed you have, but I have told you, when Allah confers power on us, He shall tell us what we should do and how we should do it. As I said, we are instruments of His will."

"Can I make a suggestion?"

"One does not make suggestions to Allah!"

"To his representatives, then, so they can pass it on."

"I'm listening."

"They way I see it, you round the *kaffirs* all up into camps surrounded by electric fences, you gas all the useless ones straight off, the rest of them, you divide into groups based on their skills and their gender, and you work them till they drop dead. Anyone who disobeys, you gas them. What do you think?"

"I think you're dreaming."

"I'm not dreaming, it's been done before."

"The methods you suggest are barbaric, Allah commands that we kill the infidels according to Muslim rite."

"You don't get the point, imam, killing six million infidels isn't like burning some girl like Nadia, or slitting the throats of forty villagers in Aïn Deb. Half-arsed methods just won't work, it takes productivity. When you've worked it out, let me know, I'll drop by. *Salam.*"

"Allah has cursed you, son of a dog."

"Yeah, well fuck you, and you too, Emir! You want genocide? Well bring it on! Me and my mates, we'll be only too happy to roast some Nazi jihadist fuckers, and we'll invite all the kids on the estate to the barbecue."

"You're asking for trouble . . . "

"And you're getting it."

Now that war has been declared, I have to do the hard bit: tell my mates everything. They'll hate me, reject me, they'll go ballistic, but truth is truth, it should be known. I'll take it in stages, I suffered from finding it all out at once. I'll tell them who my father was, what he did, then later, when they're ready, I'll tell them about the Nazi killing machine, I'll lend them Rachel's books, explain that papa never told us anything, that that's why Rachel killed himself. And if they ask me, "What about you, what are you going to do?" I'll tell them, "Tell the truth, all over the world. After that, we'll see."

I t was in August 1995, nearly a year and a half ago, that Rachel wrote to the Algerian minister for Foreign Affairs, and there's still been no answer—at least not while I was living in Rachel's house, and I didn't find any sign of a letter among his books and papers. The fact our parents' names were changed has been bugging me since the start, like it bugged him. Given what I've learned since, it feels like they were buried with numbers tattooed on their forearms. I thought about going back to Rachel's house and asking the new owners if there's been any post since I left, then I thought that if the Ministry hadn't replied over the past sixteen months, they're hardly likely to send a reply in month seventeen. Maybe the letter got lost, I thought, in Algeria, everything ends up in the hands of the police, but I couldn't believe they'd treat a ministerial letter the way they'd handle an ordinary letter; diplomatic letters are sent by couriers on special planes. I felt I had to send a follow-up to Rachel's letter, so I wrote another letter. "To whom it may concern," like when you write to the police. And while I was at it, I wrote to the French Minister of the Interior about what's been going on at the estate. It won't do any good, but like Rachel says, you have to do what you have to do. Here's what I wrote:

Minister of Foreign Affairs, of the People's Democratic Republic of Algeria.
On 16 August 1995, my brother, Rachid Helmut Schiller,

sent you a registered letter in which he asked you to rectify the names of our parents, who were murdered on 24 April 1994 by an unidentified armed group. They were buried by the local authorities, my mother under her maiden name and my father under a pseudonym. You have not done so, nor have you bothered to reply to his letter. My brother is now dead and, as the last of the Schiller family, I am writing to you again. I'm guessing that this letter won't achieve anything, but that's no reason not to try. Don't worry, Monsieur le Ministre, after this nobody else will come to bother you. I wouldn't wish it on you, but if someday, someone tells you your parents have been murdered by persons unknown and buried under the name X, you might begin to understand our grief. For now, you're the one holding the gun, you don't have to worry who died, who disappeared, and who suffers in silence.

Yours, insincerely, ashamed of the fact that I am half-Algerian.

This was my second letter:

Monsieur le Ministre,

You, more than anyone in this country, must know what's going on on the H24 estate. I'm sure our commissioner, Monsieur Lepère, has written to you more than once, because he is committed to his work, he is doing his best, and I know that he feels terrible that there's nothing he can do. He's a by-the-book kind of cop, that's his problem. Jihadists have taken over our estate and are making our lives hell. It's not an extermination camp yet, but it's pretty much ein Konzentrationslager, as they said during the Third Reich. Gradually, people are forgetting that they live in France, half an hour from Paris, and we're finding out that the principles France talks about on the world stage are really just political bullshit. Even so, and in spite of our flaws, they are principles we believe in more than ever. Everything that we as men, as French citizens, refuse to contemplate, the Islamists are more than happy to do and we're not even allowed to complain because, they tell us, it is the will of Allah, and Allah's law trumps everything. At the rate things are going—since the adults are too pious to open their eyes and the kids are too innocent to see further than the ends of their noses—the estate H24 will soon be a full-blown Islamic Republic. At that point you'll have to declare war, just to keep it within its current borders. We won't fight with you in that war, we'll emigrate and fight for our own independence.

I'm not expecting you to do anything, I just think that there are some things that have to be done, so I'm writing to you. I expect you'll reply quickly and comprehensively, that's one of the things the French civil service is proud of. You'll tell me how impressed you are by my civic mindedness, and you'll give me a whole spiel about the steps being taken by you and by the government to restore law and order on the estate. If that's what you're planning to say, and I'm pretty sure it is, then don't bother, I've heard it all before.

Yours,

A furious citizen notionally under your jurisdiction but forced to live under Islamic law.

February 1996
Auschwitz, the end of the journey

This was how I planned it, I wanted to end my journey in Auschwitz. I arrived in the early morning, I wanted to be on my own before the busloads of tourists showed up. It was going to be a long day. The camp is vast, over 45 square kilometres, more than 11,000 acres. It is a city, like the gold-rush towns that sprang up in far-off countries in an era of rampant capitalism, booming cities sprawling out from a small encampment, motivated by greed and haste, funded by new finds, new wealth; a city both orderly and chaotic, with well-defined boundaries, broad avenues, parade grounds vast enough to intimidate a marathon runner, ugly administrative buildings, posh neighbourhoods with ridiculous houses, baroque castles, opulent cathedrals, cookie-cutter working-class slums stretching out forever, rococo theatre, extravagant cinema, trendy nightclubs, bustling brothels and dreary bars, industrial estates, train stations and shunting yards, warehouses, anaemic parks, astonishing wastelands, the hectic markets, and the sports grounds that show the city is dying of boredom and inaction, the frightening barracks and the rudimentary runway flanked by a control tower that will soon be an aerodrome worthy of a capital. This is how they are, these vast, mushrooming cities, electrifying and monotonous, full of potential and doomed, they create wealth and poverty in equal measure and in the end, they make poverty and violence a daily occurrence, they are madness in search of apotheosis. Here, life is sparkling, free, clever, a constant spectacle, while in the underbelly, in the measureless *favelas*

that ring the city, people's lives are cramped, teeming, shameful, nameless and they die with disturbing ease, *die at a yes or
a no*. These unplanned cities, carved into the logic of the totali-
tarian system that created them, flourish based on a myth, and
based on that same myth they die. One day, nature reasserts
itself and everything silently disappears, swept away by the
absurdity that created it. It was not gold that spawned this
oppressive city, born out of the ashes of a poor remote village in
the heart of Poland, it was not oil, or coffee, or rubber or rare
metals, but the systematic extermination of the *Lebensunwertes
Leben*, Jews preferably, and gypsies, but also political prisoners, antisocial elements, and all possible types of *Minderwertige
Leute*. To tell the truth, this city was a powerhouse prepared to
burn anything it could lay its hands on—there was no question
of shutting down the furnace just because the supply of Jews
dried up. In hell, everything burns, tramps and traitors, enemies
and resistance fighters. Auschwitz was the largest, the most dismal, the most deadly and the most rapacious of the Nazi death
camps. In four short years, 1,300,000 men women and children,
ninety percent of them Jews, were tossed into the furnaces—an
average of a thousand souls a day, the equivalent of a village
wiped off the map, house by house, family by family, between
daybreak and sunset.

It was still dark and terribly cold, a grubby snow was falling
and the wind from the east cut through me. If I had been hoping
for the worst welcome to punish me for returning to the scene of
my father's crimes, I got my wish, but it was still far from enough.
For a prisoner arriving here on the death train, there were many
things that made their arrival infinitely more cruel, the exhaustion
of having had to stand for days in crowded cattle trucks: the
hunger, the thirst, the filth, the panic, the fear, the torture of the
selection process, the pomp and ceremony, the contemptuous
orders, the barking dogs, the brutality of the soldiers, the humiliation of having to undress outdoors, the shaving of their hair,

the tattooing of a number on the forearm, and, through everything, the overpowering sense that something incalculable and
terrible has happened here: it was here that humanity ended,
betrayed by God himself. Were they still men when they arrived
in the camp? Arriving here on a tourist train on a bright spring
day would have been obscene. I am not just any visitor, I am
Helmut Schiller, son of SS Officer Hans Schiller, and in this place
lie my father's share of 1,300,000 dead, gassed for the most
part, shot in the head if they were lucky. I had only one choice,
to arrive as my father had, in a warm car, calm, perhaps preoccupied by some technical problem, or arrive like a prisoner, terrified, starving, numb, soaked to the skin, more alone than anyone in the world, traumatised by what was going on, not knowing what was expected of him, of him in particular. I wanted to
approximate the reality of a prisoner arriving here, wanted to
know how far my father had come. But I know that this atrocity
beggars belief, that nothing and no one could bring me even a
fraction of an inch closer to understanding it. I am free, I came
here of my own free will, I stand here a free man, I have my hair,
my teeth, I have my papers in my pocket, and, barring some
accident, murder, a fatal illness or suicide in a moment of madness, I know that I will be alive tomorrow, and the day after, and
the day after that and so on to the end of my days. I cannot
make myself a camp prisoner, a guinea pig in a Nazi laboratory,
a *Sonderkommando* or a *Kapo*, all I can do is slip into my
father's thoughts, retrace his footsteps, try to follow his terrible
path; I can do nothing but try to empathise with a prisoner, try to
feel as he must have felt as death, mysterious and degrading,
sweeps over him. I can do nothing. But I am here, I had to come,
and I must go on to the end.

I followed the tracks for the death train from the Jewish platform, the *Judenrampe*. In the distance, barring the horizon, is the
building that appears in every book, a long, low, red-brick build-

ing with a red-tiled roof and a watchtower in the middle, strad-
dling the tracks. This is Auschwitz II, *Konzentrationslager*
Auschwitz II-Birkenau. Past the entrance arch, barracks stretch
out endlessly in serried ranks. On one side is the women's camp,
on the other, the men's, and everywhere you look, watchtowers,
barbed wire, electric fences. There can be no mistake that hell
was once built here, not long ago: everything is still as it was,
everything is ashes and solitude just as it once was. Here, in
Birkenau, evil reached its apogee. To the east is Auschwitz-I, the
wrought iron gate crowned with the famous motto: *Arbeit macht
frei.* Work shall set you free. Inside, in what was once a high-
security area, is the Krupp armaments factory, the DAW, the
Deutschen Ausrüstungswerke factories, the *SS Werkstätten*—
workstations, the general pharmacy and a number of hospital
blocks known as the HKB, the *Häftlings-Krankenbau* for soldiers
and *Arbeiter.* Three kilometres to the north is Auschwitz-III
Monowitz. The great, grey complex of buildings you can glimpse
through the mist was occupied by *IG Farbenindustrie*, which spe-
cialised in making Zyklon B, fertilisers and detergents. You have
to imagine all these things: the buildings are no longer there, they
were bombed in 1944 and later razed. You can still see the foundations. In the *Buna-Werke*, another complex which was
bombed, synthetic rubber, essential to the Third Reich, was
made. Ten thousand prisoners worked in gruelling shifts. I don't
believe a single one emerged alive, they knew too much, the
secrets of production, they had had contact with military secrets
far ahead of their time. The last *Arbeiter* were massacred during
the chaos after the Soviet army marched into Poland and its units
advanced on the camps at breakneck speed, trying to get there
before everything was destroyed or removed.

I went into Birkenau and let myself be guided by instinct. I
tried to forget everything I knew, I wanted to know what it felt like
to step into this camp for the first time, knowing only its mon-

strous reputation. It was difficult, it was impossible, I knew too much, I had spent so much time studying this place, I could have moved around it with my eyes closed, the map was burned onto my brain. I could have moved around like a diligent soldier, anxious to get from A to B to execute his orders promptly. I could retrace his footsteps, walk boldly as he did, wrapped up in a thick greatcoat against the blizzard: bringing a wounded worker from the infirmary to his workstation; dragging some human wreck to Bunkers I and II, where French Jews were gassed; picking up the daily productivity reports from one of the four ultra-modern complexes—the famous K II, III, IV and V, marvels of extermination designed, they say, by Himmler himself, to function both as gas chambers and crematoria—and dashing back with it to the SS Administrative Building, allowing myself a quick visit to the *Kapos'* brothel to see the new arrivals or, out of morbid curiosity, peeking through the window of the experimental clinic run by Carl Clauberg, or the one run by the sinister doctor Josef Mengele, the Frankenstein of monozygotic twins, swing by the laboratory where chemical engineers like my father—who, given he was a SS-*Hauptsturmführer* by then, was probably in charge—worked on their magic potions, their treatments for "lice"; everywhere in fact, except the baleful area of Block 11, where lunatics unlike any on earth experimented with tortures and methods of execution that were bizarre even in Auschwitz. I could just as easily move from the parade ground to where the prisoners assembled at dawn and lead a group to wherever they were assigned to do forced labour.

I've learned to follow my father in my mind: I could have wandered around the Lager as though I had grown up here. There is not a single detail of his working day I have not imagined. Papa was a methodical man, regular as a metronome, he spent his whole life obsessed with timing things. Our life in Aïn Deb was regulated by his watch. While my childhood friends needed only a ray of sunshine, a sudden whim to go from place to place, there I was, champing at the bit, watching the big hand on the house clock, waiting for my fifteen minutes of freedom.

I found myself standing in front of the K Complexes, my father had probably worked on the development of K IV, he may even have inaugurated it. Why that one in particular? The dates fit. My father was posted to Auschwitz-Birkenau between January and July 1943, work on the complexes began early in 1942 and was completed in late 1943. By the time he arrived here my guess is that the first two were already operational and the third was in the testing phase, the foundations were probably still being dug on K V. In fact, I knew this was true, I had read so many books, so many survivor accounts, I knew all there was to know. This is why I know that papa was working under the orders of the first *Kommandant* of Auschwitz, the sinister SS-*Obersturmbannführer* Rudolf Höß, who would later be arrested by the Allies in Bavaria living under an assumed name; he would be tried and sentenced to death by the Polish Supreme National Tribunal in 1947 and hanged in front of one of the *Kremas* of his beloved Auschwitz. In the summer of 1943, when my father was taking up his new post in Buchenwald, Höß would be replaced by Arthur Liebehenschel and Richard Baer. The first would be arrested and executed in '48 with the creepy *Kommandante* of the women's *Lager* in Birkenau, Maria Mandl and her deputy, "The Beautiful Beast" Irma Grese, whom papa probably flirted with between shifts. Richard Baer died in prison awaiting trial in 1963. Josef Mengele, known as the Angel of Death, escaped via the Franciscan ratline in Italy, and took off first for the clear air of Perón's Argentina then to Paraguay and Brazil to invest his part of the immense Mengele family fortune, live it up and die a natural death in 1979 at the age of 68 somewhere in Brazil, leaving behind him the myth of an Übermensch whom even death could not touch. When asked, "Why does your father not turn himself in?" in an interview in New York, Mengele's son replied,

"That has nothing to do with me, that's his business." If I'd been his son, I would have turned him in and would have demanded to testify at the trail as one of his victims.

The further I have gone on my journey—which I wanted to be instinctive, the better to penetrate the mystery—the more I understood the implacable system that regulated this place down to the last second. I was a prisoner of what I knew. I was trapped in my books, my technical reports. In reality things did not work like that. Behind the cold logic of the Machine was the savage mystery of death which pervaded the camp, the cruel laws of random chance which, here more than anywhere else, stalked the prisoner's every step, watched him, made certain that the selection for this task, this punishment, fell to him, which decided that illness should strike him rather than another, which meant instant death; things conspired magically such that trivial incidents snowballed to become great catastrophes which jammed this splendid, unstoppable Machine, panicking the *Bonzen,* humiliating them, unleashing reprisals, terrible fury, wanton acts, unending punishments; there were the days and nights of privation; there was the mystery of time, stretching out to infinity until it broke the will, destroyed all hope, even all regret, then suddenly contracting, choking the world, making every movement seem hurried, a pitiless garrotte that made each minute weigh more heavily, each second more uncertain; and there was the weather, its shifting moods, its tortures, its sudden fevers; there was the lack of privacy, the shame and the animal instincts that accompanied it; there was the hunger, end-less, frantic; the smells that turned your stomach; there was the terrible loss of awareness that made the prisoner his own worst enemy, *each having signed a pact with hunger, with the instinct to survive, with madness*, and there were the thousand tiny everyday events which could at any moment turn to tragedy; my God, the tragedy that might result from a stolen shoe, a cap lost in the dead of winter, one glance too many at an officer, a second of inattentiveness, a bowl shattering, a twisted ankle, a bout of dysentery or lumbago, an infected wound; there was the gruelling preoccupation with constantly having to look busy, to never raise suspicion; there was the turmoil you carried around in your head all day, all night; there were the suppurating fears, the endless questions, the morbid moments of elation, the childish fears, the excruciating needs, the impossible dreams, the fleeting memories of another life in a world where the sun existed, where day and night were a mercy shared with others. A trivial thing could mean death, could make life unbearable, everything was uncertain, everything doomed to failure, to darkness, to decay. It must have been so bad that we hoped this splendid, unstoppable machine would keep on turning. Perhaps we even prayed to God to forget us and to watch over the Beast. Ensure she had her dead so she might gorge herself on them and leave us in peace. When everything runs well, we might snatch a moment of peace here and there. When everything runs smoothly, we can bide our time and die in peace.

My mind too is filled with mysteries. One of them haunts me, I think about it all the time, it is the mystery of the survivor. How is it possible to live after the camps? Is there life after Auschwitz? Of all the accounts I've read, particularly those written in the heat of the moment, when the camps were liberated and during the first war trials, not one expressed hate or anger, not one clamoured for revenge. I didn't understand, I don't understand. It is a mystery to me. Calmly, shyly, these women, these men, simply explained what it had been like, answered the questions asked of them by investigators, by judges. "My name is X, I arrived in the camp on such and such a day, month, year . . . I was posted to the clothing workshop . . . yes, I knew prisoners were being gassed . . . yes, I was beaten by the *Kapos* . . . I witnessed punishments . . . one day they had us all assemble for the execution for five prisoners accused of stealing a remnant of material . . .

another day, a friend of ours, Y, threw himself against the electric fence, we were all beaten for not stopping him . . . He wanted to kill himself, we could understand that." What about you? "Me? I was lucky, I was posted to 'Canada.'" Can you tell us what you mean by "Canada"? "That was the name for the huge warehouses near the camp where they sorted through the belongings of new arrivals, we'd put all the money in one pile, jewellery in another, and we would sort the clothes and make large bundles of them that the trucks took to the station. The work was exhausting, but it's wasn't so bad . . . Canada was like paradise for those who had to slog away outside in the cold and the mud." I read and reread the books of the famous survivors of Auschwitz—Charlotte Debo, Elie Wiesel, Jorge Semprun, Primo Levi—and I didn't find a single word of hatred, the hint of a desire for revenge, the least expression of anger. They simply described their day-to-day life in the camp with all the detail they could remember, and this is their artistry, they related what they saw, what they heard, what they smelled, what they touched, the heaviness and the tiredness in their backs, their legs. They replicated it as a camera replicates an image, as a tape recorder replicates a sound. When they talk about their torturers, they say, "Officer X said this or that on such a day at such a time." When they talk about their companions, they say, "So-and-so said this, he did that, one morning he was gone, we never saw him again." Why this detachment? Where is the rage? Where is the hatred, the cry for revenge, where is the longing to destroy everything, to reject humanity, to turn your back on God, to run and keep on running, to stop listening? The experience of the camps is unlike any other, all the noise in the world cannot drown out the suffering that rose up from this place. This is how we talk about it, like a sunless day that by chance was visited upon the world. We talk about pure evil, about the incalculable suffering it inflicted on us. "Kuhn is out of his senses. Does he not see Beppo the Greek in the bunk next to him, Beppo who is twenty years old and is going to the gas chamber the day after tomorrow and knows it and lies there looking fixedly at the light without saying anything and without even thinking anymore? Can Kuhn fail to realise that next time it will be his turn? Does Kuhn not understand that what has happened today is an abomination, which no propitiatory prayer, no pardon, no expiation by the guilty, which nothing at all in the power of man can ever clean again. If I was God, I would spit at Kuhn's prayer." This is the only note of anger I can find in Primo Levi's book *If This Is a Man*. He notes that nothing, not prayers, not pardon, not the expiation of the guilty, nothing that is within man's power to do can ever make this right, nothing more. I don't understand. In my own way, I am a survivor, but I cannot find the words, I have not the strength within me to express my rage, my shame, my hate, and I know that nothing can ever stanch the longing for revenge I carry inside me. To discover that you are the son of a murderer is worse than being a murderer yourself. The murderer has his justifications, he can hide behind language, he can deny, he can brag, he can take responsibility for his crime and proudly face the gallows, he can claim he was only following orders, he can run away, change his identity, find new justifications, he can mend his ways, he can do anything. What can the son do but enumerate his father's crimes and drag that millstone with him all through life? I hate my father, I hate this country, the system that made it what it was, I hate humanity, I hate the whole world, I hate all the famous people who coldly wrote their books describing what my father did as though it were a job, nothing more, a job he was being paid to do, they stripped him of what humanity he might still have had and portrayed him as a witless automaton obeying the orders of the Führer, I hate them for sparing him, for not hating him as one should hate a tormenter, for not insulting him, I hate them for their detachment, I hate them for their restraint. I know my father—he was aware of what he was doing, he was a man of conviction, a man of duty, he deserves all the anger in the world. *You are scum, Hans Schiller, you are the vilest murderer that ever lived, I*

loathe you, I despise you, I would have your name obliterated, I
would have you burn in hell until the end of time and those you
gassed come and spit in your face! You had no right to live, you
had no right to give us life, I want nothing to do with this life, this
nightmare, this unending disgrace. You had no right to run away,
papa. I have to take it upon myself, I will pay for you, papa. May
you be cursed, Hans Schiller. I sat down and, like a camp prisoner who has witnessed too much in a single day, I cried water-
less tears.

It had stopped snowing. The wind had died away. The cold
was not so biting. A small unseen sun brought a faint warmth.
Perhaps only one degree, but to me it felt like a breath of life. I
got to my feet. I ached all over. I stretched and continued to wander around the camp. I wanted to go back to the station, all
things considered it is the most important place in the camp, the
most cruel, the place where everything is decided. It was here
that the men, the women, the terrified children, the babies sleeping in their own filth arrived at the end of the line. They are still
dressed as they were in the city, they carry a suitcase, a bag, a
briefcase, a toy, the women carry their babies, hug them to their
breasts, fingertips gently stroking their cheeks, sheltering them
from the cold, from the sun, they have their papers on them, their
watches, their jewellery, money in their pockets. And that yellow
star on the lapels of their jackets, true, the *Judenstern*, a badge
of shame, but it signifies only that they are Jews; it is possible to
dislike them, it doesn't matter, no one can be expected to like
everyone. Others are shamefaced, the Gypsies, the dark-
skinned people, the sick, with their strange pallor and their frail
voices, the old men and women pitiful to see so far from the life
they once led, and what of the children who can neither grow up
nor pretend to be grown-ups nor understand what is going on
around them, what is being done to their parents. But this station is not like any station in the world. And this star is not like

any star in the heavens. It is here, on the *Judenrampe*, on this wasteland around the station, that the selection took place, that they were separated, registered, tattooed, where they dressed in camp clothes, lined up, and here they waited for someone, some *deus ex machina* beset by terrible fears, some *Bonzen*, to give the order. They wait for hours and every minute is endless. For the old, the sick, the children, this is where it ends. They will see no other day. They do not know it, some of them suspect, but something that has not yet happened, something you have not seen with your own eyes is simply a speculation, life is still possible: the doors to the gas chambers are already open and the *Sonderkommandos* are waiting for them, standing to attention, by their wheelbarrows, the stench of rotting flesh and the stony silence helping them to forget what they have come to. In a few hours, they will be smoke rising into God's heaven, the deaf, blind, cruel God to whom they have been praying all their lives. How is it possible to believe in such a God? A cat, a rat, a cold-blooded snake affords humanity more warmth. It is a life rubbing up against another life. For the able-bodied men and women, this is where it begins. In this place they are forever stripped of their autonomy, their dignity, their memories, their humanity. Everything. It is at this moment that they truly become *Abgewandert.* Death is a formality that will come later, when they earn it through good, honest work.

She was standing at the gates of Birkenau. A frail old woman, her legs slightly bowed, a handbag dangling from her elbow, wearing a ridiculous little hat. Her coat had seen better days and was shiny with wear. She stood alone, motionless, staring fixedly at something in front of her feet. She looked like an elderly housekeeper standing at a bus stop in a chalk white, windswept housing estate waiting for the first bus of the morning. She glanced left and right, then turned again and for a long time she stared at the train tracks that stretched out towards the horizon, at the banks on either side, at the sky wrapped up warm in its heavy clouds, before turning to look again at the building and the watchtower. She took in every detail. I could feel something inside her cry out as she stood frozen before this threshold which was once crossed only to die. She steeled herself and walked forward under the archway where she stopped dead—I think even her breath stopped. Her head jerked from side to side as though twisted by some malfunctioning machine. It was fear, the all-consuming fear that is Auschwitz. I stood transfixed by this strange, piteous ballet in this theatre of horrors beneath a sky which left room only for grief and silence. I could tell that she was searching her memory, searching for landmarks, reference points. Memories. She stood, thinking. I would say that she was feeling things inwardly, evil and its mysteries scattered by time, she moved like an animal that instinctively senses the reverberations of some distant earthquake and begins to panic. But she, she did not move, no longer moved, she looked as though she could stand there forever, waiting. Then she shuddered, and, as though resolved to face her suffering, stepped through the entrance into the camp, a single step, then stopped again. She scanned the place, then turned to her right and, taking small steps, walked slowly, her head down. She had stepped into another world, this world I know so well on paper I could guide her, predict her every reaction in advance. I realised that she had lived here in this loathsome place. How I knew, I'm not sure, but in her I saw a star in my dark sky. I followed her.

She went into the women's *Lager*. She stopped, took a handkerchief from her bag, rolled it into a ball, wiped her eye then pressed it to her nose. She moved forward, read the number on the first block, then the next, and the next. She was walking faster now, darting ahead in jerky little steps, the block she was looking for was not far. Then she stopped and for a long time she stared at the block on her right, then stepped towards the entrance, climbed the three steps, reached out and put her hand on the doorknob. She hesitated, then turned it first one way, then the other. The door was locked. She did not try again. She sat down on the top step. I watched her. She did nothing, she did not move. She was off somewhere in her mind, in some dark place. I felt a surge of affection for this woman. She seemed so frail, so alone.

I hid in the shadows so I could watch her. Head tilted to one side, she was toying with her handkerchief in her lap, folding and unfolding it, rolling it into a ball and unrolling it again. In her mind, I thought, she was very far away. After half an hour, she got up, gave a little sigh and headed east towards the gas chambers and the crematorium. There was a crowd. Tourists. A group of kids, schoolchildren, and an adult group. They were listening to their respective guides. The kids were taking photographs, whispering to each other. What they wanted was to shout, to ask real questions, but this was not a place where conversation was customary, those who came here were gassed, incinerated, rose in a column of smoke, they knew that. The older group said nothing, they stood motionless. The woman joined the older group. She said something to the man standing next to her, who put his arm around her shoulder and kissed her on the forehead. The gesture of a friend. I joined the group. The guide was talking, explaining. I didn't like his voice, there was something wrong about the tone. What irritated me was that he was trapped in his books, in his technical reports, what he was describing was a process. That is not what extermination is! Not just that. It cannot be brought down to its final act. There is everything else, the most important part, the part that is nameless, the everyday evil that you quickly grow accustomed to, that you never grow accustomed to, that thing which the old woman instinctively understood, that thing that I have been trying desperately to understand for months without even coming a fraction of an inch closer. I had felt this from the first: I could know my father, know myself, by following his path to the end, to the heart of the Machine. But no knowledge, no insight, no compassion, no imagination can achieve what experiencing the genocide has etched on the minds of the prisoners, and they, the survivors, have no means of communicating it to us. My father will forever be a mystery, and my pain will know no end.

The group moved on. I positioned myself so that I would be walking beside the little old woman. We struck up a conversation. She spoke English with a thick Mitteleuropean accent I couldn't quite place. She told me she was born in Czechoslovakia, in Bratislava, but had been living in New York since '48. I told her I was French and that I lived on the outskirts of Paris. When I felt we were getting on well, I said, "Were you in Birkenau?"

She blushed and said, "Oh, no, not me, my sister Nina was sent here. I was at Buchenwald . . . with my parents."

"Your sister . . . did she die here?"

"Yes. I found out from a friend who was at Birkenau with her . . . She died last year."

"Mmm-hmm."

"They were at school together in Bratislava. One day, they didn't come home. Later on, they came for us . . . for the whole family."

"Mmm-hmm."

"What about you?"

"Me? I . . . well, I . . . "

"One of your parents?"

"Yes . . . my father . . . My father was at Birkenau and at other camps . . . miraculously he survived. I never knew, he never said anything . . . I only found out recently, by accident, after he died."

"I understand . . . You mustn't feel bitter . . . there are things you cannot speak of to your children. Believe me, it is almost unbearable to speak of them even with those who were here."

We came to a crossroads. Her group was heading towards their bus, I had to follow my journey to the end. As she was getting on to the coach, I suddenly rushed up to her, I gripped her elbow and said, "I wanted to apologise . . . "

"But what have you to apologise for, young man?"

"I . . . life has been cruel to you . . . to your family, your parents . . . I feel somehow responsible . . . "

She looked at me, her old, beautiful eyes had known too much pain, and taking my hand she said, "Thank you, child, I'm very touched. No one has ever has ever said sorry to me before."

I leaned and kissed her on the forehead. A gesture of friendship, of solidarity across the gulf that separated us.

I was overwhelmed by the encounter. This woman did not deserve for me to lie to her. I had the sickening feeling that I had robbed her of her life, her dignity. But I told myself perhaps she had long since done her mourning and that it would have been cruel to wake the dead. In fact, I realise the only person I have lied to is myself, *no propitiatory prayer, no pardon, no expiation by the guilty, which nothing at all in the power of man can ever clean again.* If I were her, Helmut Schiller, I would have spat your apology into the dust.

It was time I left. I had no business being here, I have no place here. I should never have come, I have defiled it.

After Rachel came back to Paris in February 1996, he holed up in his house and never came out again. Two months later, on April 24, he killed himself in his garage. I found out he was back from Momo, who always knows everything. He said, "Hey, I saw your bro down at Prisunic. Jesus, the fucking state of him! Has he got AIDS or what?" "Leave it," I said. "It's just some middle-class bullshit, problems with his wife or his high-powered job." At the time I didn't suspect anything, but what Momo said got me thinking and I decided to go round there. I made out like I was just passing. It was pretty choked up. He looked like a walking corpse, he was all hunched and confused like an old man, and Rachel had always been sharp, well turned-out, always plugged-in, always had his shit together better than any CEO. He was wearing these creepy striped pyjamas I'd never seen before and he had his head shaved like some convict. The house was upside down, the whole place was filthy, it reeked, the blinds were closed. It was like a cell in solitary. He sat on the arm of the chair and he said in this little voice, "I was going to come and see you on the estate . . . I will come . . . I will, I'll come . . . " I asked him if everything was okay. He shrugged like it was nothing serious. "It's fine." We drank cold coffee in awkward silence. I kept looking at him out of the corner of my eye, he was staring at the floor, his hands on his knees. If I didn't know him, I'd have thought he was some junkie who'd woken up in our place. He wasn't there, he was off some place in his head, I could hear him thinking. It looked like he could feel everything he was thinking. He looked so frail, so alone. And so strange. I was moved. Then suddenly, doing his best to sound serious and persuasive, he started giving me one of his little lectures about reliability, honesty, decency, studying hard. I got up and said, "Okay, all right, I can see you're fine, I'll leave you to it." He called me back! First time ever, he was never the kind to be pushy, to keep people hanging around if they wanted to head off. He said, "I wanted to say I'm sorry." He hesitated and then he said, "I haven't been a good brother to you, but never forget that I'm your big brother, and I love you more than anything in the world." I guess I shrugged, I hate that sort of soppy shit, I found it really embarrassing. He said again, "Don't forget that . . . whatever happens." What he said had me so choked up, I got angry. I got up and stormed out and didn't look back. I regret it now. I should have stayed, talked to him, asked him what was going on, taken him in hand, moved into the house so I could keep and eye on him. I could tell he was losing it, it was obvious. But back then, the way I looked at it, I had my shit and other people had theirs. I'm ashamed to admit it, but I didn't go back there, I wouldn't let myself, I was pissed at him for not keeping his word, he'd said he'd come and see me on the estate. I'd even told aunt Sakina, and she was so happy. And I'd told my mates so they could "accidentally" drop by while he was there, they're pretty useful for filling up space and giving the impression that life's spur of the moment and everything's a party.

In his diary, there are three pages about his suicide. To Rachel, it wasn't suicide. He never uses the word. He talks about retribution, about justice. He calls it an act of love for papa and for his victims. I don't know if it's just to try to link two things that can't be linked, to make a single gesture for both victims and executioner. I don't think I'll ever really understand what was going on in his head. It's probably the same with anyone who commits suicide. Faced with their lifeless bodies, we're dumbstruck, asking questions to which there are no answers. Now I've read and reread his diary, I can understand the mental process that led him to kill himself, but the act itself is beyond all understanding. I can understand thinking about suicide, everyone does it, on the estate it's like an epidemic. I can even accept that there might come a time when you do something, when you plan, when you decide how to do it, when you run through it in your head, when you play at being a desperate man putting a bullet through his brain, falling back, holding your breath to see what it feels like but it's a long way from there to actually going through with it. That moment is beyond imagining. Even the person committing suicide can't imagine it, at some point there's a click and it's all over. Rachel didn't choose the easy option, didn't put a bullet in his brain, swallow poison, jump off a bridge, throw himself under a train, he killed himself slowly. It was nothing to do with suicide, he wanted to atone, he wanted to be gassed to death like papa's victims, like it was papa who was gassing him. He watched himself die and I think he probably tried to stay conscious right up to that last second. This was the price he wanted to pay in papa's place for the victims of the camps and probably for me, to relieve me of the burden of our debt. Yeah. "Suicide" is not the word.

I'm not trying to make excuses, but back then, life wasn't exactly a bed of roses on the estate. Had it ever been? I think so, I remember a time when people were happy there. You came and went, you had no worries, no fears. And if you had, usually round end of the month, you got through it and if you couldn't dodge the people you owed money to, you tightened your belt, lived on credit, the women would go to the pawn shop. Looking back, I think people were more relaxed, they struggled, but they didn't think of their lives as a sort of hell they'd never get out of. You'd hear them say: "Tomorrow's another day"; "*Vive la République, vive la France*"; "Where there's life, there's hope." Or things like "He who sleeps forgets his hunger"; "We'll eat better tomorrow"; "Suck your thumb if you still feel hungry"; "Pretend it's Ramadan"; "Have a glass of water and get a good night's sleep" and we'd laugh. If things were really bad, you made like a soldier from the First World War, talking to himself in the trenches: "We'll just have to make the best of things," or "You have to die of something," or "There's people worse off than us," or "A man dies with his boots on . . . " That's what I always heard, you could compile a dictionary of sayings like that, most of them brought back from Africa by war veterans. We didn't give up hope, when we were at our wits' end, we'd get out our secret weapon: Allah, Jesus, Mary or the local *griot*. Back then, the estate was like a village that wasn't on the map, it had its ups and downs, one day we'd be helping each other out, the next day we'd be at each other's throats and the day after that we'd be sitting round the fire, all friends again. That was all we had to keep us going: arguments about fences, squabbles between neighbours, kids fighting and family histories that twisted and tangled all the way back to darkest Africa. Apart from the old women who pulled the strings and were constantly whining about something, no one had the patience to untangle them so everyone pretended that they knew, that gossiping and running people down was just another form of conversation. But maybe I only think that because I was young, we were always off somewhere getting up to some shit, we didn't think about the big picture, who was stirring things, what was going on in people's heads, we'd picked up on snatches of conversation that sounded mysterious and violent, that smacked of heroism and great rewards in heaven or on earth. When the first Islamists showed up, we were happy, they had faced up to the dictator and his men back at home, back in Algeria, *Taghouts*, they called them, big shots with big guns who were going round murdering and looting and it was all completely legal. I saw a thing or two back in Algeria, every step I took I thought I was about to be deported and exterminated like an *Untermensch*, an inferior person. They looked funny in their old-world suicide-bomber getups, with their martyrs' belts, their scruffy beards, their battered faces, their staring eyes, their all-terrain sandals, we liked the way they talked, like Allah's rap crew, the way they were always available, the way they were like superheroes fighting for the poor. There were only about a dozen of them, but there were hordes of us and we were all itching to be their right-hand men. We'd do anything, they only had to ask, they had Allah's ear, he was on their side. We were all wet behind the ears but they had us all fired up, they taught us how exciting it was to have people to hate, people you wanted dead so much it kept you awake at night. We'd talk about this stuff at night in the cellars and the stairwells, muffled up in our Mujahideen-issue parkas while the poor souls who had only their poverty to worry about double-locked their doors to the truth of the Prophet and moral certainty and slept like happy morons. During our initiation, we despised abstract creatures, people without names, it was mystical enough to intoxicate a saint. The vague and the inexplicable were your basic ingredients if you wanted to become a fanatic, and we wanted it right then and there. These loathsome abstract creatures, we called the infidels, the *Kaffirs,* the tyrants, the *Taghouts,* you could imagine they were whatever you wanted, the cat, the dog, the kitchen sink. Once we were deemed worthy of *jihad,* the imam opened the big sack of *Kaffirs* and in a solemn, incontrovertible voice, gave each of them a name: this one is the Jew, *Lihoudi,* he is scum, the worst of all, this one is the Christian, *massihi,* the hypocrite, the accursed, this one is the communist, *el chouyouï,* the monster reviled by Allah, these are the secular Muslims, the westernised Arab, the liberated woman, dogs and bitches who deserve to die a cruel death, these ones are the queers, the junkies, the intellectuals who must be crushed by any means necessary. Most of them were people that we knew, our neighbours, friends from school, work colleagues, local shopkeepers, teachers, people on the TV. Suddenly we saw France in all its horror, rotten and corrupt to the core, a whole pack of *Untermenschen,* filthy poisonous bastards in league with Israel, America, and the vile Arabic dictatorships who exterminated their own people to prevent Islam from spreading. It was high time to exterminate. As the months went by, and we organised rescue operations, we all escaped as best we could, but there were a lot of people who were still in it up to their necks. People who don't rise above fundamentalism are doomed for centuries to come.

As you've seen in the previous chapters, things have got a whole lot worse these past few months. Ever since Nadia was torched by the emir on the orders of the imam, and Cyclops and Flicha showed up with their new *Kapos,* this isn't my estate anymore. They've already turned it into a concentration camp, we're dying slowly but surely, we lock ourselves in, they keep files on us, watch our every move, we're constantly harangued about the rules of the *Lager,* what we should wear, how long our hair should be, how we should behave, the things we shouldn't do, there are daily rallies, a general mobilisation on Fridays, the harrying sermons, the trials, the punishments, and in the end you're signed up to the death *Kommandos* and shipped of to the camps in Afghanistan. All we need now are some gas chambers and a few *Kremas* and we can start the mass extermination. And no sign of a Righteous Person on the horizon. Rachel doesn't explain it, but I've found out that Righteous Persons were non-Jews who risked their lives hiding Jews from the Gestapo and the police. He had a file about them and another one about Righteous Persons who were German, who were at the heart of the Machine and used their money, their intelligence and their courage to save thousands of innocent people. Some of them are famous and respected: Oskar Schindler, Albert Battel and others. Why couldn't you have done that, papa? Rachel would still be alive and we would be the sons of a Righteous Man. Rachel says that the Holocaust is a historical aberration, that humanity would never allow such a thing to happen again. Rachel was educated, he was knowledgeable, he knew what he was talking about, but I think he forgot that people only realise what's going on after the event. One minute before his death, he's alive, but a second later, there are shocked people grieving for him. Aunt Sakina liked to say, "The difference between yesterday and tomorrow is today, because we don't know how it will end." And Monsieur Vincent, who's a real stickler for tightening wheel nuts, used to look over our shoulders, cross his fingers and say: "So good so far, if the wheel nut shears, we'll all know about it." And Rachel also forgot that humanity is always failing, it never learns, it's too much hassle. Everyone on the estate knows that it's too late. The Islamists are already here, they're settled and here we are, bound hand and foot, caught in the trap. If they don't exterminate us, they'll stop us from living. Worse still, they'll turn us into our own guards, deferential to the emir, merciless to each other. We'll be *Kapos*.

How things change. In a few months, the estate has become unrecognisable. What was a Sensitive Urban Area, Category 1 has become a concentration camp. In a few short minutes, the time it took to flick through a military record that should never have been there, Rachel fell into history's black hole. In two years, he lost his health, his mind, his job, his friends, his Ophélie: the girl he'd loved his whole life. And me, in ten months I've gone from dumb apathy to a state of permanent panic somewhere between madness, anger and the urge to rush halfway across the world and drown myself. I don't know what to do or what will be done tomorrow. I feel terribly alone.

More alone that anyone in the world. My parents are dead, Rachel is dead, uncle Ali is not much longer for this world and I have no idea what will happen to aunt Sakina. Life is unutterably sad.

Me and my mates have been saying that maybe it's time to get the fuck out, to go die somewhere else. Then again we've been talking about hanging in there and fighting. One day, we'll swear it's all worth it and the next day we're saying it's not worth shit. We can't see what kind of miracle could set it off.

24 APRIL 1996

T ime has seemed so slow to me these past few months. I've lived through a whole century, and not the easiest of centuries, one filled with horror and shame. It has been long and painful, I have paid a price for every step, every word, every scrap of information to know my father, to know in myself the meaning of the extermination and his part in it. I followed his path from start to finish, slipped into his thoughts, set my foot in his footsteps. At no time did I flinch, not before the gas chambers, not before the unbelievable everyday horror of the camps, not even before the grief that every day ate away at my heart. If the walls of the camps, the ghosts of the prisoners, if the men and women I met on my journey into the heart of the Holocaust, if the books I have read could bear witness they would say: this man has given all he can give, he may speak, he knows.

I think I have been honest, I think where possible I have weighed things carefully, nothing is ever absolutely black and it is rarer still that things are white as snow. I have neither tempered the responsibility my father bears, though he was only a tiny cog in a fantastical machine, nor considered that blind machine could have functioned, even for an instant, without the determined commitment of each and every man who was a part of it. I could be wrong, but because I know him as well as any child can know his father, I believe he was never deliberately cruel. He was what he was: stern, exacting, inflexible. A bit of an opportunist too, from what I know of his time in Egypt and Algeria. He had to live, he took whatever was offered: spy, weapons instructor, anything.

In Algeria at least he did enough to earn the title of veteran *Mujahid,* a title of great glory to Algerians. In the village where he lived he was a respected Cheïkh, he was a loving husband to maman and a good father to us, devoted enough to deprive himself of our presence and send us to France to be educated so that we might have a solid future. He was the victim of a barbarous act and was elevated to the status of *chahid,* a martyr of the nation. To the people of Aïn Deb, he was a Righteous Person.

You do not choose your life. My father did not choose, he found himself on a road that led to infamy, to the very heart of the Holocaust. He couldn't leave the road, all he could do was close his eyes and keep on walking. No one dreams of being a torturer, no one dreams of one day being a torture victim. Just as the sun releases its excesses of energy in sporadic sun spots, from time to time history releases the hatred humanity has accumulated in a scorching wind that sweeps away everything in its path. Chance decides whether one is here or there, protected or exposed, on this side of the channel or that. I chose nothing, I chose to live a quiet, hardworking life and here I am before a scaffold that was not built for me. I am paying for another's crime. I want to save him, because he is my father, because he is a man. This is how I choose to answer Primo Levi's question in *If This Is a Man.* Yes, no matter however far he has fallen, the victim is a man, and however terrible his shame, his executioner is still a man.

And yet at every moment of our lives, we all have a choice. We have a pact with life, it can leave us when it chooses, if it should judge us unworthy, too obsessed with our power, and we have the luxury of leaving it when we choose, the moment it takes a direction which does not conform to our ideals. We make our decision and we choose an amicable separation, however painful and permanent it may be. If one is to die, one might as well do so with a little self-respect, a little respect for others. My father chose his path and each time life presented him with an alternative, he persisted in that path. He did not kill one person, he killed two, then a hundred, then thousands, tens of thousands, he might have killed millions. He was caught between hatred and servitude and such chasms of the mind are bottomless. And in the end, when the day of reckoning came, he chose to turn his back on his victims and run away. To do so was horrifying, it was to kill them a second time. Later still he knowingly made the mistake of fathering children, aware that sooner or later the truth would come to light and that his children would suffer. To say that such a man is not a man is to strip him of his responsibility, his guilt, it is a way of offering him his quietus, to suggest that he has nothing to atone for, no forgiveness to ask. But even for God in all his glory, or Satan in all his power, such impartiality does not exist, they must earn their thrones and protect them, it is we who have made them kings. And even if "nothing at all in the power of man can ever clean again," we can at least agree to this: we must pay, pay in full. We must not leave our debts behind us.

So, for my father, for his victims, I will pay in full. It is simple justice. Let it not be said that all the Schillers have failed. May God, that blind and senseless *thing* that majestically roams the heavens, forgive my father, and let Him take note that for my part I expect nothing of Him. May his victims forgive us, that is all that matters to me. My death does not atone for anything, it is a gesture of love.

My dear Malrich, my beloved brother, if you should read this diary, forgive me. I should have told you, should have shared this terrible burden with you. You were so young, so ill-equipped. But I have made amends, I have written this diary as much for you as for myself. Be strong and steer your course. I love you. Give my love to aunt Sakina and uncle Ali. If you see Ophélie, tell her that I love her and ask her to forgive me.

It is 11 P.M. It is time.

THE END

P.S. I wish this diary to be given to my brother Malek Ulrich Schiller. Thank you for respecting my wishes.

Carmine Abate
Between Two Seas
"A moving portrayal of generational continuity."—*Kirkus*
192 pp • $14.95 • 978-1-933372-40-2

Salwa Al Neimi
The Proof of the Honey
"Al Neimi announces the end of a taboo in the Arab world:
that of sex!"—*Reuters*
160 pp • $15.00 • 978-1-933372-68-6

Alberto Angela
A Day in the Life of Ancient Rome
"Fascinating and accessible."—*Il Giornale*
392 pp • $16.00 • 978-1-933372-71-6

Muriel Barbery
The Elegance of the Hedgehog
"Gently satirical, exceptionally winning and inevitably
bittersweet."—Michael Dirda, *The Washington Post*
336 pp • $15.00 • 978-1-933372-60-0

Stefano Benni
Margherita Dolce Vita
"A modern fable...hilarious social commentary."—*People*
240 pp • $14.95 • 978-1-933372-20-4

Timeskipper
"Benni again unveils his Italian brand of magical realism."—*Library Journal*
400 pp • $16.95 • 978-1-933372-44-0

Massimo Carlotto
The Goodbye Kiss
"A masterpiece of Italian noir."—*Globe and Mail*
160 pp • $14.95 • 978-1-933372-05-1

Death's Dark Abyss
"A remarkable study of corruption and redemption."
—*Kirkus* (starred review)
160 pp • $14.95 • 978-1-933372-18-1

The Fugitive
"[Carlotto is] the reigning king of Mediterranean noir."
—*The Boston Phoenix*
176 pp • $14.95 • 978-1-933372-25-9

Francisco Coloane
Tierra del Fuego
"Coloane is the Jack London of our times."—Alvaro Mutis
176 pp • $14.95 • 978-1-933372-63-1

Giancarlo De Cataldo
The Father and the Foreigner
"A slim but touching noir novel from one of Italy's best writers
in the genre."—*Quaderni Noir*
160 pp • $15.00 • 978-1-933372-72-3

Shashi Deshpande
The Dark Holds No Terrors
"[Deshpande is] an extremely talented storyteller."—*Hindustan Times*
272 pp • $15.00 • 978-1-933372-67-9

Steve Erickson
Zeroville
"A funny, disturbing, daring and demanding novel—Erickson's best."
—*The New York Times Book Review*
352 pp • $14.95 • 978-1-933372-39-6

Elena Ferrante
The Days of Abandonment
"The raging, torrential voice of [this] author is something rare."
—*The New York Times*
192 pp • $14.95 • 978-1-933372-00-6

Troubling Love
"Ferrante's polished language belies the rawness
of her imagery."—*The New Yorker*
144 pp • $14.95 • 978-1-933372-16-7

The Lost Daughter
"So refined, almost translucent."—*The Boston Globe*
144 pp • $14.95 • 978-1-933372-42-6

Jane Gardam
Old Filth
"Old Filth belongs in the Dickensian pantheon of memorable characters."—*The New York Times Book Review*
304 pp • $14.95 • 978-1-933372-13-6

The Queen of the Tambourine
"A truly superb and moving novel."—*The Boston Globe*
272 pp • $14.95 • 978-1-933372-36-5

The People on Privilege Hill
"Engrossing stories of hilarity and heartbreak."—*Seattle Times*
208 pp • $15.95 • 978-1-933372-56-3

Alicia Giménez-Bartlett
Dog Day
"Delicado and Garzón prove to be one of the more engaging sleuth teams to debut in a long time."—*The Washington Post*
320 pp • $14.95 • 978-1-933372-14-3

Prime Time Suspect
"A gripping police procedural."—*The Washington Post*
320 pp • $14.95 • 978-1-933372-31-0

Death Rites
"Petra is developing into a good cop, and her earnest efforts to assert her authority…are worth cheering."—*The New York Times*
304 pp • $16.95 • 978-1-933372-54-9

Katharina Hacker
The Have-Nots
"Hacker's prose soars."—*Publishers Weekly*
352 pp • $14.95 • 978-1-933372-41-9

Patrick Hamilton
Hangover Square
"Patrick Hamilton's novels are dark tunnels of misery, loneliness, deceit, and sexual obsession."—*New York Review of Books*
336 pp • $14.95 • 978-1-933372-06-8

James Hamilton-Paterson
Cooking with Fernet Branca
"Irresistible!"—*The Washington Post*
288 pp • $14.95 • 978-1-933372-01-3

Amazing Disgrace
"It's loads of fun, light and dazzling as a peacock feather."
—*New York Magazine*
352 pp • $14.95 • 978-1-933372-19-8

Rancid Pansies
"Campy comic saga about hack writer and self-styled 'culinary genius' Gerald Samper."—*Seattle Times*
288 pp • $15.95 • 978-1-933372-62-4

Seven-Tenths: The Sea and Its Thresholds
"The kind of book that, were he alive now, Shelley might have written."
—Charles Sprawson
416 pp • $16.00 • 978-1-933372-69-3

Alfred Hayes
The Girl on the Via Flaminia
"Immensely readable."—*The New York Times*
160 pp • $14.95 • 978-1-933372-24-2

Jean-Claude Izzo
Total Chaos
"Izzo's Marseilles is ravishing."—*Globe and Mail*
256 pp • $14.95 • 978-1-933372-04-4

Chourmo
"A bitter, sad and tender salute to a place equally impossible
to love or leave."—*Kirkus* (starred review)
256 pp • $14.95 • 978-1-933372-17-4

Solea
"[Izzo is] a talented writer who draws from the deep, dark well
of noir."—*The Washington Post*
208 pp • $14.95 • 978-1-933372-30-3

The Lost Sailors
"Izzo digs deep into what makes men weep."
—*Time Out New York*
272 pp • $14.95 • 978-1-933372-35-8

A Sun for the Dying
"Beautiful, like a black sun, tragic and desperate."—*Le Point*
224 pp • $15.00 • 978-1-933372-59-4

Gail Jones
Sorry
"Jones's gift for conjuring place and mood rarely falters."
—*Times Literary Supplement*
240 pp • $15.95 • 978-1-933372-55-6

Matthew F. Jones
Boot Tracks
"A gritty action tale."—*The Philadelphia Inquirer*
208 pp • $14.95 • 978-1-933372-11-2

Ioanna Karystiani
The Jasmine Isle
"A modern Greek tragedy about love foredoomed
and family life."—*Kirkus*
288 pp • $14.95 • 978-1-933372-10-5

Gene Kerrigan
The Midnight Choir
"The lethal precision of his closing punches leave quite a lasting mark."
—*Entertainment Weekly*
368 pp • $14.95 • 978-1-933372-26-6

Little Criminals
"A great story...relentless and brilliant."—Roddy Doyle
352 pp • $16.95 • 978-1-933372-43-3

Peter Kocan
Fresh Fields
"A stark, harrowing, yet deeply courageous work of immense power
and magnitude."—*Quadrant*
304 pp • $14.95 • 978-1-933372-29-7

The Treatment and the Cure
"Kocan tells this story with grace and humor."—*Publishers Weekly*
256 pp • $15.95 • 978-1-933372-45-7

Helmut Krausser
Eros
"Helmut Krausser has succeeded in writing a great German epochal
novel."—*Focus*
352 pp • $16.95 • 978-1-933372-58-7

Amara Lakhous
Clash of Civilizations Over an Elevator in Piazza Vittorio
"Do we have an Italian Camus on our hands? Just possibly."
—*The Philadelphia Inquirer*
144 pp • $14.95 • 978-1-933372-61-7

Carlo Lucarelli
Carte Blanche
"Lucarelli proves that the dark and sinister are better evoked
when one opts for unadulterated grit and grime."
—*The San Diego Union-Tribune*
128 pp • $14.95 • 978-1-933372-15-0

The Damned Season
"De Luca…is a man both pursuing and pursued. And that makes him
one of the more interesting figures in crime fiction."
—*The Philadelphia Inquirer*
128 pp • $14.95 • 978-1-933372-27-3

Via delle Oche
"Delivers a resolution true to the series' moral relativism."
—*Publishers Weekly*
160 pp • $14.95 • 978-1-933372-53-2

Edna Mazya
Love Burns
"Combines the suspense of a murder mystery with the absurdity
of a Woody Allen movie."—*Kirkus*
224 pp • $14.95 • 978-1-933372-08-2

Sélim Nassib
I Loved You for Your Voice
"Nassib spins a rhapsodic narrative out of the indissoluble
connection between two creative souls."—*Kirkus*
272 pp • $14.95 • 978-1-933372-07-5

The Palestinian Lover
"A delicate, passionate novel in which history and life are
inextricably entwined."—*RAI Books*
192 pp • $14.95 • 978-1-933372-23-5

Amélie Nothomb
Tokyo Fiancée
"Intimate and honest...depicts perfectly a nontraditional romance."
—*Publishers Weekly*
160 pp • $15.00 • 978-1-933372-64-8

Alessandro Piperno
The Worst Intentions
"A coruscating mixture of satire, family epic, Proustian meditation,
and erotomaniacal farce."—*The New Yorker*
320 pp • $14.95 • 978-1-933372-33-4

Eric-Emmanuel Schmitt
The Most Beautiful Book in the World
"Nine novellas, parables on the idea of a future, filled with redeeming
optimism."—*Lire Magazine*
192 pp • $15.00 • 978-1-933372-74-7